Acknowledger

C000171958

Thanks to my writing friends In Arun Scribes who offer so much advice, encouragement and support.

Thanks also to Dr Jill Barber at the Engelsea Brook Primitive Methodist Chapel and Museum for her input and information and also allowing me to use an image from their archive on my cover.

Thanks to Hull City Libraries and Hull Maritime Museum. The staff at both were exceedingly helpful, as were the staff in Grimsby Reference Library and Wendy Ellison, my ex-colleague at the University of Chichester.

Thanks also go to the participants on Rod Collins's Blog about Grimsby and Cleethorpes http://www.rodcollins.com/wordpress/ a mine of information on all things to do with Grimsby and Cleethorpes history.

Thanks to Karen Wells at Verité CM Ltd for my cover design.

Thanks to my beta and proof readers John, Angela, Julie and Patricia.

Thanks to Mary Elmhirst, this is also your story.

Thanks, as always to my family for their support.

Part One

Betsy

1798-1799

Chapter 1

William shivered, the patched smock offering little protection against the cool autumnal air. His toes twitched on the bare earth, wanting to run, anywhere rather than staying here. Tasting the faint tang of wood smoke from the nearby cottages, he groaned as the men lowered the box into the earth. He wanted to scream 'Mama', but bit his tongue to stifle any sound escaping. The painful image of his mother lying in the pine box, twisted his stomach into knots. He had seen her in it that morning before his father nailed down the lid; her skin pale and bloodless; her hair flowing around her shoulders like a raven's wing. Dada had told him to give her one last kiss and he had leaned over to press his mouth to her cheek, flinching as his lips touched her icy, unyielding flesh.

She looked so peaceful and still, but Mama had never been still. From the time the sun woke until it set, there were things to do she said. He longed to climb in the box to lie against her and stared with jealousy at the small bundle in her arms. For eternity, that baby would lie with her but William, would never feel her hands yanking the wooden comb through his knotted hair; never hear her complaints about his torn and mucky clothes, nor feel her dig around in his skin with a needle to find the splinter in his hand. The worst thought of all, the one which caused his eyes to water was that he would never again have the comfort of her gentle hugs and kisses.

His little brother, Joe, attempted to climb up on the bench, startling him. 'What's in the big box?' he asked.

William hopped down and held him tight. 'It's the pirate princess,' he said. 'We need to save her from the wicked witch.' Mama had drummed into him how he must always protect his younger brother.

Dada nodded to him. 'Take him outside, William.'

With an excited whoop, Joe ran through the door, followed more reluctantly by William, to battle with the witch as their father hammered in the nails, tap tap, tap. Each tap pierced William's heart although it was no hardship to play Joe's favourite game and it occupied them until it was time to leave. Joe remained in his sisters' care while their father thought William old enough to see his mother buried. After all, next harvest he would old enough to work in the fields.

Salty drops formed in William's eyes. He screwed up his eyes. Crying was forbidden, had he not he been told by Mama that crying was only for babies. He looked around at his older brother and father, shocked to see tears dripping down their freshly scrubbed faces, as the vicar spoke his words 'Dust to dust, ashes to ashes'. William, unable to swallow for sadness, tasted the dust and ashes in his throat.

His father stooped to pick up some dirt from a pile of earth beside the grave and dropped it with a clatter on to the coffin, now so deep William felt sad that the sun would never reach her. Mama always complained of the cold. His brother, Tom, bent down in turn to gather dirt and William copied, his fingers closing around a lump of claggy soil. His older brother walked to the edge of the grave and scattered the soil and pebbles, running a sleeve over his eyes as he turned away. William moved forward in his turn, teetering on the edge of the grave, the rough planks of the coffin lid far below. His arm extended and he opened his hand to watch as his tiny handful of earth fell splattering into the grave. Stepping back, Dada give him a half smile from a face screwed up with pain. William ran to him and clasped his hands around his thighs, as his father patted the top of his head. The mourners turned to depart once the gravedigger began to shovel in earth from the mound beside the open grave.

As they walked the short distance down the lane to the cottage, an unseasonable icy wind from the north, blew into their faces. Even the clouds look sad, thought William, as he clung to his father's hand. A smattering of rain hit the mourners and the men pulled on their woollen caps, which they had held throughout the service. Mama had always told him that women cover their heads in church while men take off their caps. She called it 'respect' but he did not understand why. It seemed daft to him.

Back in the cottage women bustled around preparing food. It was good to be busy so you did not have time to grieve, thought William's older sister, Elizabeth. She expected to take up her mother's duties to keep house for her father and brothers. It would be no hardship to leave her place as kitchen skivvy for the vicar's wife. She tried to shake off the guilty pleasure she would feel in saying farewell to her mistress, who never failed to pull her up for any failing. But her mother had trained her well and she felt able to manage the household and the neighbours would always be there for advice. The village of Frodingham was small, but that was good, because everyone mucked in to help whenever needed.

She glanced out of the single window and saw the men walking down the lane from the church. It's done, she thought, Mama is buried, and she choked back a sob. Little Uriah sat on the earthen floor playing with a stick. Elizabeth scooped him up to bury her tears into his chest, but the child protested so much she set him back down. Lucky him, he won't remember this day or his real mother for I will be his mother now, she vowed.

As William walked through the door of his home, the warmth of his family's love greeted him. He was petted by Granny Leaning and his Aunt Lizzy. Both women had walked from Broughton to be there. They knelt to hug and pet him, their affection a salve for his wounded heart. He knew them well. Mama took her youngest children on visits to his aunt in the summer and he looked forward to playing with his cousins in the woods. They always wanted him to be the Frenchie or the traitorous Irish, which he didn't like so much because he never got to be on the winning side. William took comfort from his Aunt Lizzy's likeness to his mother, could almost believe she was still with him as he snuggled up close to her. She even smelt like Mama, a mixture of wood-smoke and onions. He wondered if he would continue to visit with his cousins, but dare not ask.

As some of the neighbours drifted away, leaving the family to mourn in peace, a pony and trap drew up in the village. The erstwhile mourners looked at the driver with curiosity; it was odd to see a stranger at all, let alone a solitary woman. She appeared to be of middling years, her coat black, as though in mourning, her hair dark and curling under a fashionable, feathered bonnet. How peculiar! They knew all the ladies around the village and none would have worn a bonnet so dashing. They stumbled over a better word to describe it. Only gentry might wear such a thing, and yet she did not appear as grand as one of the Nelthorpe ladies. Hailing the man closest to her trap, the stranger asked for directions to William Holtby's cottage. When he pointed it out, she thanked him, instructing the pony to walk on. The neighbours continued their speculation as they made the way to their own cottages, a Lincolnshire accent, they agreed. She must be related to Bill, the ruddiness of her cheeks a signal of kinship.

Elizabeth opened the door to the stranger letting her mouth hang upon in surprise, as the woman shouldered her way in to the cottage, stooping so as not to damage her plumage on the lintel.

Once inside she looked about her. One room downstairs by the look of it and a ladder to another room above; a labourer's cottage, plain to see, with its sparse, home-made furnishings. Earthenware pots littered a plank table along with the remains of a meal of cheese, plum bread, sliced apples and beakers of ale. Bill, her younger brother by a year, took a step towards her in surprise. His face looked grey and careworn. Was he only thirty-six?

'Betsy, is it you. How did you know it was Mary's funeral?'

'I didn't. I had business in Brigg so I thought to surprise you. I have been meaning to come for some time. I am sorry for your loss, brother. I wish now I had visited earlier.' A polite mistruth as the fact of his recent loss made her plan easier to accomplish.

'Sit down and take some refreshment. Elizabeth, this is your Aunt Betsy. You're named after her. Fetch her some ale will you.' Elizabeth dropped a quick curtsey and left to do as she was bid.

Betsy perched herself on a low, wooden bench and, after delivering further commiserations, she asked Bill the names of his children.

'Well let's see, there's Elizabeth our eldest, then Tom, Hannah, William, John, we call him Joe, and our youngest Uriah. James, the baby died soon after his mother.' Bill counted them out on his fingers. 'That makes six, doesn't it?'

'If you don't count James,' Betsy concurred. 'That's the reason I came to visit. I have a proposal to take one off your hands. I have a very

9

comfortable income and I need an heir. The doctor, I kept house for, left me a good-sized house in Grimsby and a respectable annual income.'

Bill did not know what to say. It did not feel right to give away one of his and Mary's children. He thought for a moment and said. 'Our Hannah will be a good mother to the youngest, we can just about manage. They don't go hungry; Elizabeth is in service and brings in a little and Tom works on the farm with me. It's better now than it was at the start of the war. At least there's no shortage of bread now.'

'That's good. In these dismal times, I wondered how you'd been faring. I wrote to the vicar in Broughton and he told me where you were living.'

Bill looked baffled. To be honest it had been a few years since he had thought much of his sister. Times were hard and he had enough problems of his own to concern him, without thinking of his sister's situation. It must be nigh on fourteen years since he had last seen her, the day of his wedding.

'Just consider the advantage for the child. He will have an education and be able to choose any profession.'

Bill continued to look puzzled until he dragged his mind back to Betsy's proposal. 'One of my sons then; you want a boy?' He studied the tamped down earthen floor for a long moment, turning the offer over in his mind. 'I suppose Uriah will not remember us if you take him.' Bill swallowed hard; perhaps it would be best for the child. He was barely two years old and it would free up Hannah for service in another year or two.

'No I want one that's old enough to be biddable and young enough to learn. What about that one?' She pointed to William.

'Not William. He's his mother's favourite.' Her brother checked himself and said 'was,' in a way that caused Betsy to pat his hand.

'He can be my favourite then.' Betsy liked the look of William and she disliked the name Uriah, an unlucky name, for did not David have him killed to claim Bathsheeba? She was indifferent to John. Had not Salome demanded his head on a plate? William, however, was a strong name, a lucky name, the name of their father, another William Holtby. Yes, she liked that. As she studied him, she began to see a likeness to his grandfather, maybe not in his colouring, but in his green eyes which were set wide apart and the long, thin nose and the square set to his chin. He would grow up to be handsome and she was not averse to handsome.

Betsy also noted the way William sat still on his aunt's lap, not fidgeting like Joe, or picking his nose like Uriah. William appeared to be listening to the conversation going on around him. She could see him thinking. He would do very well and she made up her mind.

'I'll give you twenty pounds as a dowry for your daughters. The younger one has an eye that wanders; she will need money if she is to find a husband.'

Bill sighed. His sister had always been bossy but how could he turn down a fortune, more money than he earned in a year? It was true, Hannah's squint was going to be a burden to her. He rubbed his head as though it would make his thinking clearer, but tiredness, grief and resentment muddied his mind. Why did Mary have to die and leave him with all these problems? He'd been content with his lot but within forty-eight hours his world had blown apart. Betsy tapped him on the arm, impatient for an answer.

He took the safest option. 'Mary was never one to mollycoddle the children but she thought William special, said he would amount to something. Maybe it's you who will make that happen, Betsy, because all I can see for the future is more poverty. If the fields are enclosed and we must work for a pittance, how will we cope? Then there's all this talk of invasion. Tom and I have been called to train for the militia, although we only have pikes for weapons. I often worry what will happen to the children if I am killed fighting. Pray God it never comes to that.'

Bill swallowed hard again and shook his sister's hand to seal the deal and she passed him a bag of sovereigns, not that suspicious paper money the government had introduced, but gold. More money than he had seen in his life. He would need to find a good hiding place for it.

'Well if we are to reach Brigg by dark we ought to set off. You'd best make your goodbyes brother. We'll not visit again; it will unsettle the child.'

Chapter 2

William did not like this day one little bit. He felt sick with disbelief. What had he done wrong? He could not figure it out as he sat beside the woman who called herself his aunt. The only aunt he knew of was Lizzy and he had left her behind, along with the rest of his family, forgoing even the chance to say goodbye.

Dada had held him by the shoulders and knelt to speak to him so quietly he had to strain to hear him above the women's chatter. William ran the words through his head but they still made no sense. He was to be a good, brave boy and was lucky to be chosen by Miss Betsy Holtby, his aunt, to be her new son. He would want for nothing and even go to school. William did not want anything other than for his mother to rise from her grave telling him it had all been a mistake, and he certainly did not want school, whatever that was.

Dada had taken him out to the trap and lifted him on to the seat beside the strange woman. Had shaken his hand as though he were a man, then turned back into the cottage and closed the door with a finality that shocked him. William looked at the door in desperation even as his aunt turned the trap around and set off, the horse moving at a brisk pace. He began to cry well before they left the village and Miss Holtby handed him a handkerchief, no rag but a clean, white square of soft cotton. She told him to cry as much as he liked but when they got to Brigg he should cry no more. Her voice was firm but gentle and he stole a look at her between his tears and she smiled down at him with his father's eyes, a mixture of green and brown, which his mother called hazel.

She began to talk and he strained to hear over the clip-clopping of the pony's hooves and the raucous cry of starlings in the stubbly fields.

'How old are you William? I would guess five years old.' In spite of himself, he could not help but correct her with all the indignity of a six-year old being thought younger than he was.

12

'Ah then you must be of an age to get into mischief. Your father and I got up to plenty when we were your age.' She proceeded to tell him of misdeeds from her youth.

Gradually William's tears ceased and he looked at her with curiosity for she had a way of telling the story that made him forget his sadness. His father never talked about his childhood and William could hardly credit the antics he was hearing. It was the same kind of mischief that he and his sister Hannah got into, like scrumping apples from a neighbour's tree or painting their faces with bramble juice to make Mother think they were ill, and the tales they told on All Fools Day to try and trick his parents.

Betsy looked at William and noticed how his eyes shone bright and round with interest, the remains of his tears no more than salty streaks across his cheeks. They were driving on a track through the edge of Broughton Woods, the rooks' harsh cries and the lengthening shadows casting a gloomy presence about them. William caught a glimpse of Grandma Leaning's cottage in the distance, pointing it out to Betsy with excitement.

'Can we stop?' he cried. 'I want to see Bobbin.'

'Who is Bobbin?' asked Betsy, puzzled.

'Grandma's cat.'

'Do you like cats?' William nodded enthusiastically.

'Would you like one of your own?'

His nod was even more enthusiastic. 'A ginger Tom, just like Bobbin.'

'Well I'll have to see what I can do.'

William looked at his aunt in wonder. In his short life, he had never dared express a wish for anything. They all had to make do with what they had or 'woe betide', his father used to say. Did his aunt mean that there was a chance he might have a cat? William did not own enough words to express his confusion.

Betsy glanced at the cottage William had pointed out. it was tiny and mean, with an untidy and dilapidated thatched roof. She remembered that William's mother had been brought up on parish relief after her father died. Granny Leaning was evidently still as poor as a church mouse.

13

A slight shiver travelled up her spine as she thanked God for her luck in sidestepping such a fate for her old age. She felt no guilt in taking William from his family. She had already developed a real liking for the lad and meant to do her best for him. In return, he would recognise that and be grateful for it. Of that she had no doubt.

They drove out of the woods and into farm land; the harvested fields bare and black since fire had burnt the remains of the wheat, the smoky smell lingering in the air. She thought with sadness of her brother, widowed at an early age, and burdened now with a young family in a time of great hardship for farming communities.

Unlike most of her sex Betsy did not see marriage as security but a trap, unless lucky enough to marry money. She smiled grimly at the thought of her would-be suitors back in Grimsby who had made her life such a misery these last months. She was their prey; a spinster with means, still of an age to bear children. Well the laugh would be on them when they came to realise she had settled her money on William and, by God, she intended that the contract be watertight. They would soon leave her alone in peace.

She felt William's body slump against her and as she looked down at him saw that his eyes were closed, the dark lashes fringing his tear-stained cheeks. A sudden lump came in her throat and tenderness threatened to bring teardrops to her own eyes. I have a son, she thought, maybe not of my own body, but he is my flesh and blood, and I will love him, as long as my breath remains.

Chapter 3

William did not know where he was when he woke the following morning. He knew that his belly was empty. His stomach gurgled and groaned and there was a hollow, achy feeling inside. He lay in a truckle bed in a room larger than he had ever seen before. There was a thin sliver of light where the curtains did not meet. He did not know they were curtains for they were a rich, heavy material rather than the thin sacking which hung at the window at home. He moved a fraction, feeling the crisp, cotton smoothness of a sheet and a pillow at his head, but again he did not have the words for these. He was used to sleeping on his brother's straw mattress between thin scratchy blankets.

There was a sound at the door, a shy knock, and then it opened. A young girl walked in carrying a jug.

'Here's more hot water, Ma'am,' she said, as she placed it on a cupboard, before disappearing.

'William, are you awake?' His aunt shook the curtains aside, letting light flood into the room. She was already dressed but poured the water into a bowl and dipped her hands in to test the heat before drying them on a towel. 'Come here and I will wash you.'

William began to climb out of bed and realised he was bursting to relieve himself. He crossed his legs, looked down and was shocked to see he was not wearing the clothes he had on yesterday; instead he was dressed in a long shirt of fine material which almost reached to the floor.

'Take off your nightshirt, dear. It's a bit long, I was not sure of your size.'

As he did so, he hopped on one leg and clutched at himself in distress. His aunt pulled out a pot from beneath her bed and covered her eyes while he peed into the bowl in relief. When he had finished, she peeped through her eyes and laughed.

'Come here, little one, you must have been desperate. Let me give you a good wash down.' What he really needed was a bath: she could see the dirt ingrained into his pores.

He stood timidly before her as she took a cloth and ran it over his face, the water dripping onto the floor. He looked down as she scrubbed at his neck and his ears, surprised to see that he was not standing on an earth floor, but on wood. That must mean he was upstairs somewhere.

'Where are we, Ma'am?'

'The Angel Inn in Brigg, dear. There's no need to call me Ma'am, Aunt will do nicely. We'll take the coach from here to Grimsby where I live. We have a few hours until it arrives to do some shopping, and before that we can eat breakfast. You must be starving.'

The thought of food cheered him up. His aunt helped him into his clothes, although she tutted as he put on the torn, patched smock and ragged breeches. She imagined they used to be light brown, but were now a colour hard to describe, somewhere between the green of grass and the colour of the deep loam of Lincolnshire fields.

Leaving the bedroom, William followed his aunt down a wooden staircase. The solid wooden balustrades gleamed with polish. Scattered in the dining room were small tables covered by crisp, white cloths. The large table at the end of the room contained dishes of fat bacon, fried eggs and crusty, fresh bread and butter. He took a slice of bread, looking for a wooden trencher. His aunt seeing that he had only taken bread, piled a shiny, white dish with food until his eyes widened with anticipation and his mouth watered.

She had to show him how to use a knife and fork when all he wanted to do was pick up the food and cram it into his mouth. The saltiness of the bacon was indescribable and the yellow butter on his bread so creamy, he had to lick his lips and then stretch his tongue towards his chin to lick up any remaining juices.

His aunt smiled to see his pleasure. His table manners were appalling but never mind for today. She understood that everything was new to him, remembering her first day in the big house with the servants sitting down for breakfast, her eyes bigger than her mouth to see the amount of food on offer. As the housekeeper showed her around the house and explained her duties, Betsy noticed furnishings and comfort she could never have dreamt of. That morning cemented her vow never to go back to living in a labourer's cottage, with all the hardships that entailed. The long hours of menial work in the big house were preferable to the longer hours of a labourer's wife and with little enough comfort at the end of it. What would she have had to look forward to, other than endless pregnancies and a probable early death, like her mother, who died giving birth to twins. The bleakness of that time and the desperate attempt to keep the twins alive preyed on her mind, but milk soured so quickly in the summer months. She shook her head at the memory and offered William a beaker of tea to try, but he preferred the bitter taste of the mild ale he was used to.

'Well, Child, if you're finished eating we will go shopping. It is market day and I cannot have you arriving at your new home in those tattered old clothes.'

His aunt opened the door on to a bustling street. People were streaming towards the market place, some with baskets of wares on their head, others with empty ones in their hands, all impatient enough to knock over a small, bemused child. He grasped his aunt's hand tight as she dodged the horse mess and the stinking town drain running down the centre of the road, and guided him into a cobbler's shop.

The door opened on to a rich smell of leather, hanging in ghostly tendrils from hooks in the ceiling. The only light came from a small bow window where the cobbler sat at a battered wooden table.

'Am I to have boots, Aunt?' William asked in surprise. Even his oldest brother Tom never wore boots until he began work as a labourer like his father.

'No child, you are to have shoes. Sit on the stool there, by the window, and let the cobbler measure your feet.'

Shoes, only gentry wore shoes. The old man stood and came towards him with a piece of string and a wooden rule, an old clay pipe clamped firm between the dark stumps of his teeth. His hands felt calloused and horny as he measured each part of William's foot with the string. Stale, tobacco breath wafted over William as the cobbler leant over to measure the string against the rule that he had asked the child to hold.

'Can you have them ready within two hours?' his aunt asked, as she chose some brown leather. The old man hummed and hawed, but when he saw the gold of her sovereign, he demurred and bowed, knowing he had a sole prepared of approximately the right size, otherwise there would not be a cat in hell's chance. Two hours, he sniffed, what did she think he was? Did he have elves and fairies as helpers?

'Let's see if the market has some good second-hand clothes. I can't expect a draper to make up breeches for you before we leave.' They left the cobbler and made their way over to the stalls packed into the market square.

It seemed to William that everything was for sale. Housewives thronged around the stalls selling vegetables, apples, eggs, cheese and butter. If his stomach had not already been so full his eyes would have been out on stalks to see so much fare. Urchins, in rags worse than his, eyed the food for a chance to grab some, while the stall holders were talking to genuine customers. William watched as a tiny girl filched an apple while an older boy distracted the trader by jeering at him until the man threatened him with a good hiding. The girl turned towards William, her face grey and pinched from hunger. She saw him looking and stuck out her tongue, knowing he would not tell; after all he was dressed not much better than her, and ragamuffins stuck together.

Beyond the food stalls were rabbit skin sellers; attracting merchants from as far away as Hull, his aunt said. All he knew was that Hull was beyond the river, somewhere to the north. He had never seen the river in question, let alone the sea.

Finding a woman who sold clothes, William's aunt asked if she had any of the right size to fit him. As she scrabbled through a pile of garments William noticed the redness of her hands, they looked like lumps of broiled meat. She picked out a white shirt which had ruffles at the end of the sleeves and again at the neck.

'He'll look the proper little gentleman in this,' she said, handing it to his aunt, who first inspected the seams for signs of lice.

'You'll not find any of them buggers in my clothes, Missus, I launders them all in strong lye soap before I sells 'em.'

Aunt Betsy held it against William to check the size as the woman delved back into the pile of garments and pulled out a pair of breeches and a waistcoat to match, both the colour of eggy yolk.

'These 'as come from a good 'ouse,' Betsy shook her head at the impractical colour.

'Mebbe these then.' The woman handed his aunt some the colour of holly leaves and she held them against William's legs to check the size.

'They will do nicely, thank you.' The woman's meaty hands closed around the shillings she was offered and William was dragged away again, his new clothes folded into a string basket his aunt had dug out of her reticule.

'Stockings,' she said, before moving on.

Later, as William stood in the bedroom of the Inn in his new finery, he felt out of sorts. For a start wearing shoes and stockings constrained his movement. His feet felt heavy. How could he run in the stiff leather? His shirt was too white and clean. How could he climb trees without tearing it? When his aunt took him to a mirror, a small gentleman appeared in front of his eyes; the breeches and waistcoat had turned him into something he did not recognise. How would his family recognise him? But his aunt praised the changes and he wanted to make her happy after spending so much money, so he tried to smile.

A sudden hullabaloo put a stop to everything else.

'The stagecoach has arrived.' His aunt pushed him towards the window to look down on the most thrilling sight he had ever seen. Four splendid, sweating horses pulled a mud-splattered coach, piled high with luggage. Two uniformed men rode upfront and from within the coach several people peered out, their faces smiling to have reached their destination in safety.

'Let's go downstairs. We'll have about forty minutes to eat luncheon before we need to board the coach ourselves.'

Over the days to come William regretted his eagerness to see the horses and his abandonment of his rags lying discarded on the floor. Throughout the next few lonely nights he longed for a smell of home and family and the comforting thought that his mother had washed and touched his clothes. He was left with no reminder of his family but a sense of laughter and sadness left far behind.

Chapter 4

'Poor old Grimsby,' said his aunt as they trudged along a narrow lane to her house. 'It's seen better days.' They were passing a dilapidated thatched cottage, but to William it looked no worse than any other in his village.

He was weary after the excitement of the morning and the ride in the coach along deeply, potholed lanes. Aunt Betsy tried pointing things out to him on the journey but he felt a little sick after a luncheon of soup and steak and kidney pudding. He had eaten more meat in one day than he had seen in a year and it swirled around in his stomach, threatening to force its way back to his mouth. If it did, he knew he would die of shame, surrounded, as he was, by ladies and gentlemen in such fine clothes. He had not been able to stop himself from breaking wind but neither had the old gentleman sitting opposite, the other occupants wafting away the rich meaty smell with only a polite wrinkle of the nostrils and a hand to guide it elsewhere.

Before he knew, they stood at the door of a brick built house while his aunt fished around in her bag for a key. Upon finding it she drew it out with a flourish and unlocked the door.

'Well here we are, William. Welcome to your new home.' She pushed him gently forwards through the door into a spacious hall, with heavy oak doors off to both sides. The floor, tiled and polished, gleamed in what remained of the afternoon sunshine until the front door was pulled to behind him, plunging the house into gloom. His aunt led the way to the back of the house. The lack of noise and bustle from elsewhere in the house confused William. His aunt opened a door into a bright and airy room, with a door in the far corner leading to a scullery.

'Is this our room? His aunt looked surprised. 'Who else lives here Aunt?' William tried again.

'Why just you and me, William, then there's Lottie who comes in to help in the mornings. It's not such a big house. Shall I show you to your bedroom before I prepare some supper?'

'I thought there would be a family in each room. Aren't there any other children in the house?' William looked crestfallen.

Betsy gathered him in her arms. 'It's just you and me, my dear. We'll keep each other company, don't you worry.'

William was not convinced. As he lay lonely in his bed that night he longed for his family. This house was big enough for them all and more. He wondered why they could not all come to live with his aunt. He found the silence and the strangeness of the last two days unnerving. Tears came readily to his eyes and he longed for the warmth and smell of his brother's body and the snuffling breaths of his younger siblings, a comforting lullaby guaranteed to shush him to sleep. When he awoke the following morning, he found himself lying in wet sheets and not knowing how to hide the evidence, shame crimsoned his cheeks. His sobs summoned his aunt to the room but rather than anger, she displayed a tenderness he had not expected but lapped up like a puppy.

Once cleaned up, his arms snaked around her neck and his warm breath stirred the fine hairs on her cheeks. She and William sat still on the floor of his bedroom, his body wrapped in a blanket, rose scented soap on his skin. They drank each other in, silently; no words could describe the protectiveness she felt towards him and at last she understood the pain of loss which he was feeling. Why had she not thought of this in all her scheming? They were doing each other a favour that was all. But he must think that she had stolen him away from his family. How could his affection be earned by new clothes, a bedroom and good food alone? What was she thinking of?

'Shall we try getting you that pussycat you wanted?' she said, as she peeled him away from her neck and began to dress him. His eyes, which were more green than brown, studied her face and seeing a faint smile, he nodded.

'Can he stay in the house?' he whispered. His aunt pretended to consider the question and then laughed and ruffled his hair.

'Of course, he can, my love.' She was rewarded with a grin of delight. 'Let's go down and see what Lottie has prepared for breakfast, shall we?'

Lottie's love for small children oozed from her pores. No sooner had she caught sight of William than she enveloped him in her comforting, pillowing chest. Her slackening cheek gently slapping William's own as he breathed in the scent of the sugar and spices she had used to bake him a special treat. She held him away from her to take a good look, the deep lines covering her face crinkling, as she ran her eyes over him.

'Why you're a fine fellow, but you could do with a bit more meat on your bones. Never you mind; Miss Betsy here will feed you up. You're a very lucky boy having such a fine auntie.'

Lottie was around the same age as his Granny in Broughton and every bit as motherly and William took that as a good sign. But where his granny was taut and thin, Lottie's skin almost appeared too big for her body dimpling in all the wrong places. Likewise, her hair; It sprang from her cap in a grey balloon of curls, giving her a wayward appearance. William fell in love with her at once.

'Lottie, William wants a cat. Do you know of anyone who has any kittens?'

Lottie pondered for a several seconds. 'I'll have to ask around. Most people don't keep them, if you know what I mean.' She didn't want the poor little mite having nightmares about drowning kittens. She had seen his eyes light up with expectation when Miss Betsy asked her question.

As they ate their breakfast Betsy rethought what she had planned for the day. Starting his tutoring might be a step too far at this stage. It would do William no harm to be shown the town, such as it was. There was not much to discover. If the weather was fine tomorrow she could hire a pony and trap and explore further afield, perhaps visit the hamlets by the sea, a mile or two further South.

It was a cloud-free morning as they set off from Betsy's house in Chantry Lane. Looming to the right lay a large church framed by trees, the leaves beginning to change colour from green to russet. As they approached the centre of the town Betsy was greeted coolly by ladies and more warmly by the odd gentleman who wanted to be introduced to William, standing patient but curious by her side. One man in particular, shot William a frown when Aunty Betsy introduced him as her nephew and ward.

'I don't think that man liked me, Aunt,' he said, as they continued walking into the Bull Ring. She did not answer but a smile played around her lips.

An enticing smell wafted from a bakery on the corner and a gaggle of ragged boys and girls hung around it. If anything, they were more pinched and filthy than the children in Brigg. They looked expectant when they saw Betsy and she did not disappoint, scattering a few halfpennies at their feet while other customers looked askance.

'You really should not encourage them,' one of them said.

'Maybe you have never been hungry,' Betsy replied, standing her ground.

'There's far too many of them. Something should be done,' another opined.

'There's talk of building a bigger poor house. The one in Bethlehem Street is full to bursting,' said the first. Betsy shuddered and walked away, pulling William with her.

'What's a poor house?' asked William.

'A roof over their heads, scraps to eat and unremitting, pointless labour in return, while what the poor really want are jobs. Maybe this new dock they are building, will provide some.' William did not understand what she was talking about but did not like to ask more. He sensed she was irritated, but with him or the women in the bakery he could not say.

Changing the subject, his aunt explained, 'Years ago, they baited bulls here before slaughtering them for meat. Those days are gone now, thank goodness, but can you picture it William? Crowds of people watching and cheering, the bulls raging and the dogs wildly snapping at them, blood everywhere; it was considered entertainment, just like a hanging or throwing fruit at someone in the stocks.'

He tried to imagine, but it looked too peaceful. There were shabby houses all around and a three- sided fenced off area, which he imagined to be the Bull Ring, but all it contained now was a water pump.

Did you ever see it, Aunt? He asked.

'No, never, it had ended by the time I came to live here. Now it's just a fish and pig market.'

Moving on, they came to the narrow market place, scarcely more than a street, where the town's stocks stood. There were no market stalls that day but a few ragged children played around the stocks, shoving their hands through the holes whilst others threw whatever filth was to hand at them. William longed to join in their game and grinned at their squeals of laughter. Would his aunt let him outside to play? He hoped so.

On the east side of the market place was the Black Swan coaching inn where they had been dropped the previous evening. Walking towards it William could see only pastureland beyond it.

'Who would guess that the sea is only a few hundred yards away over there?' His aunt pointed away from the Market Place. 'To the east and west, all is marshland.' William saw sheep grazing in the distance. 'This was once a busy port, way back in history, but it silted up over the years. But now the town grows poorer every year,' she sighed, 'Pray God, not for much longer.'

'Can we go to the sea?' asked William in excitement, not listening to all the other things she was saying. The word 'sea' had a magic about it. He longed to see it.

'Tomorrow, if it is not raining, I will order us a pony and trap from the inn.'

After they had retraced their steps his aunt stopped in front of the new Town Hall.

'There is a schoolroom in there, William. Not yet, but in a year or two, you will come here to learn. What they teach you will open a door to a world where anything is possible, if you work hard and apply yourself.'

He decided his aunt spoke in riddles because nothing she said made sense to him. Perhaps his father had let him go to some mad woman. Homesickness fell over him like his mother's shroud and he started to drag his feet and look down at the muddy ground littered with stones, surprised that he could not feel them beneath his feet; maybe there was a point to shoes after all.

Betsy felt his sudden misery, but did not understand how his mood could change from one second to the next. I am going to have to learn to think as a child does, she thought. This was all harder than she expected, but her determination to win him round remained undaunted.

They walked home in silence with William only cheering up when Lottie presented him with a cup of milk and a sweetmeat to munch on. Why was it, he wondered, that rich people seemed to have lots of interesting things to eat? His tongue licked at the sweet biscuit in his mouth; it had a flavour he had never tasted before, both sweet and sour at the same time.

'Do you like that, William?' asked Lottie. 'Have another one, they're called Nelson's Balls, after our great admiral.' She chuckled and handed him another sweet before catching sight of her employer's face. She looked tired and dispirited. 'Why don't you play a game of cards with him?' whispered Lottie, hoping to ease her distress.

'He does not know his numbers?'

'Well maybe it's a way of learning?'

Betsy could have hit herself. She beamed her thanks at Lottie, who smiled to herself. Lottie may have no learning herself, but she knew how children's minds worked.

After dinner, Betsy took William into one of the rooms at the front of the house. He stood at the open door, peering in, not really believing his eyes. He had few words to describe the colours and objects within the room. The walls were painted a deep, rich cherry red with matching curtains at the window. On the polished wooden floor, rugs in jewelled colours, lay beneath small tables set around the room, one holding a globe, another, a lamp. On the mantel-piece, something gold ticked softly.

'Come, in child.' Betsy spoke gently, understanding his trepidation.

'Are you rich, Aunt Betsy?' his words mere breaths of astonishment.

'No, William, not rich.' She laughed and took a hold of his hand, drawing him in to the room, indicating a highly-polished chair beside an equally polished table. 'I like to think of myself as comfortable.'

'Why are you comfortable and my father so poor?'

'I am lucky and some of that luck I made myself. This house belonged to an elderly doctor. He needed a housekeeper and I applied for the job. What I did not know was that he had no relations, beyond an old and childless cousin in Halifax. When he gave up doctoring because his sight was going, he decided to teach me to read, so I could read to him all these books you see lining the shelves. Over the years, we grew close until he told me that he looked upon me as a daughter and I cared for him as a daughter should. He left me everything you can see and more beside. Not just the house and all its contents, but an income and a love of books. That is what I want to pass on to you, William, learning; it is the route out of poverty.'

She picked up a small book and opened it. Inside was a picture of an apple with two squiggles above and more below. 'What is that a picture of, William?'

'An apple, Aunt'

Yes, and do you see the letter, that is the letter A, A for apple, and this word underneath spells Apple. Once you have learnt these letters, and there are only twenty-six of them to learn, you can read. What do you think about that, William?'

He did not know what to think but nodded at his aunt because she seemed as though she wanted some confirmation of his ability to learn these letters. The thought frightened him. What if he should prove unworthy or stupid?

'Those lessons can begin another day. What do you say to a game?'

Games he loved so he nodded, this time with enthusiasm. Betsy walked over to a desk and opened a drawer, taking out a pack of cards. She spread them on the table face up so he could see the numbers and the pictures.

'Let's find cards which make a pair William?'

Picking one up with a picture of a king she asked him to find another card which also pictured a king. That's easy William thought. Within half an hour he was matching all the cards on the table and saying the name of the card as he picked them up to show her.

'Find me two cards with the number three on them. Oh, well done, William. Now find me those with a number eight.' Betsy was delighted with his progress and congratulated herself on choosing him. They would do well by each other.

'Tomorrow or the day after we will play the real game,' she told him. That's when we place all the cards face down and then try to make them into pairs again. But for now, come sit by the fire with me and I will tell you a story.'

William was enjoying himself and was happy to slip down on to the soft Turkey rug beneath the table and climb on to his aunt's knee as she sat in a rocking chair by the fire. Shadows were beginning to play in the room as the light began to fade, but his aunt lit a candle placing it under a coloured glass lamp, adding more warmth to the already sumptuous room. He lay back in her arms and she began to talk.

'Once upon a time there lived a giant...'

Chapter 5

The October sun shone weak amidst ash coloured clouds. As the hired nag breasted the hill and turned onto the cliff top lane, Betsy turned towards William, hoping to see wonder and excitement. All the way he had chattered about wanting to see the ships, but now his lips were pulled down into a frown of disappointment. Before them lay the wide river estuary; entrance to the German Ocean beyond. In the distance the Spurn of Yorkshire, a flat ribbon of land, snaked into the sea.

Why had William thought the sea would be blue? It wasn't, it was as brown as a ploughed field, the ripples of the waves not dissimilar to ridges of muddy earth, ready for planting. He saw a tiny sail on the far horizon. Was that a ship? It looked so small. Sometimes he and his brother, Joe, played pirates. That thought made him sad. He missed Joe more than anyone. How long would it be before he saw him again? They used to imagine ships as large and stately, with cannons and brave companies of sailors to see off Blackbeard, a name his mother conjured up to threaten her children with if they misbehaved. Just two weeks ago, after the church bells had rung to celebrate a great victory at the Nile, their game had turned into a battle between Nelson and the French. That single, tiny sail out there, so far away, was not what he had imagined a ship to be.

A few fishermen's cottages lined the low cliff where ragged children wove baskets as their mothers tended to holes in the nets. Smoke wafted from a nearby chimney where, his aunt explained, fish hung on hooks to cure. William wrinkled his nose at the pungent smell. He was not sure that he had ever seen a fish, other than tiny sticklebacks in the stream close by his house. Down on the muddy beach, a woman and two children bent double as they picked something from the mud, wicker baskets by their side.

'The tide is out,' said his aunt. 'We can leave the trap at the inn and go down onto the beach.' William looked unsure but his aunt jollied him along as they reached a brick building that grandly called itself the Dolphin Inn. A few fishermen sat outside smoking clay pipes and one of the younger men stood and held the horse as Betsy and William climbed down from the trap. She reached back up to take a hamper Lottie had packed for them, as an ostler appeared from the stables to take charge of the horse. After paying the man a few pence to feed and water the nag, she led William towards a path down to the foreshore.

At the bottom of the low cliff lay fine, pale sand. His aunt instructed William to sit and take off his shoes and stockings. Still unused to the feel of shoes, William needed no further encouragement and he was delighted to feel the soft, cool grains beneath his feet. As he began to look around he saw pale glints of something hard and shiny not far from his toes. He bent down and picked up one of them and then another, all different shapes and sizes, some pearly pink, some whorled with lines, some curved, others long and slim.

'Look at these, Aunt Betsy,' he stretched out his palm as she spread a rug on the sand for them to sit on.

'They're shells William.'

'Shells?' he queried.

'They're the homes of tiny sea creatures. They're all empty now, but there you have a razor shell, an oyster and there a cockle and this one is a winkle.'

He ran his finger over them, feeling the smoothness of the winkle, the sharpness of the razer shell and the roughness of the oyster.

'If you put the cockle to your ear, can you hear anything? Some say you can hear the wind and rippling waves. Do you see the women in the distance?' William nodded, his ear catching the sounds of waves lapping the shore. 'Well they are gathering cockles to sell. Shall we go and look?'

His aunt gathered her skirts to avoid the mud. She was wearing some scuffed, leather boots but William felt the hard ridges of cold, wet sand beneath his toes. He laughed as he stamped on worm casts, which scattered the muddy sand. As they neared the water the sand became squelchy and pulled at his feet, his heels sinking deeper into it. When he lifted his feet, they came up with a plopping sound which made him giggle.

He looked back at his footprints seeing pools of water settle into them. The shore was retreating into the distance.

'The tide goes out a long way here, William. It's dangerous to be too far out when it turns. You see the sand banks around us?' He turned his head and saw areas of the beach which were slightly higher than others and nodded. 'When the tide come in it swirls around these banks and sometimes strangers get cut off from the land and drown. Always be careful of an incoming tide.'

The cockle pickers were not far now, as was the water's edge. The woman began to stretch her aching back and called over.

'The tide's turning, Ma'am, best get back.'

His aunt shouted her thanks and was about to turn when William saw a ship sailing from the ocean. It was a real ship, as he had imagined, tall with two masts and sails that billowed in the winds. It appeared to ride on the waves like a great white horse. He jumped up and down with happiness, spattering globules of wet sand all over Betsy. She was about to admonish him before she caught sight of his face, rapt with delight.

'A ship, a ship,' he cried, looking around for his brother to share the excitement. Disappointment doused his spirits as he remembered he was alone with his aunt.

'Yes, it's a merchantman sailing to Hull, and there's another. They're queuing to catch the high tide. One day soon, we might get such ships sailing into Grimsby again.'

They stood and watched a moment longer as a line of sails appeared from the east. William was entranced. 'They will anchor there until the tide is high enough. Pilots will row out to guide them into the river. They don't want to hit any sandbanks,' explained Betsy.

The cockle picker, her wet skirts dragging in the sand, reached them. She carried a basket on her head, while two children, as young as William, almost sank under the weight of the basket they carried between them.

'You have had a good day, I see,' said Betsy, to the woman and received a cheerful smile in reply.

Betsy chivvied William to turn around and told him to run back to the shore as it was time for their picnic, while she strode smartly behind him.

They sat and ate a lunch of bread and cheese. William did not like the gritty sand invading his mouth. He tried to wipe it away with his tongue until Betsy gave him some cold tea in a jar to wash it out. William still preferred ale but his aunt did not. It was one more thing he supposed he must learn to like.

They watched the sea creeping across the sand towards them. Some parts of the beach became small islands for a few minutes, before eddies of water swirled over them until they finally disappeared, swallowed by the muddy waters.

'Sometimes a sea fret comes in with the tide,' Aunty Betsy told him. 'That's when it's the most treacherous time to be out on the sand. You can lose your bearings easily enough and head out to sea rather than back to shore.' William shivered. He was not sure again if he liked the sea. 'The fishermen never go out if it looks at all foggy.'

As if on cue, fishermen began to make their way down to the shore and their small upturned boats. William's body quivered as the wind got up and his aunt suggested it was time to go, but not before she had bought some fish for supper.

Beyond the Dolphin inn was a market place. It was nothing like the bustling market at Brigg, but there were half a dozen stallholders in front of some thatched, cob cottages. Betsy walked towards one that sold fish. An old man, his face wrinkled and weather-beaten sat on a stool beside it.

'How fresh is this whiting?' asked Betsy, pointing to one of the fish. William studied it. Not as big as some of the fish on the stall, it lay silver and gleaming and smelt of the sea.

'Caught this morning, Ma'am.' Betsy bent down to sniff, and with her nose satisfied, told him she would take it, along with half a dozen oysters, as long as he dressed the fish.

'When we get you your cat, William, we'll take the head, but as for now, I have no use for it.'

The man took a knife, wiping it on a piece of grimy cloth before deftly cut off the head and tail. He then slit open the stomach and removed the insides, tossing them to the ground. Whereupon, seagulls, screeching overhead, swooped and flew off with their prize before William had time to blink. Betsy produced a cloth from her hamper for the old man to wrap the fish.

As they turned away from the stall Betsy took a hold of William's hand and finding it cold to the touch, said. 'Now let's have a warming cup of tea before we head off for home.'

Betsy pushed William towards the fire in the Dolphin's back parlour and he ran to warm up his hands while his aunt ordered tea and a curd tart. When it arrived, she cut it in two and invited him to take half. William took a bite and his eyes opened wide. The light pastry crumbled as he bit into it then his tongue found the delicate, creamy curd filling and he licked at it, trying to make it last. He savoured it in silence and guilt as his aunt chatted to the landlady.

He wished he could share the tart with his brothers and sisters. It dawned on him that his life would never be the same, because his aunt meant to raise him up to be more than a labourer. How he wished that she would do the same for the rest of his family; it was unfair that she had singled him out for favour and he was certain he did not deserve it. His body shrank into itself with loneliness and guilt. What if he asked her to take Joe as well? The more he thought about it, the more he missed his brother. If he told her that, would she relent and write to his father? He imagined a scene where his brother stepped down from the coach and he would run to greet him. They would have such fun and he could show him real ships.

Running his finger over the plate to catch all the crumbs, he looked up at his aunt who wore a patient expression on her face as the landlady rambled on about her plans for the Inn.

'Times are hard Ma'am, especially since those Methodists stopped the follies. Every Sunday in summer we'd have crowds of farmers and labourers turning up for the fun. But them Methodists, they don't like people to enjoy themselves, do they? What's it come to if you can't have a little drink after church, hey?'

William wondered what a Methodist was. He would not like to meet one if they stopped you having fun.

'But I've had an idea and I would like your opinion, Ma'am. Bathing Machines!' A look of triumph appeared on the landlady's face. She expected some reaction from Betsy and seeing a slight nod of interest she carried on with her explanation.

'If only my Lord and Lady Yarborough would deign to come and give their blessing to the town, I'm sure we could make this the very finest of seaside watering places. We've ordered two of those machines; I have heard they are all the rage with the ladies in Brighton. Would you use one, Ma'am?'

Aunty Betsy looked rather horrified at the thought, but this did not deter the landlady. 'We could make our little village the Brighton of the East Coast, don't you think? After all it was nought but a poor fishing village before the Prince of Wales visited, and I am sure the air here is every bit as healthy.'

Betsy doubted that Cleethorpes could ever be a possible match for Brighton, so near to London. It was too difficult to get to Cleethorpes for anyone outside of the county. She smiled and wished the landlady well with her endeavours. Betsy finished her tea and tart within seconds and stood to discourage any further conversation.

She was pensive and quiet on the way back. Several times William tried to pluck up courage to ask his aunt to let Joe come to live with them. Each time he ran his tongue over his lips and opened his mouth to speak, he took fright, seeing her expression so distant and dour. His courage seeped away like water flowing from a bucket. She stopped the trap not long after they had passed a post mill and were nearing Grimsby.

'Do you see this, William? This may change our fortunes.'

Men were busy shifting mud in the marshy ground but it looked an impossible task. Wherever they dug, water filled the holes in an instant. Oxen dragged huge oak timbers towards men waiting to begin the hard labour of hammering them into place.

'What are they doing, Aunt?'

'We must look to the future, William. Never cleave to the past.' William did not understand her and once again he began to think her wits were addled.

'Once this war with France ends,' she continued, 'then we'll see changes. Mark my words, William, with a new dock, Grimsby will see better times and you must be ready, my boy. Do you see those men? Irish navvies brought in to build us wharves. Ships will be arriving here once again, bringing wealth and prosperity back to our little town, God willing.'

Chapter 6

It was two weeks since William had come to live with Betsy and high time his position as her heir be made official. She had no doubts on that score because her heart had been won over by him. Her barren womb had never betrayed her before. There had been no hankering for a child, no sleepless nights of yearning, no tears and no sign that she missed anything in her life. But now she could not countenance sending him back to his father and would fight if her brother asked her to do so. Not that he would, because she was sure that he had his hands full with the rest of his motherless brood.

Betsy had come to love William as if he were her own. Her passionate nature freed itself from the reserve she showed the world, allowing her whole body to respond with joy to his smiles, with misery to his tears and a fierce desire to protect him. How this had happened she had no idea, but she did not resist it. It gave her life a meaning she had been unaware was lacking.

Little William now had his kitten. Not the ginger one he had hankered after, but one mostly white with distinctive markings. Its face divided diagonally by a streak of black gave it a quizzical look. He named it Socks because of its black paws and white legs. It was amusing to watch William play with his kitten and then stroke its silky fur, because it mirrored her own reaction to the boy. She enjoyed teaching him and made most of it into games and she loved nothing better than sitting him upon her knee to tell him a story, her fingers often creeping towards to his dark, curling locks.

The kitten had certainly settled him down. There were no more night-time accidents. He smiled much of the time and was happy to go along with whatever lessons she had planned for him each day.

There was only one caveat. He had to get out and run around outside after lessons. She had discovered this the hard way. One afternoon she could not find him anywhere in the house and began to panic. She grabbed her cloak and ran out into the street but could not see him. It was only when she got to the market that she found him playing with ragamuffins near the stocks.

Outraged, she had marched him home. His sullenness, as she rebuked him for his behaviour, further upset her.

'But it's not fair,' he'd cried. 'I don't get to play with any children now. It's only you. And I hate being indoors all of the time.'

'You are going to be a gentleman and as such you don't get to choose who you play with. I will not be shamed after I have worked so hard for my place in this town.' She softened. Was it his fault that she had taken him from his brothers and sisters.

She began to take him out to the grounds of the old abbey every afternoon. He chased around the stones and played hide and seek with her. There they met a mother with a son around William's age, Robert, who came with a hoop and stick and William begged for one of his own. She was happy enough to oblige and content to sit with Mrs Sutcliffe as they watched the boys play together. Betsy was as delighted as William was to have discovered a friend. Robert was tall and fair while William was dark and small for his age. They played well together, avoiding the squabbles that so beset brothers and with William often taking the lead.

'Robert tells me that you are teaching William to read and write, Miss Holtby,' Mrs Sutcliffe had said the day before. 'Would you consider teaching my Robert too? I will pay of course. He will be going to the Grammar School at eight, but must know his letters by then. My parents neglected to teach me, being just a girl, and my husband lacks both patience and time. I had thought of sending him to the vicar but he's very deaf and by all accounts, is rather too fond of the cane.'

Betsy had floundered and was reluctant to give a definite answer. She decided to discuss it with Mr Dawson, her lawyer. Conscious that her status in the town was ambiguous, especially with the ladies, she did not wish to alienate them further. Mrs Sutcliffe, was a newcomer to Grimsby, although married to a Freeman. The other Freemen's wives often looked at Betsy askance. They believed that the position of Freemen in Grimsby, passed down from father to son ever since the days of a King in some bygone century, raised them above the hoi polloi. They appeared to judge her as no more than a servant, who had somehow wangled her way into a fortune by scheming or, heaven forbid, by providing more comfort than she ought. She knew the gossip, as unfair as it was, but she did not wish to cause tongues to wag further.

Betsy's appointment with her lawyer was opportune. Mr Dawson had been her employer's attorney too, as well as his friend. He had often called of an evening to take a glass of brandy with Doctor Taylor, sometimes interrupting whatever they were reading together. She had never minded because she was pleased that the doctor had company. Since his sight began to fail, he rarely got out, unless to church, where he clung on to her arm, sure that he would trip on the uneven street.

Mr Dawson treated her politely enough, but there was always the scent of disapproval which hung around him whenever he had to do business with her. He assured her that he would like to be of assistance in dealing with her affairs, and as an executor, he had that right. It wasn't distrust exactly, but there were hidden reservations when he greeted her. His pale, blue eyes appeared to look down, away from her face, though they were near enough the same height. It made her uncomfortable, as if she were a lesser being, or was it just that she was a woman? She had an inkling that he did not approve of women. His wife had died many years before but he had a spinster daughter, Alice, who kept house for him. There was no love lost between Alice and her father, that was apparent every time she saw them in church. Alice pretended to be the dutiful daughter but there were hidden depths in her eyes and distaste in her frown when she glanced at him. Betsy sensed the lawyer preferred a glass of brandy with the doctor than the company he had at home.

Betsy was sitting with William in the study when Mr Dawson arrived. Lottie showed the visitor into the drawing room, a room mostly unused now as few people called on Miss Holtby, or at least, few that were welcome. She left William to work on his letters and went to greet the lawyer.

'Miss Holtby, you are looking handsome today.' Betsy was nonplussed, it was not his usual form of greeting to her.

'Thank you, Mr Dawson. It must be all the fresh air I am getting, taking William out each afternoon.'

'William is your nephew?'

'Yes, and I wish to make him my heir.'

The lawyer frowned. 'Are you quite sure, Miss Holtby? How long have you known the boy? What if he does not turn out as you hope? Or you may marry and have children of your own.'

'I am quite certain, Mr Dawson. I have no wish to marry and want to make that clear by settling my money on William. He is already showing signs of natural intelligence and with my guidance he will grow to be a fine gentleman.'

With a slight shake of his head the lawyer made his disapproval known. 'Forgive me, Miss Holtby, I should like to meet the boy.'

Betsy stood to fetch William. As she re-entered the room she pushed him gently towards Mr Dawson.

'Come here young man,' he said. 'Let me have a good look at you. Do you like living with your Aunt?'

William turned towards his aunt, looking for some guidance. Finding none, he nodded almost imperceptibly, lacking the courage to speak to the old gentleman.

'Cat got your tongue, hey? I don't bite. What do you like about living here, young William?'

William coloured and looked once again at Betsy, this time she smiled and nodded her encouragement.

William drew a deep breath. 'I have a kitten. He's called Socks, Sir. And Aunt Betsy plays games with me and we eat meat.' His words ran together so fast that he wondered if the man had understood him, but he smiled and patted him on the head.

'Run along, young fellow, your Aunt and I have business to discuss.' William turned and ran from the room in relief.

'Well, Miss Holtby, he does appear to be a likeable, if unmannered child, but children grow up and we cannot always tell how they will act as adults.

A will can always be changed and if you marry it will be void, so my advice to you is to make a will.'

'No, that's not good enough, I'm afraid. Since my employer died, I have been plagued by a few so- called gentlemen calling and making their desire for my hand scarcely a secret. I want William to be my heir and I want it irrevocable. Then they will leave me in peace. I will soon be out of mourning and I expect offers to be imminent. You know Mr Fellows, he's the most persistent. He comes here with his insufferable sister and they both make my flesh creep.'

'That worthless scoundrel!' Mr Dawson looked at Betsy with some sympathy. She was a striking woman with her high cheekbones, a shapely-figure and a modest income. Oh, yes, she was bound to attract men, but he did not understand why she was averse to marriage. It was not his business, but he knew that his friend in leaving her the money had hoped she would find happiness, and, in his view, for a woman that surely meant marriage, didn't it? She needed the guidance of a husband or a father; all women did, but certainly not Mr Fellows. He would get through her money in no time, being far too fond of the ale house.

'Doctor Taylor knew full well my intention never to marry and he wanted to give me that independence. However, he did tell me he wanted me to do something good with the money. I choose to offer that to William. I want him to have the opportunity to make something of his life.'

Her firm and considered tone made the solicitor realise she was serious and, while he could not admire her attitude, he began to feel a little respect for her.

'Very well, I will draw up a deed of trust for the boy. In the meantime, please think carefully what that means. Until you sign nothing is fixed. I believe you should delay your decision-making for as long as possible, to give you a chance to change your mind.'

She thought it best to agree, although nothing would change her mind, of that she was sure.

'There is another thing I wanted to ask you, Mr Dawson. It has nothing to do with the estate but I ask for your advice as my late employer's friend. Is that acceptable?' He nodded, smiling, flattered to be asked. 'A lady I met recently asked me to teach her son his letters and I wondered about opening a small school, here in this room. It is rarely used. However, I am worried about the reaction of some of the town ladies. Do you think they will turn further against me?'

'A dame school!' Mr Dawson's feathery eyebrows rose to an unprecedented degree and Betsy had to stop herself from smiling.

He must think that she was rising way too far above herself. Ten years ago, she had been nothing more than an illiterate housemaid until Dr Taylor recognised something in her and gave her the chance to become something else entirely. While she could no longer remember that uneducated girl, she worried that many others still saw her as little more than a jumped up serving wench.

'Yes, I thought to start with just William and this other boy, Robert and then see how we got on. If the boys learn under my tutelage and if I enjoy the work, then I could advertise for other boys.'

'But you do not need the money!'

'I know that, Sir.'

'Well there is no doubting the need for a school for the younger boys, but are you..?' he struggled to find the word.

'Qualified to teach?' she asked, innocently. 'How many governesses are qualified? How many dame school teachers know more than their letters? Dr Taylor not only taught me to read and write but, whenever I read a book to him, he questioned me on the subject and taught me to love learning for its own sake. I may not speak French, nor can I draw but I have an understanding of plants and animals, the world around us, our nation's history, basic mathematics and so much more.'

Mr Dawson was shocked. He had no idea that his friend had taken things so far as to educate his housemaid. He knew she could read, sign her name and deal with household accounts, but so could many women, his own daughter one of them. But he discouraged Alice from reading anything other than the Bible. There was an article he had read some years before which suggested that reading novels could send women insane. They became too emotional, too hysterical for their own good. He tried to think of the town's reaction when Miss Holtby's learning became known.

41

Tongues would wag for sure, but with time the gossip may cease, if she acted with humility.

'I would not advertise,' he warned. 'By all means teach this other boy up to the standard needed for entry to the grammar school. If you succeed in that and do not draw attention to yourself then you may find the town clamouring for your dame school.' He believed she would fail, and in all probability, had an elevated opinion of her abilities. Doctor Taylor, his great friend, had been too kind to his servant and most likely praised her too much.

Betsy considered this and decided it was sound advice. Slowly, she might win people around, and if the other wives did not interfere with Mrs Sutcliffe's wish for her to teach Robert, it may work.

'Thank you, Mr Dawson, I will do as you suggest.'

The following day she told Lottie to mention to some of her servant friends that Miss Holtby intended to put all her money in trust for her nephew.

'Tell them it's going to be watertight, Lottie. Then see how the word spreads. I expect to see no more of Mr Fellowes and his sister after they hear that gossip.'

William woke one morning in December feeling more happy than sad. He could not consciously put that into words, but it was a feeling that made him warm inside, like a dish of hot chocolate that Lottie had made him when he had a head cold. Socks, despite his aunt's admonishment, always snuggled down in his bed and he felt the warm fur against his chin, his rough tongue lapping his neck. It ticked and he giggled. It did not feel so lonely in bed now that he had Socks.

He enjoyed Robert joining in with his lessons, and when they wrapped up warm and walked to the abbey grounds to play, he felt like bursting with happiness and energy. His aunt said he was like a dog straining at the leash and he pretended to be a dog, yapping and jumping up until she told him to stop, pretending to be cross. He knew she was laughing inside. He liked Robert as much as his brother, Joe, maybe even more, because Joe could be annoying at times. Robert had no brothers or sisters and he was as happy as William to have someone to play with.

William wondered how his family was getting on, but with less sadness because his aunt made him feel special in a way his mother never had time for. Betsy could not replace his mother but he was beginning to love her. He thought for a moment and realised that if his father came to take him home he would be sad to leave. He liked learning to read. Now that he knew all the letters and the sounds they made, he was beginning to put them together into words and he felt proud of himself.

On Sundays, he and his aunt went to church and the familiarity of the songs and the prayers soothed and anchored him to his previous life. Even the sermons sounded familiar, although he often got bored half way through. The vicar's preaching had a monotonous tone and his aunt sometimes had to shake him to stop fidgeting. It was the only time his aunt got annoyed with him. She sat up straight, in a pew towards the back of the large church, and expected him to do the same. Her face took on a stern and unyielding look, something she was not, but he noticed the frowning glances from other ladies, but didn't understand them. When she first wore her new grey dress and pelisse, the stares found their mark, but it only made his aunt sat up even straighter and her face showed no reaction. It was a shame because she was so proud of her new clothes. She told him that she had never worn anything but black since she left home to become a servant, and although her new dress was plain, it made her look like a duchess in his eyes.

St James's church was much grander than the church at Frodingham. It even had an ancient reclining statue of a knight by the door. When his aunt explained about knights, it led to all sorts of new games with Robert. They would pretend to charge around the abbey grounds on their mighty steeds, chopping at each other with stick swords. Sometimes they were Crusaders fighting the heathens and at other times they rescued princesses from castles, where they had been imprisoned by evil uncles. All from stories woven by Aunt Betsy as she settled William down in bed for the night, and reworked by William and Robert in games during the following days.

Outside the church were always plenty of beggars, especially since the weather had turned so cold. Most people shunned them as they left church. His aunt never did, but instead of scattering halfpennies, she gave them to William and asked him to share them amongst the neediest children. While he did this, she stopped to talk with Miss Dawson or Mrs Sutcliffe, to deflect attention from William.

At the end of November there was a day of thanksgiving for Nelson's victory at the Nile. The Town Council decided to hold a feast and an ox was duly slaughtered and roasted. William remembered it as a day full of joy and laughter. Following a church service of thanksgiving, the people streamed out to be greeted by the Town Cryer. Mr Robinson, the town barber in his day job, rang his bell summoning everyone, church and chapel goers alike.

'Come one, come all, our town awaits

Nelson's victory to celebrate'

The crowd laughed and clapped his cheerful doggerel, whereupon mummers in costumes made of colourful strips of cloth and wearing tall hats with paper flowers danced and sang the revellers into the Bull Ring. Serving girls, with hog-sacks of ale poured into tankards, offered it to the men. The women and children were given a weak but warm punch to savour.

The smell of roasting meat attracted the poor and comfortable alike and for once they mingled, happily content to enjoy the feast and festivities. Having eaten their fill, the mummers once again played their music and people began to dance. His aunt grabbed a hold of William's hands and pulled him into the centre of the Bull Ring where the remains of the bonfire, now little more than embers and bones warmed his feet. An occasional dog darted in to grab a bone and was kicked away by any dancing boot able to make contact. People moved to no recognisable dance but twirled and jigged around until giddiness overtook them. Those who could not dance, through age or disability, leant against the walls of the old tithe barn and clapped or cheered to see the fun. William noticed that some of them wore tattered uniforms. There was one man with a peg leg who tried to stand straight and tall with pride, but William watched him dab at his eyes with a rag, leaving smeary stains down his cheeks.

As darkness began to fall, William's aunt drew him away as the party become more raucous. Ale was flowing freely and the faces of the revellers, lit by the braziers, took on a more sinister appearance. William, tired but happy, held on to his aunt's hand as they walked the short distance back to their house. If anything, the music and laughter grew shriller, only ceasing when the substantial oak door closed behind them.

The snow lay thick on the ground by Christmas. Trees around the church glimmered with frost, their bare branches silver against a bright blue sky, but the beggar children huddled together in their rags, their faces grey and pinched in misery. When his aunt gave him some coins to distribute, he saw that they were pennies rather than halfpennies. She put her finger to her lips. When he had finished his task, and walked towards her, he overheard her lending support to the building of a house of industry. Ever since a child had been found dead of starvation and cold in an unheated hovel she began to change her mind.

'As much as I dislike the need for one, it is preferable to the situation we have now. Every Sunday we see more beggar children and no threat of putting them in the stocks will stop them.'

'It would be kinder to help them back to their own parish,' said Miss Dawson.

'But if they are from this parish, what then? The relief the town gives to its poor is just not enough in these difficult times. No child should die of starvation.' Seeing William beside her, Betsy broke off her conversation.

Miss Dawson looked stricken at Betsy's scolding. Betsy was not sure if Alice was a ninny without the capacity to think for herself. Her statements appeared to come straight out of her father's mouth, despite her apparent dislike of him. On the other hand, Betsy could not help but feel sorry for her. She suspected disappointment in her spinsterhood lay at the heart of Alice's trouble. She rarely saw her smile but she detected genuine warmth when her eyes gazed at William. The poor woman obviously longed for a child. Betsy wondered if she had ever had a suitor. Her father's need of a housekeeper may have caused him to chase any away. All she had was a boorish brother, an intolerant father, and her resentment of both.

William loved the Christmas carols they sang in church. His aunt reminded him of the story of the baby Jesus and he knew Christmas Day was special. At home his mother always put some meat in their pottage. She saved up for months to provide a little extra food and then the day after, they would walk up to the farmer's house where they would receive a gift, a few shillings for his father, a twist of sugar for his mother and maybe a pastry for the children. After receiving the gifts, the children would line up and sing a song of thanks and their mothers bob a curtsey to the farmer's wife. As they left, William would always glance back to the enormous yule log, which his father and the other labourers had helped cut. The warmth and glow from it enticing him to linger a moment longer.

His aunt's yule log was much smaller, more like the one his father brought to the cottage, but welcome all the same. Before lighting it on Christmas Eve, Betsy anointed it with oil, salt and wine,

'Will you join me in prayers, William?'

They stood together in front of the log and prayed that its fire would protect them from evil and the next year would bring prosperity. William thought of his family doing the same. He wondered if it was the wine which made the difference, because his mother had not been protected from evil. And, if he understood the meaning, prosperity had forever been absent from his family's life.

At sunset Betsy lit the yule candle, and they sat to eat Betsy's traditional supper of fish pie. 'Are you looking forward to Christmas Day?' Betsy asked William.

'Will we get to eat the pudding tomorrow?' It was a whole month since Lottie had called him in to the scullery to help stir the pudding with a wooden spoon. His eyes had opened wide to see everything that went into it.

'Thirteen ingredients in all to represent our Lord Jesus and his apostles,' she said as she showed him how to stir clockwise. 'It must be done from east to west just as the Magi journeyed to visit the baby in his manger.'

'Why is there a thimble in the pudding, Lottie?'

46

'There's more than a thimble, whatever you get on your plate will tell your fortune for the next year. Now make a wish, young man.'

William closed his eyes, the fragrance of the pudding assailed his senses, making it difficult to think. What was he to wish for? Should it be to see his brother again or for a ball. Robert had said he wanted a bat and a ball for Twelfth Night. William thought he might like one too, not that he'd ever received a present on Twelfth Night.

Lottie scooped up the pudding mixture into a muslin cloth and put it in a pan to steam. 'Now for the best part, William? Would you like to lick the bowl?' She presented him with a small spoon and he scraped the remaining mixture from the bowl into his mouth. It was even more delicious that he had expected.

When he woke up on Christmas morning it felt like a special day, although it started like a normal Sunday. In church, he gave thanks for the birth of baby Jesus. Outside, he inwardly repeated those thanks as he distributed the handful of coins his aunt had given him to children, white with cold and haggard from hunger. It was strange how their faces looked old and wizened underneath the grime and yet they were mostly no older than he. He thanked the Lord he had a warm home to return to.

Before they left for church he had sniffed some enticing smells coming from the scullery and he had seen Lottie preparing food the day before. He felt sad that she would not be eating with them, but celebrating the day with her own family. When they arrived home, his aunt sent him into the study to practise his reading while she finished the meal.

At last, with his stomach groaning its hunger, she called him through. William's eyes opened wide to see the deal table covered in a sparkling white linen cloth. On it rested a golden, roasted chicken, still steaming from the pan, with dishes of carrots, turnips and crispy potatoes. Decorating the table were strips of holly leaves with bright, red berries and a pair of silver candlesticks where fine, tapering candles gave off a flickering, magical light. He never failed to be surprised by his aunt's wealth. At best, his mother used to conjure up a turnip and potato soup with a few shreds of beef for Christmas dinner and they had been grateful for it. If one of their hens ceased to lay, she sold it for someone else to eat, the money being used for bread or cloth or tallow. If they were lucky, his father snared a rabbit. So long as the farmer was given the skin, he did not mind them having the meat, but there was little enough meat on a rabbit to feed all his brothers and sisters. Despite that, no one complained when it was rabbit stew day.

'Come, William. Sit and I will carve you some breast,' said his aunt. 'One day, when you're older, you will carve.'

The taste of that chicken, in rich gravy, with potatoes cooked in the meat fat was so delicious that he asked for more, but his aunt warned him that he might then not have room for any pudding. She went into the scullery to collect the dark, plump confection that he'd helped stir so many weeks before. He could see the steam rising from it, a holly leaf decorating the top. His aunt took a small bottle of brandy from the dresser and poured some over the pudding. William wondered what she was doing and was more mystified when she took a thin sliver of paper and put it to the candlelight. As soon as it caught she held it against the pudding and it burst into flames of blue and purple and orange before his eyes.

'Ooh!' cried William in delight, and again he cried 'ooh' when he put the mixture of fruit, nuts and candied peel, together with brandy butter in his mouth.

'Do you like it? Be careful, you might find a surprise in there.' William looked at his aunt with his mouth full of the sweetness of sultanas and currants and could only nod his head. Just then his teeth crunched down on something hard. It must be that thimble he'd seen. He took it out of his mouth and found not a thimble but a silver sixpence. After wiping it on his napkin, he held towards his aunt in puzzlement.

'It's a lucky sixpence!' exclaimed Betsy. 'That shows you will have a good year in 1799. It's yours dear; you can keep it.'

He had never owned a coin in his life and he could not believe that he had some money of his own.

'What will you do with it, dear?' asked his aunt.

'I think I must send it to my father. He needs luck,' said William.

'Don't you worry about that, my sweet, I have given him plenty of money.'

The pudding turned to gluey sludge in his mouth. He hesitated before asking in a plaintive voice, 'Did my father sell me?'

She looked at his stricken, tearful face and her heart contacted. How could she have been so unfeeling?

'No, no, don't ever think that.' She rushed to his side and took his face in her hands. 'Your father did not want to let you go. I needed an heir and I chose you. He took a lot of persuading but came to believe it was in your best interest. I compensated him for the earnings you would make when you became old enough to labour with him and I provided a dowry for your sisters. He is not so poor now, as long as he uses the money frugally.'

William thought about this, his mind churning to try and digest the information. It was difficult for his brain to grasp all that she had said, but he liked the thought that his brothers and sisters would have more to eat. He began to feel proud that he had been the one to help them.

'What's an heir, Aunty Betsy and why did you choose me?'

'It means that when I die you will have this house and my money. I want you to do something good with it. I chose you because I saw something in you that led to me believe you would do well in your life, given some help, which I can offer. As I said before, you could be a doctor or a lawyer, if you work hard.'

Why did she want him to work hard? He knew what he wanted to do, what he had always wanted, what his father and brother did. He wanted to work on a farm. He daren't say it. If he did she might send him back to his father and then he would have to give back the money.

Chapter 7

The snow showers of December turned to blizzards in January. Being so close to the sea usually meant that the coastal towns escaped the worst of the winter weather, but not that winter. It was so cold that William found the hairs in his nostrils and eyebrows froze whenever he ventured outside. It almost hurt to breathe, despite the woollen mufflers and hats they wore. There were days when it was too cold or the snow too thick on the ground for Robert to attend their lessons and for William to go outside to play in the afternoon. He became fretful and sometimes his whining made Betsy impatient and he caught the sharp side of her tongue, which she regretted instantly. She did her best to make amends with a game of snap or some other pastime.

As the war against the French demanded ever more men, Mr Pitt, the Prime Minister, demanded ever more money to pay for it. In January Betsy was horrified to learn that a new income tax was to be introduced. While she had an income that was comfortable, it was not excessive. Now she must pay an additional two pence in the pound to help fund this dreadful war, and all the while prices were rising. She had totted up the amount she would need to keep house for the year and had given her brother what she felt she could spare. This new tax and the increasing prices of meat and bread made her situation much more precarious and her miscalculation weighed heavy on her mind. A dark cloud enveloped her in worry every morning when she woke and grew thicker throughout each bitter, snowy day.

After the third day of thin vegetable soup, William threw a tantrum. Betsy lost her temper and smacked him.

'Don't you come that tone with me, young man,' she snapped. 'You should thank your lucky stars you're not still in that hovel I rescued you from.'

William held his hand to his smarting face, his eyes wide with shock.

Betsy did not apologise or try to comfort him. She pointed to his plate and told him to eat. He picked up his spoon, twirling it listlessly around his bowl, tears falling onto his shirt sleeve. The meal continued in silence. Betsy did not feel ashamed of her actions. The boy was in danger of becoming too spoilt. She had overindulged him, giving in to the pleasure of his smiles. Her happiness fed on his. If that continued he would become too weak, she saw that now. He must grow up strong and able to cope with hardship and setbacks, just as she had to. This winter was proving to be one of those times.

Betsy was thankful for the few shillings that Mrs Sutcliffe paid for her son's lessons every week. It meant she could keep Lottie on. She had kept the house running while Betsy nursed the doctor during his last months of illness. The one thing she could not countenance was losing Lottie, who depended on her scant wages to feed her family.

Everyone was suffering from the weather. Progress on the new docks had come to a temporary standstill and little by little the town began to take on an air of desperation as it sank into hibernation. People did not venture out if they could help it and traders and shopkeepers also began to suffer. Mr Brown, the ironmonger, was desperate enough to hold a closing down sale. The panic on his wife's face at church spoke of a future which was unthinkable. Betsy could hardly look her in the eye.

One Sunday the vicar announced that the King had declared a day of fasting for the war effort. There was a snicker of wry laughter amongst the groans of the congregation. Afterwards it was all anyone could talk about.

'He wants us to eat barley bread, even the poor won't touch that,' declared Mr Dawson. 'I'll be damned if I'll eat it.'

'The price of white bread is becoming extortionate, Papa,' Alice said.

Betsy saw the look of annoyance flash across her eyes. 'It is and I wouldn't be surprised if the baker isn't mixing chalk with it. The last loaf I bought was distinctly unappetising.' Betsy thought it important to take Alice's side these days. She knew how tough she was finding it to manage on the housekeeping allowance her father gave her.

'Did you hear about the food riots?' Alice asked.

'It's hardly surprising,' Betsy sighed, then caught the look of disgust on Mr Dawson's face. 'I mean it's reprehensible, but if people are starving... Oh!' She tried to keep a straight face as a snowball landed on Mr Dawson's chin and dripped down on to his muffler. His expression of shock and fury made even his daughter turn her head, as she attempted to disguise her smile.

All conversation died as snowballs began to rain down on them. No one could run fast enough on the icy path to catch any of the vagabonds to deliver a deserved wallop.

Billy laughed aloud, wishing he could join in. His aunt silenced him with a glare. Although he knew that his father would have done the same or worse for complaining about the food, he still felt stricken about her reprimand two days before. He was so dependent on his aunt's goodwill that her harsh words unsettled him and for the first time in a few weeks, he longed for his family's comfort, wondering how they were getting on without him.

Betsy also wondered how her brother was doing during this frightful winter and was thankful he had the money to see him through it.

Spring brought little let-up in the weather. Where snowdrops should have appeared in the churchyard, they hid beneath the ice. Daffodils struggled to show their leaves let alone any sign of their welcome yellow trumpets. Cherry blossom buds fell, unopened and desolate, onto the frozen ground while Betsy listened for birdsong and found it sparse and desultory. She put out crumbs each day hoping to keep the robins and blackbirds alive. Each morning she scraped away the frost from the inside of her bedroom window, on the chance that she may glimpse of a tiny, red breasted bird. The snowman which William and Robert had made by the back wall in January remained standing, its shape softened and blurred by further snowfalls but its coal pebble eyes stared out, bleak and accusing. Betsy shivered to see it. Had God forsaken his people? The church was fuller than ever on Sundays, everyone praying for deliverance from this dreadful winter. Their voices raised in songs of hope and contrition. The sermons making it clear that this winter was a judgement from God.

Some snow continued into April and the east winds blew in with a biting force. Men and women both huddled into their cloaks if forced to venture outside. A nod of greeting to their neighbours, rather than a pleasant stop for a gossip was the order of the day. It seemed to Betsy that the town was closing in on itself; soon all motion would cease as it began to die, slowly around her.

Betsy kept silent and strove not to make her money worries known. She did not want to upset William or Lottie, whose very existence depended on her wages and the little parcels of food Betsy gave her. The halfpennies she gave away on Sundays dwindled to farthings, although it broke her heart to see the looks of despair on the children's faces. They rarely ventured out of whatever hovel housed them, smokeless chimneys allotting them no warmth or comfort. Instead toothless crones stood peering out of grimy windows, hobbling outside to approach any foolish passer-by, crippled hands outstretched, "For the chillen, Mistress" they whined. Betsy never failed to give a farthing or two; the grey, pinched faces of the children haunted her dreams. She wondered how many had survived this appalling winter. There was no doubting that the pauper's area of the graveyard showed evidence of recent activity. How the gravediggers managed to chip through the frozen earth, she did not know.

Secretly she walked around the house at night looking to see what she could sell if things got too bad. It pained her to betray her benefactor who had built up his collection of objects over so many years. She fingered his collection of oddities, a tiny circular shell that looked like a snail, a piece of amber, the skull of a bird; these she would keep for William. Her glance moved to the mantelpiece, the gold carriage clock, a jasperware vase, a silver christening cup. No not the christening cup, it had been the doctor's dead son's and one day it would belong to William's son.

She remembered the doctor's excitement when any new parcel arrived from London and he demanded a knife to cut the string. Even though his sight was failing he would stroke the leather bindings of new books, and gently slit the pages, then tell Betsy she had no need to dust or prepare his dinner but must sit down and read to him. She read of many things. Each time she hesitated over new words or passages, he would explain with utmost patience about philosophy or natural science or history. His interests were wide and his bookseller knew it. She scanned the bookshelves, often pausing to take a favourite down only to replace it knowing she could not let it go. They had become her friends.

There were so few people in the town who would want to buy any of the curiosities the doctor revered. Amongst the Freemen were only a handful of professional people; for the most part they were small shopkeepers or tradesmen and many were labourers. Most grazed a few animals on the marshes to eke out their wages. Who of them would want to read these books?

Doctor Taylor always told her that it was a good job he had an inheritance from his own father because he would never grow rich from treating the Freemen of Grimsby. Most could only afford a doctor when in dire need and would neglect to send a bill or chase those who did not pay. Having said that, he was also scathing about the venality of the town, especially at election time and Betsy often wondered why he had never chosen to go elsewhere, somewhere he would be more appreciated. Being no Freeman himself, he had no vote or say in the affairs of the town he liked to criticise. She suspected that he had long given up on ambition and settled for an easy life surrounded by his books.

One day in March, when they began to use the study again for lessons, William noticed that the gold clock on the mantelpiece was no longer there. He missed the soothing rhythm of its ticking. On a shelf below the books had been a glass decanter and a set of brandy glasses, but they too had gone. He wondered what had happened to them.

In April, Colonel Loft with his militia arrived in town, their red coats bright against the remains of the snow in the Bull Ring. William was excited to see them but Betsy knew they had one aim in mind, to recruit Freemen with the promise that if they voted for Colonel Loft at the next election, they would be excused military service. He was a rogue, and who would dare risk signing up? There was no guarantee they could avoid military service.

The day after, she came upon Lottie in the scullery sobbing quietly into the stew she was preparing.

54

'That's not an onion making you weep so, Lottie. What's the matter?'

'It's, Sam, Miss Holtby, he's gone to be a soldier. He said there was nothing for him around here.'

Sam was Lottie's youngest son, just turned twenty-one and now a Freeman, though a poor one. Betsy's heart bled for her, knowing how she idolised him.

'He said he wanted to give me the bounty but once he'd accepted the King's Shilling they told him he would need most of the bounty for his uniform. He managed to give me ten shillings, as if that could stop my heart from breaking, Miss.'

Betsy took Lottie in her arms and hugged her. Like any mother, Lottie would be worn down with worry until the boy returned.

'He probably won't be sent to war. It's another of Colonel Loft's tricks.'

'I hope you're right, Miss. He's a good boy. He promised to come back one day.' Lottie snuffled and blew her nose into a rag from her pocket.

One advantage that Grimsby had over Hull was that the Press Gang never made an appearance. Sometimes Betsy wondered that the town survived at all, its population dwindling to the hundreds rather than the thousands it once boasted.

In late May, a terrific storm heralded the end of winter, although anyone witnessing it believed it to be more likely the end of the world. William woke, terrified to hear roaring and howling from outside. He felt the bed shaking and so too, the floor. He grasped Socks and cried in such fright that his aunt ran into his room.

'Shush, William, it's a strong gale. Don't be afraid. It will pass soon enough,' she soothed, despite her own misgivings. The wind rattled the doors and the windows, searching out any gaps so that the air in the bedroom stirred like an invisible hand, shaking the curtains, the bed clothes and ruffling the thin rag rug on the floor. At that moment, a gust blew so strong that a crunching, sliding noise above convinced William that some monster was running across the roof and he cried out again.

'It's just a tile moving. Listen, there's another one,' she confirmed as a second tile dislodged. She mouthed a silent prayer that the whole roof wouldn't go. She had no money to replace it.

'Shall I get into bed with you, William? We can look after each other.'
He nodded, grateful for his aunt's protection.

'Budge up then.' She put her arms around him and he laid his head on
her chest and as the wind at last began to die down, they fell asleep.

Everyone was up late the following morning. When Lottie arrived, they
had still not dressed.

'It's a sorry sight outside, Ma'am. There's many a thatch gone, a tree
down and branches blocking the lane by the church. I was that scared in
the night, I thought 'Old Nick' had come for us all. I've never known a storm
like it.'

As Lottie raked the ashes in the hearth of the back room, Betsy looked
out on her garden. Last week she had delighted to see signs of returning
life. Now, the burgeoning leaves had blackened and shredded in the
furious gale and branches, snapped from the cherry tree littered the
ground. She worried about her brother. The harvest this year would be
poor, which meant higher prices. She sighed, wondering what else she
could sell.

At last the weather improved and the congregation gave thanks to God
and the people celebrated by walking outside and greeting friends with
smiles of relief and gossip. Betsy took Robert and William to the new docks
to see how they were coming on. Some progress had been made and there
was talk that the docks may be opened in less than two years. It was a relief
for William to be out of the house and he begged his aunt to go to the
abbey fields; he wanted grass and open skies; trees and hedges. He was
sick of the narrow, winding, barren streets of the old town and most of all
he wanted to run and play with Robert, screeching, shouting, laughing,
chasing, anything that did not involve sitting at his studies. Aunt Betsy
agreed, having missed watching him play.

Mrs Sutcliffe arrived one morning with two thin booklets.

'My husband thought that these would be suitable reading matter for
the boys. He bought them from a peddler and was impressed by the
message they contained. He asks that you use them in your lessons. I think
he intends to question Robert on them.' She looked apologetic.

Betsy took the pamphlets and thanked her for the thought, inwardly grimacing at the thinly veiled instruction.

'I will read them and decide how best they may be used.' Betsy always thought it prudent to give herself time to judge how she should react.

Later that evening, when she had time to herself, she sat and opened the first poorly printed volume; its paper cover and title instinctively made her suspicious. Are these what Doctor Taylor called chapbooks, she thought? He had not been against them, at the cost of a penny they brought reading to the masses.

BLACK GILES THE POACHER: CONTAINING SOME ACCOUNT OF A FAMILY WHO HAD RATHER LIVE BY THEIR WITS THAN THEIR WORK, BY HANNAH MORE.

As she read the moral tract her cheeks flamed. Was it directed at her by the Freemen for handing out coins to the beggar children? Black Giles was every bit as bad as he was painted in the story and died a penitent death for his sins. But not all Grimsby's beggar children were products of evil, wastrel parents. What about those whose fathers had died serving their country, or from illness, perhaps? She sighed, recognising the awkwardness of her situation but wishing she could shout out her feelings of frustration.

Neither the poor nor women have rights, but must wait for their reward in heaven. She knew that, had always known it, but was it wrong to want something different? For William, it will be better, she promised herself. All her ambitions would be directed through him. He would be a doctor and as the doctor's aunt and housekeeper she would obtain an unquestionable position in society.

Gingerly, she picked up the next booklet. The title was *Village Politics* and took the form of a dialogue between two men; a blacksmith and a mason. One propounding the ideas in The Rights of Man, the other refuting them and he, naturally, was the winner of the argument. Why? You only had to look at France to see the results of 'liberty' and the folly of allowing the populace to have a say in government.

Her heart hammered in her chest. Did the town think she was a radical? What could have given them that idea? She was always careful in her speech and words. After all, the terror of the guillotine remained fresh in everyone's minds. No, she should stay in the place allotted for her, the message from these two booklets, was clear. Throwing the booklets back on to the table, she wished she could talk to Doctor Taylor. She missed their conversations and felt so alone with her thoughts.

'Betsy,' he would say. 'Believe in a merciful God. Do what you think is right and just. Let God judge you, not others. Care not for gossip and prattle. She sighed, it was easy for him to say that, not so easy for her.

These were no books fit for six year olds and she would not use them in her lessons. She would tell Mrs Sutcliffe that she preferred teaching the boys to read Bible Stories, the word of God being all the guidance young children needed. No one could argue with that.

Sighing, she stood and walked to the bookcase and took down her copy of Paine's The Rights of Man. She meant to read it once more and then hide it. If someone were to see it, William would suffer and that she must not allow. One day, when the war was over, she would like to read it with him and see his eyes open just as hers had.

Betsy realised that she did not know when William's birthday was. Probing him she found that he did not know either. It was a good excuse to write to the vicar of Frodingham and enquire about her brother and to ask for William's baptismal date. She received an answer within the week. It seemed William would be seven in the first week of July. His family had all survived the winter. Although many villagers had to apply for poor relief, the Holtby family had not. Betsy smiled; her brother had been sensible and used the money she had given him. She decided to hold a birthday tea for William and invited Robert and his mother, Lottie of course and Mr Dawson and his timid daughter; a poor gathering for a boy, but who else was there?

The day dawned bright and sunny for a change and Betsy wondered if a trip to the seaside would not have been better, but it was too late to alter her plans. At three o'clock the guests arrived and William greeted them as his aunt had instructed, with a bow and a 'Welcome, thank you for coming'. She was proud of him; his manners were now impeccable in comparison to the boy who had arrived here only nine months before. Robert gave him a spinning top as a present and the boys ran off into the garden to see if it would work on a flat stone.

'So how is the teaching going?' asked Mr Dawson.

'You had best ask Mrs Sutcliffe,' replied Betsy.

Mrs Sutcliffe smiled and said, 'Very well, I believe. My husband only last week required Robert to read a verse from the Bible and the boy managed it very well.'

'Will he be ready for the Grammar school by the time he is eight, Miss Holtby?'

'Oh yes, Mr Dawson, I think so. I am also teaching them to add and subtract and some elementary geography, using Doctor Taylor's globe.'

Miss Dawson looked at her father with annoyance. 'Why is it, Father, that if book learning is acceptable for Miss Holtby, that will you not let me do a little reading? I hear that the novels by Miss Burney are very entertaining.'

Mr Dawson frowned at his daughter, shuddering with distaste. Betsy was keen to bring the subject back to the boys' education.

'I intend to go to the Grammar School shortly to ask what else is needed before the boys enrol.'

'You mean before Robert enrols.' he said.

'William too. He will go as well.'

'Oh, my dear Miss Holtby, he will not be allowed to attend. The grammar school is only for the sons of Freemen. I thought you realised that.'

Betsy looked at him in confusion and panic. It had never occurred to her that William would not attend the only school in Grimsby.

'I will pay of course. I know the Freemen's sons receive free education, but surely, they will accept William, if I pay. Doctor Taylor told me that he paid for his late son to attend.'

'They changed the rules when the new master was appointed before the war.' Mr Dawson shook his head with some embarrassment. His daughter cast her eyes down; she understood how disappointment felt and she felt sorry for Miss Holtby.

'Could you not ask Mr Sutcliffe if an exception can be made?' said Betsy turning towards Robert's mother with pleading eyes.

'I will ask, but I think they keep strictly to the rules,' she said, quietly. She had realised months before that Betsy wanted to send William to the school with Robert, but had never dared to say anything. The shame brought pink to her cheeks. She had not wanted to upset the arrangement she had with Miss Holtby; it was too beneficial to Robert. She flinched from the accusing look in Betsy's eyes.

The tea party was ruined. Betsy did her best to stay cheerful for William who came running back into the room at that moment, with Robert in tow.

'Is it time for tea yet?' The boys chimed. Betsy nodded, unable to speak, and they sat down at the table to gorge themselves on bread and pastries, before Lottie brought in a cake, decorated with sliced strawberries and sugar.

Betsy was not a woman to be thwarted, so she visited the school on the following Monday. She would never have dared to open the door to the schoolroom, let alone, march in when she was in service, fearing the scholarship she would find inside would overwhelm her. Lessons were finishing as she walked into the classroom and boys were scrambling to exit into the street and the remains of a hot, summer afternoon, leaving behind an unmistakable odour of maleness. The schoolmaster, Mr Wilkinson, was gathering up slates from the ancient desks.

Putting down the slates, he greeted his visitor shyly, unused to women barging into his classroom.

'I have come to enquire about my ward beginning school when he turns eight,' Betsy began. 'I am willing to pay as he's not the son of a Freeman. He is a good boy and will not be any trouble and is reading already.'

The schoolteacher looked apologetic. 'I am bound by the rules of the Corporation, I'm afraid, Ma'am. Only Freemen sons are allowed.'

'A headmaster can always do with more money for the school. You could buy more books.'

'They will not agree and it's not up to me,' he smiled sadly. 'They are not that interested in the school or education either, for that matter.'

Betsy was puzzled, but she tried another tack. 'Perhaps you would give my ward some private tuition?

'You say he can read already, I can teach him grammar and accounts, my Saturdays afternoons are free.' He looked hopeful. His salary of twenty pounds a year could always do with supplementing.

'That I can do myself; it is Latin and the sciences which he needs. I would like him to become a doctor.' She watched the interest drain from his face.

'I do not have that knowledge myself, dear lady. This is a small town and the Corporation pays me to teach what they want, which is reading, writing, grammar and accounts. There is no call for Latin or Greek here. Have you tried the vicar?'

Betsy left the school disheartened and furious with herself. Why had she not thought to ask before? She had raised the boy's hopes. She did not approach the vicar; he was old and they were waiting for a new curate. She knew she could not afford a private tutor who would demand an annual salary. What did she know of schools elsewhere and could she afford their fees and his keep? She stopped off at the apothecary's shop as a last resort. Would Mr Marshall be interested in taking William on as an apprentice apothecary and surgeon when the time came? He would not, the boy's age and his own advancing years were against it.

The sunlight had disappeared from his aunt's face, thought William over the following weeks. He could not understand why a permanent frown replaced her smile during lessons; Robert noticed her sharp looks too and felt they were often directed at him. When William could bear it no longer, he asked her, as she tucked him in for the night, why she appeared sad, fearing it was his fault. She sat down next to him on the bed, her face shadowy in the candlelight, the thick curtains drawn against the midsummer sun.

'You know how we talked about you going to school when you're eight?' She paused, stroking his hair while she found the words. 'It seems they will not take you because you are not the son of a Freeman. It makes me very upset because it puts paid to your becoming a doctor or a lawyer because I cannot teach you to a high enough standard. I have been to the

61

school and offered to pay but they will not budge, nor does the master have sufficient skills. We could look at sending you away to school but I fear that may cost more money than I can afford, and I would miss you too much.'

William butted in, not all disappointed. 'Does that mean I can be a farmer after all?' he asked.

'A farmer, is that want you want to be? Not something more professional?'

'Oh yes, Aunt, I really do. I like our lessons but I would much rather be outside in the fields. I want to have cows and a few pigs.'

His aunt laughed in relief whilst ruffling his hair, 'And I thought you would blame me because I had deceived you into thinking you could become a doctor or a lawyer. Why William, if you want to farm, that is what you will do. I will see to it. In fact, you will be able to have your very own farm, small maybe, but perfectly possible.'

William's eyes shone in delight. His own farm! Perhaps Joe could help him on the farm or even Tom. He hugged that thought to himself as lay his head down to sleep.

Part Two

William

1813-1821

Chapter 8

William walked into the farmhouse kitchen for breakfast, having first washed off the worst of the summer dust from his hands and face.

"I'm so thirsty Mrs Hackney, I reckon I could drink my weight in ale. It's a warm day out there.'

'Here's a note for you, William,' she said, holding out her hand with a sealed letter. 'The boy said it was urgent.'

Taking the note, he recognised his aunt's seal and ripped it open. As he read his expression became grave. 'Oh, Miss Alice is dying. My aunt wants me to come and see her before it's too late.'

'You must go of course, but first have something to eat, William. Reuben will saddle the mare for you.' Farmer Hackney nodded to his young farm hand, who rose from the large pine table, stuffing the last of his bread into his mouth before leaving to do the farmer's bidding.

Mr Hackney was a good and fair master and over the last seven years he had taught William everything he knew about animals and working the land. When her ward turned thirteen, Aunt Betsy had enquired of the market stall holders if they knew of a farmer who would be willing to offer a place to William. Eventually, after several weeks of trying, she chanced upon Mrs Hackney, whose own son had recently joined the army in search of adventure. She said she would ask her husband if he was willing to help and the message came back, yes, the following week.

Betsy had driven William to Hatcliffe on a pony and trap, a bag of belongings at his feet. Both excitement and trepidation gripped him. His aunt had inspected the farm and his lodgings while he trembled with the fear that she might not let him stay. Eventually satisfied, she handed the farmer a pouch of coins for William's keep until he became useful and it was settled. He was to stay there and become a farmer. William had no regrets. From the first day, he loved the work and the surrounding countryside.

Now that the war was ending, the farmer's son had written to say he would return to help his father. When that happened there would be no place for William. He did not mind. It was time for him to strike out on his own. He had already made enquiries about taking on the tenancy of a farm near Laceby, following a tip from Mr Hackney that it was about to become available. William had saved most of his wages for the last three years by being frugal, but doubted it would be enough to satisfy the land agent. He would need to enquire about a loan with his aunt standing as surety.

By the time William had changed from his filthy work clothes the bay was ready. She was a solid and patient mare, not the fastest horse but what did a farmer want with a horse built for speed? It was a beautiful day for a ride; the early August fields promised a bountiful harvest, the first in four years. The last three had been very poor, but prices remained high because of the war and the farmers had done well.

In another week, everyone: men, women, and children would be out in the fields lending a hand. The golden wheat stood straight and tall and William offered a silent prayer for the weather to hold. On the lower hillsides around Hatcliffe, sheep nibbled their way through the sweet grass, a few lambs remaining to replace the breeding stock. He loved the Wolds: their narrow, mysterious valleys; wooded hills; the dappled sunlight playing on honey coloured stone houses and a sense of time standing still. It brings peace to the soul, he thought as he rode on towards his aunt's house.

The old mare knew her way the ten miles to Grimsby. He had been riding her there once a month since Betsy had placed him with the farmer. Through Beelsby he rode, dropping down towards Laceby, his thoughts turned to Alice. Dear Alice, whom he had not liked at first, and he suspected his aunt felt the same. Alice's pasty complexion and sour expression only added to her air of unhappiness, which never led people to warm to her while she lived with her father. She had begun to call on Aunt Betsy when Robert began at the grammar school and he was left to his solitary lessons. He still enjoyed getting out of the house in the afternoon but loneliness had threatened to consume him. He could not get used to seeing Robert with other boys, other friends, not him. Boys of his own age, who were not at school, had already embarked on working for their fathers or became beggars swept up into the new House of Industry. He missed the memory of Joe, his brother, but never brought him up in conversation with Betsy. That part of his life was over for now and no good would come of dwelling on it.

It was Miss Alice who accompanied them on their outings and slowly she won them round, or perhaps it was Aunt Betsy who drew her out. She arrived before lessons were over and Aunt Betsy always had a book waiting for her to read and they would sit and discuss it in the Abbey gardens, whilst he climbed trees and threw stones at imaginary foes.

'She's lonely, poor thing, just as I would be without you,' said his aunt, squeezing his hand. As I am without Robert, thought William. His aunt had wanted to open a small dame school when Robert left but she was thwarted by the schoolmaster's widow, Mrs Wilkinson, who beat her to it. So, William was stranded, too old for the dame school and banned from the grammar school. Occasionally he toyed with the idea of returning to his father and joining him in his work as a labourer. But his aunt held out the carrot of his own farm and now thirteen years later it was within his grasp.

'Would Miss Alice like to play a game with us, do you think?' William had asked Aunt Betsy one day, fed up that all they seemed to do was sit and talk about books. It began from there. Alice visibly softened; began to smile, began to enjoy herself. Even old Mr Dawson said to Aunt Betsy that Alice seemed happier. By that time, he was frail and slept each afternoon and was unaware that Alice visited Betsy, nor did he know about the books she was reading. When he suffered an apoplexy and died soon after, Aunty Betsy invited Alice to move in because her brother had been bequeathed the house. Her father had not left her much to live on, and Alice snapped up the offer, rather than be housekeeper to her brother and his vapid, young wife. William remembered the tears glistening on her pale cheeks as she took Aunt Betsy's hand, too overcome with gratitude for words. The first thing Aunt Betsy did to celebrate was to order copies of Camilla and Evelina by Fanny Burney from the bookseller. They read them aloud to each other after supper, giggling like children.

William's childhood maybe lacked friends, but he never lacked love. Those two, childless women heaped love upon him and in return he gave them his heart. He would miss Alice but she had been failing this past year, growing thinner and greyer every time he saw her. Pain etched her face making it sharper, but he never heard a word of complaint from her. She was always delighted to see him and always baked his favourite apple or cherry tart to welcome him home.

She had taken over the small garden and produced vegetables and fruit for the table, so they never went hungry, even in the worst of winters. Betsy called her a wizard with plants and let her get on with it, having no interest in gardening at all. When Lottie left through illness, Alice took over much of the cooking too, not out of duty, but simple love. Oh, they would both miss her. When he took over the tenancy of the Laceby farm, perhaps he should ask Betsy to visit, knowing she would be bereft without Alice. He did not want her to move in permanently, as selfish as it seemed. He was young and had an idea that he might taste the joys of being a young, single man. He needed to make some friends and acquaintances and where better than the alehouse?

Passing Nun's Corner, he saw little change in the town from the day he first arrived as a six-year-old. There were changes, of course, but not on this approach. He stabled his horse at the Inn and made his way to the house in Chantry Lane, noticing the straw strewn across the road outside to deaden the noise of carts and horses, some silent solace for the dying, and it brought a lump to his throat. Knocking gently, he wiped his eyes with his sleeve. His aunt opened the door in her slippered feet and drew him in.

'Thank goodness you're here. She's been asking for you.' He planted a kiss on her cheek, noting that her hair was threaded with silver and he stood a good three inches above her head. Had she also shrunk and grown older in the space of a few weeks?

'She made me promise that you would go up as soon as you arrived, but I hope she is sleeping.' She took his coat and cap. He begged her for a glass of ale, being hot and thirsty after his ride.

'I'll send a lad to the inn for some. Do go and see her.' He climbed the stairs and walked down the corridor to Alice's room at the front of the house. The curtains were drawn and it smelt of sickness and death. His immediate reaction was to open the sash window and let in some air and the glorious sunshine. The light fell on Alice, but he scarcely recognised her. The face staring out from the covers was shrunken to nothing, her hair thin and white, her lips smudged with dried blood. He drew the curtains again, leaving a sliver of light and went to sit beside her on the bed, taking a thin clawed hand in his thick, work-hardened one.

'You came,' she whispered.

'Nothing could have kept me away, dear Alice,' he wiped at her cracked lips with a moist cloth lying on a table next to the bed.

'I wanted you to know...' she began and wheezed piteously.

'Don't tire yourself.'

'No, I must say this. I never started living until I came to live with you.' The effort was too much and she sank back into the pillow, her pale blue eyes dull with pain. He continued to hold her hand, the pulse barely perceptible in her wrist.

Ten minutes later Betsy crept in with a glass of cool ale for William, which he downed in a second. She sat down in a chair close to the bed.

'How many hours have I sat here, first with Doctor Taylor and now with Alice,' she looked exhausted. 'I am glad you're here.'

'You need some sleep. Why don't you lie down while I sit with her?'

'No, there'll be time enough when she's gone; I would not want to be resting when she passes,' she whispered. Alice groaned and Betsy took hold of Alice's hand and began to croon to soothe her.

'What's that you're singing?'

'The last time Alice left this house we went to St James for a concert. A full orchestra playing Handel; it was sublime. Alice said it was the best evening she'd ever spent, even though she knew she had little time left.'

'I didn't know that.'

'Well it was the weekend of the Grimsby races. If I remember correctly, you came home rather worse for wear.'

William smiled ruefully at the gentle admonishment. The races were a highlight of the year attracting people from miles around. It was a time to celebrate in that lull between planting and harvest. Horse racing, cock-fights, drink, plays and a closing ball, what was not to like?

'No need to apologise, my love. You're only young once, as they say.' Betsy patted him on the knee with her free hand.

William changed the subject. 'What did she mean that she did not start living until she came to live here?'

'Oh, she told you that, did she? Her father kept her in strict control until he began to fail, never allowed friends, or pastimes, other than sewing or Bible reading. He even turned down the only suitor she had, saying he needed her to keep house for him. Her brother's the same. Did you know that he demanded she move back to look after the house when his wife died? He came here and threatened her, but by then she had the backbone to refuse him. You should have seen the look on his face when she said no. I was proud of her. To men such as him, women are chattels, possessions to rule as they please. Her father thought that by leaving her only forty pounds a year to live on she would be forever under her brother's thumb. But her brother did not want her until he had motherless children to care for. She chose to stay with you and me, preferring you to her spoilt nephews.' Betsy sighed and planted a kiss on Alice's bony fingers. 'She loves you, William, you're the son she never had, as you are mine; two old biddies, as mothers, poor William.' Betsy smiled in a deprecating way.

'You know I don't think that. I have been blessed with three mothers. All of you are precious to me.' Betsy took his free hand and patted it.

'When you marry, William, cherish your wife and children, be they only daughters. Educate them; feed their souls with love and ideas, not just duty. Duty is not enough for a woman. It kills her soul. Any sense of oneself withers if blind duty is all a woman has to look forward to.'

'I understand that, Aunt.'

'Understand this too. I have been thinking about it a lot. Marry someone older than yourself, someone who is grateful for the chance of a family and already has the skills of a homemaker. An older woman will have fewer children and a small family with help you shepherd your resources.'

William was taken aback and did not know at first how to respond. He had not thought about marriage. His dreams were all about farming and, more to the point, a farm of his own. There was a girl in Hatcliffe he had a fancy for, but she was too young and he had no intention of marrying for several years.

'I am thinking about taking on the tenancy of a farm near Laceby, Aunt.' He thought that this might steer the subject away from marriage, which made him uncomfortable.

'I can visit you, it's not far. You will have need of a wife and I will not get in her way.'

Damn, she had brought back the subject of marriage and he had no wish to discuss it, but he knew what his aunt was like when she got an idea. It was like trying to prize a dog away from a bone.

'Alice is leaving you her money, William. It's not much, but a little better than the sum her father left for her. I have stewarded our money well. I realised after that dreadful first winter you came to live here that we must spend our money wisely and so we have. You will have just over forty pounds a year from Alice.'

'She's not in her grave yet,' shushed William, but with his heart pounding. With that money, he could do much to improve the farm he hoped to tenant. 'Should she not leave her money to her nephews?'

'Her brother no doubt thinks so, but she has no liking for them, or they for her.'

'Did you ever resent her coming to live with us? You always seemed so happy to be on your own.'

Betsy smiled. 'No never. At first I felt sorry for her but I grew to love her company.' Her smile soon faded to sadness. 'I will miss her dreadfully.' She choked back a sob. 'I never wanted a husband and I would trade a thousand husbands for Alice any day.'

'Don't cry, Aunt. I have never seen you cry.' William went to kneel at her feet and put his arms around her waist, holding her tight, comforting her. She bent her head to his shoulder, breathing in the scent of the fields and the farm.

Alice gasped and they both turned towards her. Her eyes opened and her mouth tried to form a smile.

'My family,' she whispered. 'You are my family.' She closed her eyes once more and after a moment shuddered while Betsy and William each held a hand. They felt her hands slacken and watched as her body relaxed into death.

'Oh, dear Lord,' William's aunt moaned and she fell onto Alice, distraught.

He found himself standing at the foot of the bed looking down into a chasm and felt the chill of his mother's burial. He glanced to the left, half expecting to see his father and brother weeping, but it was only himself this time. Tears bathed his eyes. They stayed silent in vigil for some time but eventually wiped their eyes and hugged each other.

William needed air. Betsy, still tearful, asked him to visit the undertaker and Alice's brother and he was pleased to go. The atmosphere in the bedroom was suffocating, cloying and he did not know how his aunt could stand it. After helping her to bring a pail of hot water upstairs, he left her to the mysteries of laying out Alice's body.

He felt bereft, which surprised him. Walking up Chantry Lane he was drawn in to the church and found solace sitting on one of the pews nearest to the recumbent knight, its stone visage smoothed away over the years to a featureless face. He ruminated about life and death. His mother and Alice had never reached old age and it chilled him. Such a short time and who would remember them after he had gone? At least the effigy was a reminder of life, even if no one knew who he was. He thought about his aunt's advice to marry and it made a little more sense to him, whereas a few hours before he had never considered it. He needed to get on with his life and build for the future. No one knew their span of life until they were dying. Short or long, a wise man used his allotted time to the full. His thoughts turned to prayer; he should pray for Alice's soul. He hoped she was at peace.

Alice's brother, George, received the news with indifference. He had never bothered to visit his sister after she refused to move back to the house, barely acknowledging her in church.

'Shall we arrange the funeral or do you want to?' asked William.

'Does she have enough money to pay for it?'

'Do you mean Miss Holtby, my aunt? William was perplexed.

'Yes her, the harridan who turned my sister away from her family.'

'Yes, we can pay for it. I would ask you to not to call my aunt names. She does not deserve it.'

George ignored William's warning. 'Then do so. Alice made her bed, so she can lie in it.' The thought appeared to amuse her brother. William sickened at his whinnying laugh.

'Will you attend?' he asked, more coldly than he intended.

'Yes, as chief mourner. I was her nearest relative, after all, even if she did refuse to help me in my hour of need.' William was dismissed; the door shutting in his face.

At the undertakers, he chose the finest walnut coffin available. He suspected that her brother would have chosen a cheap pine one.

Before calling at the vicarage to arrange the funeral, he walked down to the docks. They had opened twelve years before amidst much fanfare. The whole town had turned out to greet the first ship entering the dock, cheering and waving at the sailors. He could not remember where it was from, but the town resonated to new voices and accents from as far apart as Canada and Istanbul. Each time a ship arrived, his aunt would point to the country of origin on the doctor's globe. William learnt much of his geographical knowledge in this way. He remembered the cream coloured horses which came from the Tsar of Russia, as a present for the king. They were magnificent and he had jumped up and down with excitement to see them unloaded. They had pranced around the dock excited to have escaped their confinement while their handlers clung on to their harnesses to stop them from falling into the water.

There was no ship in the dock this day. That heady time had been replaced with disappointment as the number of ships dwindled each year. How many this year, he wondered, ten, eleven, most likely no more. He knew the reasons because talk in the Queens Head where merchants and ship owners met to trade, was often enough about blame and politicking. The Haven docks were only marginally successful because the farmers of the Wolds did not send enough produce to be exported. Most ships left empty which was hardly profitable. Even after twelve years this problem had not been solved and certainly none of it had been considered when building the docks.

The Corporation lacked expertise and had blithely spent their money going along with the big farming landowners who had proposed the docks. While Hull prospered with its proximity to the Yorkshire woollen trade and Goole too, with its access to the Trent, Grimsby sank back into disillusionment. Whaling offered some hope and the whaling ship, Bernie, returned every year around June with whale-meat and seal blubber, but not this year. The talk was that it had foundered off Newfoundland.

William stood with his back to the new town, all laid out but with few dwellings built, watching the small amount of activity in the dry dock where a boat was being repaired. He did not notice the group of fisherman walking towards him until one stood directly in front of him.

'William? Is it you?' William looked at the youth in surprise; his thoughts had been miles away. He was shorter than himself, bearded with a young man's wispy growth, not yet thick or long; his upper face tanned and already weathered by the wind and the sea. It was the hazel eyes, they were akin to his father's and Betsy's; he knew them as he knew himself.

'Joe, surely not.'

'Yes, brother.'

They threw their arms around each other, hugging and laughing with delight.

'How long have you been in Grimsby?' asked William.

'A few months, no more, I have looked for you often.'

'Why did you not call at our aunt's house? Anyone could have told you where Miss Holtby lives.'

'I did not like to. I thought that I would not be welcome. Father said she was bringing you up to be a gentleman and would not take kindly to any of us making ourselves known to you.' He spoke in a cold, dismissive tone.

'That's not the case at all. I'm sure she will be delighted to see you. Only today is not a good day. We are in mourning for a dear friend, who passed this morning. In fact, I must get back as I have to help Aunty Betsy arrange the funeral.'

73

'Then you have no time for a flagon of ale?'

'No, I'm sorry but I want to hear all the news. Where do you live?'

Joe pointed to one of the new houses across the road. 'I share a room there, in the house with the black cat in the window.'

'I'll seek you out when I come back for the funeral.' William reluctantly turned away and walked back down towards the Bull Ring. He must speak to the Reverend Stockdale about Alice's funeral soon if he wanted it to be within the next three days. When harvest began, it would be impossible to leave the farm. Hunger was gnawing at his stomach and he realised that he had missed most of breakfast as well as dinner. He hoped that Aunt Betsy would have some food ready before he set off back to the farm.

As William rode out of Grimsby to the sound of the bell tolling for Alice, he ran his mind back over the events of the day. What a mixture of emotions his thoughts evoked, sadness, surprise, and joy swirled in his mind. The sun beat down and he did not know whether it was the heat or the tension of the day which caused the pain to throb behind his eyes. One thing he kept coming back to was his aunt's surprise announcement that he was to inherit Alice's money. He could scarcely believe it to be true. Surely her father would have made sure it was tied up so tight that the money did not leave the family. George would have a fit if he thought that were the case. No, he must not dwell on it because he was bound to be disappointed.

Chapter 9

Alice's brother had neither the wit nor the intelligence to consider what it meant for Betsy to pay for the funeral. The mourners were invited to a luncheon at Miss Holtby's house, rather than his own. He was left with the choice to attend and observe the disapproving looks others gave him for not paying for his own sister's funeral, or not attend and be scorned anyway. There was no doubt that word travelled fast in such a small community as this. He chose not to attend, stating pressure of business as his excuse.

Since Alice had begun to live with Betsy, she found the town far more accepting of her. Betsy was no longer a youngish, single woman on her own, whose reputation was, therefore, in doubt. Alice was as respectable a spinster as they came. Never a word had been said against her conduct, and most of the ladies felt some sympathy that her best years had been spent as a dutiful daughter and housekeeper for her father. They were inclined not to like her brother. In the ordinary scheme of things, he would have taken articles with his father and become the new solicitor in town. However, he was too idle to stick to his studies and his father had set him up as a corn merchant. He could have done well once the docks opened but success drifted like dry sand through his fingers.

Mr Dewsbury, the new lawyer in town, read the will as soon as the guests had left, without Alice's brother being present. William questioned the advisability of this, but Joseph Dewsbury assured him there was no reason Mr Dawson needed to be present. It was as Betsy had told him; the money in its entirety had been left to William, all one thousand and two hundred pounds, yielding an income of forty-five pounds a year. Two small pieces of jewellery belonging to Alice's mother were bequeathed to Betsy.

'I don't understand,' said William. 'Why was the money not left in trust for her nephews?'

'Old Mr Dawson never thought Alice would do such a thing. It did not enter his head. As far as he was concerned, Alice would either marry when he died or, more likely, live with her brother, having insufficient income to set up a respectable house by herself. He just never considered her capable of doing anything else.' Betsy laughed. 'Oh, if he's up there watching this, he will be beside himself.'

'As her brother will be, when he finds out. Is there any way he can challenge the will, Mr Dewsbury?'

'No, I drew it up myself. It is watertight.'

'I feel a little guilty, depriving her nephews.'

'Don't be,' said Mr Dewsbury. 'It was her money to do with as she wished. It made her happy to help you and happy to thwart her brother, whom she disliked heartily and with good reason from what I hear.'

Before he set off back for the farm, William walked down to the docks and called at the house where his brother lodged.

'He's not here, Master,' said the boarding housekeeper, an unkempt, dirty looking woman, her mouth a cavern of black and rotting teeth.

'They're away fishing. He said he'll be back for supper.' Her breath was so sour William took a step back.

'Please tell him his brother called,' William instructed, looking past her into a gloomy hall which stank of cat urine. As the door closed on him, he realised that he could not allow Joe to stay much longer in that filthy house. Given that it was only a few years old, he had expected it to be respectable but it had already taken on an aura of decay. He would ask his aunt if Joe could board with her. Joe would be company for her and the more he thought about it the happier he became.

However, Betsy was not as enamoured with the idea as he thought she would be. Her demeanour was cool and unforthcoming. He pressed her for a reply but she hedged and floundered, telling him it was a bad day to discuss such a matter when Alice was scarcely in her grave.

'But Aunt, he's my brother. I've missed him so much over the years.'

'No William, I will not discuss this now.' He had rarely known her raise her voice to him and it shut him up. He stood in front of her, angry and disappointed. Her mouth was set firm and her chin pointed up to his with defiance. They had never argued and he was unsure how to react. Lacking anything else to say he turned, picked up his coat and hat and mumbled that he needed to get going. Betsy put her hand on his arm but he shrugged it off.

'Don't leave like this,' she implored, hoping he would turn and face her.

Instead he stomped out of the door, feeling childish but unable to help himself. Joe was his brother and he would not abandon him for a second time. If Betsy would not let him live with her then he would ask Joe to work with him on his farm at Laceby and he could live in the farmhouse. Yes, he smiled, that was the answer. He felt calmer and regretted storming off, but rather than go back to the house and try to make amends he carried on. Harvest was beginning the next day and he needed an early night. A month of back breaking toil lay ahead.

Betsy sat in the sitting room surrounded by the remains of the wake. She had made a start on clearing up when William had gone off in search of his brother. She had not done much when he returned in a state of feverish excitement. He'd been the same when he had returned from arranging the funeral. She hadn't liked to admit her resentment at his happy mood. His brother, he had met his brother. Joy lit up his face and sparkled in the eyes she loved so much. She pretended to be pleased for him, while struggling with despair. It threatened to overwhelm her, but he could not see it. Betsy supposed she ought to be glad for him. She knew she was being unfair. He was young. He had his whole life ahead and a long-lost brother to temper his grief. She did not feel in any way guilty that she had been the cause of their years of separation.

At fifty she knew her life was slipping away and with Alice gone, loneliness and old age were all that beckoned. Alice had lived in the house for twelve years and for every one of those years Betsy had thanked God. She had never known such fulfilment. She only bore the loss of William to the farm because Alice was there. Gentle Alice, sensible Alice, Betsy felt part of her had been ripped away. Did William think it was easy to replace her with Joe, someone she did not even know? How could she grieve for her soulmate with a stranger in the house? How could she cook for someone else, knowing it was not for Alice? She found herself in tears remembering how they would sit together with a book in the evenings, understanding each other so well that sometimes there was no need for words. No husband and wife were so well matched as us, she thought and tears fell unrestrained down her face.

Someone hammered at the door. Betsy knew who it was. The hammering was sustained and violent but she was in no mood to speak to George Dawson. He could go hang.

It was an interview she could not avoid forever. He would turn up and bang on her door at odd times throughout the next few days. For the most part she barricaded herself in the back room, grateful for the heavy oak doors. Where was her strength? She felt light-headed and tearful most days. The house was beginning to look uncared for, but she had no energy to clean and cook. Perhaps she should hire a servant. Since Lottie left they had managed between them, her, and Alice. Her only comfort was the aging cat. It sat now on her knee, purring gently as her fingers tickled his neck.

She was grateful when the lawyer called to leave some papers for William to sign. She recognised his tap on the knocker, three short taps, never more, never less.

He was shocked at her appearance. Dark moons circled her eyes, her cheeks appeared sunken and hair hung around her face in limp tendrils. She had aged ten years within a few days.

'I'm not sleeping or eating and George Dawson is plaguing me by banging on my door at all hours of the day,' she said, in response to his concern for her health.

'I should send for William,' he said.

'No, leave him be. Its harvest time and he's busy,' she said with sadness because there was no one she would rather see than William. She needed to make it up with him. That was a great part of her anxiety.

'I thought I wanted to be on my own to grieve,' she said. 'Perhaps that was a mistake because I have no one to care for or to care for me. Do you know of a good woman in need of work for a few hours a day?

Hammering on the door began again. Mr Dewsbury looked at Betsy.

'It's George Dawson,' she sighed.

'Leave him to me,' he said.

She shut her mind to what was said on the doorstep, refused to listen, surprised at how weak she felt; she had braved the comments of the town with equanimity and cool reason in previous years. Now she felt helpless and alone.

Mr Dewsbury re-entered the drawing room looking grim. 'I have sent him off with a flea in his ear, but I think he'll be back. He means to have it out with you. I have told him that we could make an appointment in my office when you are feeling up to it. He knows you are ill and I have warned him against harassing you but is there not someone else who could stay with you?'

Tiredness robbed her of the ability to think. All she wanted was to sleep but in answer to his question she mentioned William's brother.

'I know little about him; but what I do know is not good. There were some bad reports. Can you make some enquiries?' The last of her strength drained away and she fell back into the chair, exhausted.

'I will ask my wife to visit. She may know of a woman in need of employment. Go to bed, dear lady, and wait for my wife. I will see myself out.'

Betsy breathed her thanks and closed her eyes. Why did she feel so drained, so unable to cope? It was not like her at all. She felt too tired to even think. Bed, she said to herself, and made herself get up. Stumbling upstairs she collapsed on top of her bed, expecting to sleep, but once there, sleep eluded her again. Her mind fought sleep, although she begged with every ounce of her being for the relief that only sleep could bring.

Sarah Dewsbury called later that afternoon and brought with her the doctor and a fresh-faced young woman answering to the name of Susan, professing her to be a marvel in her own home.

'I will lend her to you for a day or two, Miss Holtby until we can find someone suitable.'

Betsy did her best to object on the grounds of being too much trouble but that was swept aside and she gave in, grateful for any help. The doctor prescribed laudanum and gave instructions that she was to remain in bed for a week and to eat nourishing soups and possets, nothing too rich or heavy. She had never been an invalid in her life but surprised herself in the way she accepted what was advised, offering no protest; she was past all of that. The doctor escorted her back to bed where he administered the first dose of laudanum and instructed Susan to give her further drops in brandy after each meal for the following week.

Betsy retained no memory of that week. It was a black void; a nothing; seven days of her life lost and in that time, everything changed. Her mind was foggy when she awoke seven days later. Her legs felt weak as she tried to climb out of bed; they shuddered and shook as soon as she placed her feet on the floor. The room was stifling and airless in the August morning and her throat was so dry she found it difficult to swallow. She tried calling but only a croak found its way out of her mouth. She shook her head, trying to clear it from the mist clouding her mind. Noticing a small brass bell on the bedside table she lifted it and shook it, not knowing if anyone else was in the house. The bell was bright and new and tinkled softly, she shook it harder in panic. She heard light footsteps on the stairs and her bedroom door opened to reveal a young woman, no more than seventeen years of age.

'Who are you?'

'I'm Madge, Miss Holtby. Mrs Dewsbury engaged me as your help.'

Only in the dim recess of her mind did Betsy have an inkling as to why Mrs Dewsbury had done such a thing, but she was grateful that someone was in the house. Madge did not look old enough or strong enough to be of much use. She was a skinny slip of a girl; her face was pleasant enough, with pale blue eyes, hair the colour of wet sand and a pert nose.

'How long have you been here?' asked Betsy.

'Five days, Ma'am, the same as Master Joe. We both arrived on the same day.'

'Joe who?' Betsy had no idea what the girl was talking about.

'Joe Holtby, Ma'am, your nephew.' Madge looked puzzled.

Betsy sank back into the pillows. She had no recollection of inviting Joe Holtby. How had this happened? Her head began to throb.

'Can you bring me some tea and maybe a boiled egg.' Betsy needed time to think but her head was woolly and she found her eyes closing again.

Madge dipped a curtsey and ran down the stairs to comply.

She woke this time to find a cold cup of tea beside her; her thirst so great that she drank it down in one, scowling at the bitter brewed taste.

There were voices downstairs, followed by footsteps on the stair treads. Why did she feel afraid? Something had happened which made her feel uneasy, what was it? The doctor poked his head around the door and she sighed in relief.

'How are you today, Miss Holtby?'

'I wish to get up, Doctor Burns. How long have I lain in bed?'

'A week, no more. You were in such desperate need of sleep that I gave you a sedative to ensure you rested. I think it would be a good idea now to get dressed and start to resume your life, but you must still take it easy. You gave us quite a fright. It is to be expected following Miss Dawson's passing and the hours you spent nursing her.' Betsy grimaced with sadness; her grief still raw. Yes, that must be why she had become so upset, nothing more, nothing less. Surely it was enough.

Once the doctor had left, Madge helped her to wash and dress; her shaking limbs threatening to give way as she stood to put on her skirt. The mourning clothes she had worn a week ago, felt loose and baggy.

'Are you sure you feel up to going downstairs, Ma'am?'

'If you help me. Take my arm and we can go down together.' It was slow progress but they managed. Betsy was grateful to sit in the back room, where sun streamed in through the windows. Had she enough strength she would have liked to sit under her cherry tree, listening to the birds. Perhaps tomorrow, there was always tomorrow. Sadness threatened anew. There were flowers and vegetables out there which Alice had planted before she became so weak. While in time they might comfort her, now they reminded her too much of her loss.

There was a loud knock on the door and Betsy jumped in sudden fear, memories of George Dawson's harassment flooded back.

'Don't open it,' she instructed Madge.

'It's Joe, Ma'am. He's back from fishing; it was an early tide this morning.' Once again Betsy looked at her in confusion.

'Joe Holtby, Ma'am.' Madge nodded her head to remind her. The old lady must be losing her marbles, she thought. She left the room to open the front door.

Betsy smelt Joe before she saw him. The strong odour of fish clung to his clothes and hands. He barely acknowledged her as he walked through to the scullery to divest himself of wet clothes and to cleanse the fish blood and guts from his hands. He came back into the room in bare feet wearing a thin, blue jersey and grey trousers. Betsy assumed they had been in waiting for him in the scullery. The smell of fish still clung to him, permeating the room, which up to now had smelt of Alice's pies and roses from the garden. She wrinkled her nose in distaste. It no longer felt like her home with these strangers in it.

Joe sat down at the table and Madge cut a slice of bread and cheese for him, still without a word being said. Betsy stared at him, expecting him to introduce himself and make some polite recognition of her existence. She had never known such rudeness. He took a bite of the bread and cheese and only then did he glance at her with unfettered resentment.

'My father told me you would not want to meet me,' he said, once he had swallowed the bread.

'You look at me as though you hate me,' Betsy was shocked at the ill feeling in his words and expression.

'You took my brother from me. Why should I like you?' Madge hurried back into the scullery to hide amongst the pots and pans and soon could be heard clattering about so she would hear no more of the argument that was brewing.

Although there was some likeness in his colouring and eyes, Betsy could see no resemblance in character with William and was glad she had not chosen this boy to be her heir. She thought him spoilt and brutish in his attitude; his obvious lack of manners spoke volumes.

'You did not want to know me but when you needed someone to protect you, I would do,' he spat at her.

'I don't know what you are talking about, protect me from what?'

'Your lawyer came and got me, saying you were being harassed by a man, whose inheritance you stole.'

'I am sure he never said such a thing. I have stolen nothing and I don't recall asking him to bring you here.'

Had she done such a thing? She could not remember and hoped it was not true. Her mind felt so muddled. 'My late friend, Miss Dawson left her money to William because she admired him and thought of him as a son. I had nothing to do with it.'

'That's not the story George Dawson is telling in the taverns. He said you wheedled it out of his sister, just like you did the old doctor.' Betsy was stunned and angry.

'I don't need your protection. I want you to leave this house.'

'So, you tell me to leave before you even ask about my father, your own brother?'

There was a veiled threat in his tone and had been all the time he was speaking. The fear she had felt earlier came back in force. She wanted him gone. Summoning up her strength she replied in as cold and firm a voice as she could manage.

'Your vicar at Frodingham keeps me informed. I do not need you to tell me. He wrote that you left under a cloud. Money had gone missing. Does your father even know where you are?'

He stood and edged his face next to hers and snarled, 'I heard Father say you were a cold-hearted bitch. You never once let him know how William was doing.' Spittle sprayed her face. She had to summon all her strength not to wipe it off. She refused to show weakness.

Fighting tears, she replied. 'That was our agreement.' She would not bend to this odious youth, a viper who had somehow slithered into her house. 'Go! leave my house. I don't want you living here,' she cried, angry yet feeling vulnerable and alone. Please God make him go she prayed in silence, staring at his face, not six inches from hers.

At last he backed away and marched into the scullery, grabbed his wet clothes, shoved his feet into his boots and saying not a word as he passed her, he left, slamming the front door behind him.

Betsy broke into heaving sobs; her whole body shook with fear. What if he had not gone, what could she have done? Madge was useless; where was she?

Amidst her tears, she called out the girl's name. There was no answer so she called again in panic. A timid voice answered and Madge's face appeared around the door.

'Madge, Joe Holtby has gone, he is never to be admitted again if he calls. Do you understand?' The girl nodded, managing to look both petulant and scared. Was she scared of her or Joe, Betsy wondered?

'Please find me something to wipe my face, Madge, and then can you bring me something to eat. I must have missed your boiled egg this morning.' She softened her voice and attempted a smile.

Having eaten a bowl of watery vegetable soup, Betsy craved her bed again. The encounter with her nephew had stolen all her determination to resume her life. Her head felt woozy and pain began to throb above her eyes. With Madge's help she climbed the stairs and then she sent the maid to fetch some laudanum and brandy.

First, she opened the door of Alice's room meaning to seek some comfort from her friend's belongings but was horrified to be greeted by a whiff of fish and crumpled sheets. Had Joe slept in Alice's bed? If so, he had defiled it. She should have expected it. Betsy walked over to the bed. There was another smell, one she recognised from many years before when a maidservant in the big house. She flicked the top sheet back from the bed, saw the tell-tale stains then turned towards Madge, who stood outside the door with the medicine. The girl's face flushed in embarrassment before she cast her eyes to the floor. Fury grew in Betsy's breast as she glanced further around the room; drawers were slightly open when she knew they had been left shut. Betsy walked over to them, opening the one where she knew Alice's jewellery was kept but it was not there. She grabbed at Madge's arm, drawing her into the room. The girl looked frightened now.

'Mr Dawson said they belonged to him and Joe gave them to him, if you are looking for the brooch and ring,' her voice sounded scared.

'They were bequeathed to me,' Betsy protested. 'Has Mr Dawson called here?' Her headache tightened as though her head was held in a vice.

'Yes, Master Joe invited him.' The girl did not finish the sentence because Betsy sank to the floor in a stupor.

Chapter 10

Over the years, William had developed a rhythm for scything. The blade swung in an easy arc through the wheat, even as his muscles screamed after days of this work and as the sweat poured from his brow. The dust mingled with his perspiration to form streaks, as though his face and arms were painted into some primitive tattoo. He was determined to finish this field before the sun set. He had been up since four o' clock and there were two more hours until the light went. He knew he would drop into his bed and sleep without dreaming until it was time to get up and begin again. The weather was holding, thank God, and another week should see the wheat cut and then there was the barley. No time to waste.

He did not see Mrs Hackney approach until she was right beside him.

'William, a letter has come. The boy said it was urgent.'

He turned towards her, her mouth looked grim. He wiped the sweat from his eyes onto his bare arm, smudging the evidence of his graft. His hands were raw with blisters from the scythe. He did not recognise the seal but he felt a pit of dread in his stomach as he wrenched the seal apart.

'It's from my aunt's lawyer. He says she has collapsed and they fear for her life.'

The veneer of strength disappeared from his eyes leaving him vulnerable. Mrs Hackney put a hand on his elbow. 'You have to go.'

'But what about the harvest?' William cried, looking about him with anxiety.

'We'll manage somehow. Return when you can. Your aunt needs you, William.' He bowed his head, fearful that he would break into sobs. How was it possible that the two women he loved most could be taken from him so quickly? He bit his lips and blinked back his tears.

'If you leave now, you can be there before the sun goes down.' He nodded and turned to walk back with her to the farmhouse, his legs leaden with fear for what he would find in Grimsby.

He arrived at the house still filthy, the dust of the fields and the road further coating his face and hands. A young girl answered his knock.

'You must be Master William,' she said to thin air as he dived into the house and ran upstairs to his aunt's room. There was no one with her as she lay on the bed. She looked gaunt, her mouth twisted into a grimace. He took her hand and noticed how it was bent from her wrist like a claw.

'What's happened to you, Aunt? It's William, please can you open your eyes,' he cried. The girl came into the room.

'The doctor said it was apo.. something. She can't move the right side of her body.'

He turned to her, demanding to know what had occurred for his aunt to be this way. She did not answer at first but looked shamefaced. He grasped her hand tight, commanding her to speak.

'There was an argument,' she said. 'I didn't hear it all and then she came upstairs and discovered he'd taken some jewellery. Next thing I knew she was on the floor; hit it lack a sack of potatoes. I were that frit, but it weren't my fault. I'm only here to look after the house and do some cooking; I'm not supposed to be her nurse.' She grimaced with dislike as she looked at Betsy.

'Who took the jewellery, who did she argue with?'

'Your brother, Master Joe; I liked him, he was nice to me, but she made him leave,' she threw an accusing glance at Betsy.

'Stay with her,' he ordered as he ran back down the stairs and out of the house, towards the docks. He hammered on the door of Joe's lodgings only to find he was not there but at the Black Swan. Retracing his steps, he entered the fuggy bar and caught a glimpse of Joe sitting at a table with some other men. One of them turned to raise his hand for more ale and he saw it was George Dawson. Cold fury gripped William. His fingers flexed and then balled into fists. He walked over to Joe's chair and hauled him up.

'You're coming with me,' he growled, manhandling him outside. He forced Joe to stand with his back against the wall of the tavern.

'Tell me what you and George Dawson's have done.' His brother was so drunk he could scarce string two words together. William grabbed him by the shoulder and dragged him back to his aunt's house. Many years of good food and hard labour had made William much stronger than his brother, but even he was surprised at his strength as Joe struggled to free himself.

The girl was flummoxed to see them both at the door when he knocked, but she simpered at Joe, who was in no condition to notice.

'Get me a bucket of water,' William instructed as he continued to drag him through the house and out of the back door.

'I'll have to go to the pump,' the girl complained.

'Just do it,' William ordered.

It took him about half an hour to sober up his brother; the water thrown over his head had begun the work. He followed it by forcing salted water down his throat until he spewed everything up and collapsed on the ground, moaning for his brother to stop.

'Tell me what happened to my aunt. Is it true you stole the jewellery Alice left?'

'No, I gave it back to its rightful owner, for a small reward of course.'

'That jewellery was left to my aunt in Miss Dawson's will. It belongs to Aunt Betsy, do you understand? It belongs to her not George Dawson. You're a damned thief and I could have the Constable arrest you. Men get transported to Botany Bay for less. When she found that you had taken it she had an apoplexy. Do you understand what that is? You may have killed her Joe; your own flesh and blood. Have you any idea of the damage you've done?'

'She was ill way before I took the ring and brooch, George Dawson says..'

'Hang George Dawson, he's a worthless, cold hearted bastard. Betsy is your aunt. She brought me up with love and was more than my own mother to me. I have no words to describe what a good woman she is.' William looked at Joe in the gloom of the evening and saw his resentment.

'Why you're jealous, aren't you? You think she should have taken you not me. I was going to ask you to come with me to work on my farm when

87

I take on the tenancy. I would have shared my good fortune with you. Now I've no wish to ever see you again. You have destroyed her. Go! Get out before I throw you out. You should crawl on your knees to Betsy to beg her forgiveness. As for me, be sure, I will never forgive.' William sat on the ground with his head in his hands, despairing for his aunt. For his brother, he felt nothing but contempt.

For the second time that day Joe left the house, this time wounded by his brother's words but unrepentant. He had sought vengeance on his aunt and had no pity for her. He did not want to work on a farm in any case; it was the sea that called him. Ever since they had played pirates together there had been a dream that he and his brother would sail the seas. All those years yearning for his brother, longing for the time they could be together again but that woman had taken him from him again. Curse her.

William sat with his aunt all night. Never again would he allow her to be alone and he did not trust the girl. He dozed on and off but the nightmare of what had occurred kept waking him. Betsy did not open her eyes while he was watching but she knew he was there. He was sure she could sense his presence. The doctor arrived early the next morning and described what had gone on in the days he had been away. William was shocked and guilt threatened to disarm him. He had walked out on her over Joe and she was already exhausted. Had he tipped her over the edge? Was it as much his fault as Joe's?

'She has survived the night, and yesterday I thought she might not,' the doctor finished examining Betsy.

'Is that a good sign, doctor?'

'Early days, William, early days. You must be prepared that if she lives this week out, she will be an invalid. She is unlikely to regain movement in her right side and her speech could be affected. Find someone to nurse her. 'Meanwhile I'll bleed her again. It's the only medicine we have in such cases.'

William wished Lottie was still with them. Madge was a disaster and if she was all the lawyer's wife had come up with, then he should send a note to Mrs Hackney to ask for her help in finding someone suitable.

He was dog tired himself but refused to leave his aunt's side. Mid-morning, he sensed a change in her and grasped her left hand more tightly.

'I'm here, Aunty Betsy, can you hear me?' He felt a slight movement in her fingers.

Seconds later she opened her eyes and struggled to smile at him but her mouth refused to conform. She tried to speak but only gargled, jumbled sounds issued from her throat.

William saw the terror in her eyes and while his heart broke, he tried to reassure her. Slowly she became calmer as she listened to his words. Encouraged, he carried on telling her of his plans for his new farm and how they would live there together and that he would always look after her.

She tried to speak again but gave up when her ears heard the sound she made. Tears of helplessness formed at her eyes. She loved William beyond measure but she did not want to become a burden to him. What use was she now? Better to die and be done with it.

He had an idea and told his aunt to wait a moment before running downstairs to the study to seek a quill, ink, and paper. He sat down at a desk and wrote the letters of the alphabet in a strong clear hand on to a sheet of thick paper, blotted it well and ran back upstairs with it.

'Do you remember how you taught me my letters?' he asked. 'Well now we can go back to pointing and sounding out the letters. This time I will be teacher,' he grinned at her.

There was something she wanted William to know urgently so she pointed at the paper, indicating that she wanted to spell something out. He held the paper and she pointed at the letters with her left hand.

'Too fast, you're going too fast,' he cried, relieved that she was trying to communicate. She slowed down and he said the letters as she pointed at them.

'Look in top drawer,' she spelt and pointed over at the large, oak chest opposite her bed.

He walked over to it and pulled out the drawer. Seeing a bundle of letters tied up by a thin, blue ribbon, he held them up so she could see. She nodded and waved him back over to the bed. He sat back in the chair and opened one. It was from the Vicar of Frodingham giving news of his family. Why had she never shared them with him? He opened more, one for each year he had lived with her. He questioned her with his eyes and she pointed to the paper again.

'Sorry, forgive,' she spelt.

He nodded. Of course, he forgave her. He briefly scanned them, learning of his older brother Tom's death in the wars, his sisters' marriages and finally how Joe had disappeared, after being under suspicion of theft from the farm where he worked.

'You knew he was no good but you did not tell me. Did you want to spare me?' He saw the answer in her eyes. 'Do you want me to have him arrested for the theft of the jewels?' He was half afraid she might spell yes, watching closely as she pointed to the letters.

'No. Don't care about jewels,' he let out a breath in relief; at least he could spare his father that shame. She was tiring and he decided to leave her to sleep. After she closed her eyes and settled into a peaceful rhythmic breathing, he left her to go to his room for much needed rest, taking the letters with him.

The following morning saw him much refreshed. He had re-read the letters carefully and noted how in each missive, the vicar had responded to a question, presumably posed by his aunt, that his family were not in any need. How like her, he thought, if they needed more money, she would have arranged that they receive it. Uriah was the only one still living with his father but William found it hard to remember him; he must be seventeen by now but he could not conjure up his face at all. One day, he thought, I will visit them and the idea comforted him.

Betsy lived through a second night and the doctor was now very hopeful that she would survive. He was pleased to see how well she responded to questions. She struggled to make any recognisable sounds but tapped away on the paper, showing her mind remained sharp and undamaged.

William turned his mind to the future. His hopes for a few years as carefree bachelor needed to be put aside. They must sell this house and make the move to Laceby. He had seen the farmhouse, it was an old thatched affair, with untiled floors of trodden earth but it had two bedrooms upstairs and two rooms and a scullery downstairs. His aunt could sleep in the parlour which would leave the big kitchen as general living space. It would work. As soon as harvest finished he would sign the tenancy and make the move. He just needed a good, caring woman to take care of Betsy.

She arrived late in the afternoon, knocking confidently on the front door. He opened it himself as Madge was out fetching water. A full six inches shorter than him and not in the first bloom of youth but with a healthy glow to her cheeks, she stood smiling up at him. He knew her, of course, she was Mrs Hackney's cousin, Ann.

'Your cousin could not have sent anyone I would rather see than you,' he said, drawing her into the house. 'How long can you stay, Miss Hackney?'

'For as long as I am needed, Mr Holtby. With so many younger sisters, I can be spared. Indeed, I think I have become something of an embarrassment.' She gave a rueful smile.

'Are you sure you want to nurse an invalid, Miss Hackney?'

'You have always spoken so warmly of your aunt, Sir, that I long to meet her, properly. I have only seen her at market. As soon as Cousin Jane told me what had happened, I knew what I had to do. That is, if you are in agreement?'

'It goes without saying. I am delighted to see you.'

'You can leave everything to me and get back to the farm on the morrow. I brought the pony and trap here. If you would be so good as to drive it back with the old mare in tow, I would be grateful. I know they need you, the harvest is falling well behind.'

'Of course, I will. There is a maid to help you, but you will need to whip her into shape, I'm afraid. Feel free to take on someone else if she proves too difficult. I'll take you up to see my aunt, if you're ready.' She nodded her acceptance.

William rose with the sun to drive back to Hatcliffe content that Betsy was in safe hands. He could tell immediately that they would get on well together. Once his aunt found out that her new companion could read, she made William show Miss Hackney the study so she could choose a book to read aloud. Her eyes scanned the overflowing shelves with delighted awe. She selected a book that had been ordered by Alice called Pride and Prejudice by a Miss Austen. William assumed he would find it tiresome but was transported by the sound of her voice and the feeling with which she spoke.

'I've never read anything but the Bible before,' she confessed. 'I had no idea such books existed. Do you think it unseemly for me to read such a book?'

'Oh, my aunt will soon have you reading Shakespeare and Milton,' he said, laughing. 'If you stay here long enough, you will be the most educated person in Hatcliffe.'

'I shouldn't mind that at all,' a quiet smile lit up her blue-grey eyes, as his aunt nodded her approval.

She reminded him of Alice and he knew his aunt thought so too. He saw her watching and listening and weighing her up. She was the perfect replacement, if anyone could ever take Alice's place. He wondered if she would consent to move to Laceby with them but then ruled that out as her reputation would be questioned living in the farmhouse with him. His aunt was in no position to be a chaperone. The fact that she was near enough ten years older would not suffice. He sighed to himself. It was unlikely that he would find anyone as perfect as Miss Hackney to be his aunt's companion and nurse.

He set off back to the farm before sun up; there was a hint of autumn in the cool sharpness of the of the cloudless sky but with no sea mist which so often heralded a change in the season. As the sun rose so the heat returned, and before long it shimmered on the windows of a cottage as he passed.

He thought that he would like to visit the beach, as they often had, before he left Grimsby to work on the farm. It was a day for throwing himself with abandon into the water and swimming half way to Yorkshire. Neither Betsy nor Alice had ever tried out the bathing machines but people were beginning to visit the seaside villages and brought a small measure of prosperity to those who had opened their cottages as guest accommodation. That, with the less acceptable smuggling and plundering wrecks, kept the villages from poverty during the war years.

He wondered if Miss Hackney had ever been to the seaside. She was no stranger to Grimsby; often selling her mother's butter and cheese at the market, but she never mentioned having gone further afield. He would like to take his aunt and her to see the sea before he settled Betsy into her new home, thinking with sadness that it might be her last opportunity. What if he had lost both Alice and Betsy in the same month? A cold fury took over his mind to think of the damage done by his brother.

As he drove the trap into the Wolds the glory of the scenery began to soothe his skittering mind and his thoughts turned back to Miss Hackney. What a delight it had been to listen to her read, her voice so soft but direct, her smile so warm that it lit up her face. Her aunt, Jane, his master's wife often sang her praises. He wondered why she had never married; surely there must have been suitors.

He was a mere youth when he first met her and she was a respectable old maid. No that's not fair, he said to himself, the years between them appeared to lessen rather than grow. He was a man and she remained an accomplished and handsome young woman. He paused as another thought occurred to him. A woman who knew how to run a dairy. He slapped his hand on his thigh. 'Yes', he laughed aloud. His aunt's advice of a few days ago, chimed like a gong in his brain. 'Dare I?' he wondered.

Chapter 11

1816 - 1819

William was driving his cows back along the road from Laceby. It was his fourth trip that day but excitement pushed his weariness aside. His own farm, his land to do with as he wanted, how proud that made him feel.

The last three years had been tinged with happiness and heartache. He took comfort in Betsy having lived to see his son, Thomas, toddle around the house before succumbing to her second seizure. Ann had been a godsend throughout it all. There was no question in his mind that he had made the right decision in marrying her. They may not have loved each other before they sealed the knot but love had arrived unbidden, swiftly and with a gentle need that took his breath away.

Aunt Betsy had clutched his hand when he told her what he intended, the approval in her eyes more telling than any words. Over the months, she regained her voice although her words were often jumbled and like his son she had to learn to walk again. Even now there was a lump in his throat as he remembered her first steps across his kitchen. The walking stick he had fashioned from a branch of her old cherry tree becoming her constant companion.

She most loved the evenings when William or his wife sat down to read aloud. The pleasure it gave him to see her eyes light up on hearing Shakespeare sonnets brought as much joy as his son's first words. What he wouldn't have given for longer with her, but it was not to be. Ann's scream for him to come quickly, still chilled his blood, not knowing what he would find. But when he saw Aunt Betsy on the floor in her bedroom, mouthing silently and helpless at him, his heart felt crushed. He had picked her up and laid her back on the bed, knowing she was slipping away. Tears welled in his eyes as he remembered their last few minutes together.

'I love you, Aunty Betsy, more than you can ever know,' he'd told her. With her crooked hand in his, he stayed at her side, stroking strands of grey hair across her brow. She seemed to want to speak but no sound emerged from her twisted mouth. He leant closer until his ear almost touched her lips.

'Fve, fve.'

'I don't understand, Aunt dearest.' A single tear rolled down the wrinkled skin of her cheek. Ann ran to dig out the alphabet paper he had made after her first attack.

'She's too weak,' but a finger in her hand nudging his palm. He grasped the paper and guided her hand towards it. Slowly she tapped out the letters 'Forgive', then her hand flopped back into his, exhausted.

'Forgive what?' He asked, then realisation dawned. 'Joe?' He felt her finger once again in his palm. How could he forgive his brother? 'No,' he shook his head. The finger became more insistent. 'Maybe one day, perhaps, but don't ask me now, when he's brought you to this.'

With her free hand, she tried to point at the paper. William let her guide his hand as she spelt out one more word. 'Love.' The look she gave him seared into his brain with the red heat of a poker. Her eyes were pools of adoration and he fell against Ann, who knelt beside him. They kept vigil together until he felt the last breath leave Betsy's body. It was Ann's comforting body that he had clung to when work was over for days after. His pain had been so raw and unrelenting that he perfectly understood what his aunt felt after Alice died. He should have stayed with Betsy that time, not left her to cope. Despite his aunt's last wish, his hatred for his brother renewed itself. Would it ever disappear?

He looked at the sky, overcast and darkening clouds were blowing in from the west. No one could remember a summer like this one. It was if the sun had decided to take a rest and let cloud and rain take its place. Ann complained that her washing came off the line dirtier than when it had been hung to dry. She showed him the flecks of sooty ash on his best linen shirt. 'I swear', she'd said, 'the wind is blowing the fire from the chimney away from the washing line. So why is my laundry all ruined?'

The harvest this year had been late. He had intended to move at the end of September but it was mid-October and the fields on either side of the road were still covered in the remains of stubble. Any livestock which survived the lack of grass and hay had been let into the fields to graze on the dry stalks and remaining seeds missed by the gleaners.

He had suffered his own losses this year, having to slaughter female as well as male calves for lack of pasture. It had rained so much that the cattle had churned the meadow into mud and hay had rotted where it stood. William had Betsy to thank, for teaching him to always keep money in reserve and plan for bad times. He and Ann were frugal by nature and they would scrape through this autumn, hoping for better next year.

The country was finally at peace; Napoleon had been sent to St Helena from where he could not escape. Everyone expected better times but this summer had proved them wrong. The war had gone on for the whole of his lifetime. William prayed that his son would never have to go and fight in another war.

A man in a ragged tunic appeared from one of the fields ahead. William did not need to ask what he'd been doing. What kind of justice was it that a Lincolnshire trooper was desperate enough to forage for food along with the animals? These days William kept a gun at the ready in case of robbery, while resenting the fact it was necessary.

Luck played a big part in his life. That Betsy had chosen him, that the school in Grimsby wouldn't take him, that his new farm at Old Clee had become vacant when it did, all helped him to achieve what he had dreamed of. Would there be a time when he had to pay back his good fortune? That was a question he cared not to dwell on. He never forgot to thank God at the end of each day and he always anointed his yule log with wine for safe measure.

Turning his thoughts back to the farm, if next year he grew cabbage and turnips he would have enough food throughout the winter for his cattle and not be so dependent on hay. He was starting with four milk cows because he had little enough feed in the coming winter. With luck and hard work, he could grow his herd to fifteen cows, which should give them a comfortable living. Any more and he would struggle to feed them. He intended to deliver milk every day to Cleethorpes and Grimsby in the winter and help Ann with butter and cheese production in the summer.

Growing wheat was unpredictable. The previous year, with the war over, the price dropped, but this year it was already rocketing. Hunger would stalk the land, again.

His new home lay twenty minutes' walk from the sea and not much further to Grimsby. It was an ancient parish with a venerable Saxon church next door to the farm. Ann had been delighted when he took her to see it. He'd watched her face glow with pleasure as she inspected the farmhouse and the dairy. He was delighted with the pastures, un-grazed for the best part of the year, when grassland was at a premium and last year's turnips untouched and well stored in the barn. Enough to keep his cows in food until the Spring.

As he neared his destination he broke into his favourite harvest song, We Plough the Fields and Scatter. William was blessed indeed. Pride filled his chest.

Ann heard his singing from inside the dairy and came out to greet him, her belly swelling beneath her apron. She wiped her hands on a rag and walked over to kiss him.

'We are all ready for our first milking. Everything has been cleaned. Tom's been helping me.' The two-year old ran out of the dairy to be picked up by his father and swung around as he laughed in glee, his blond curls glinting in the late afternoon sun.

'Are you sure this is not the milkman's child,' he joked, because they both had dark brown hair, hers now with a few strands of grey.

'It will turn dark soon enough,' she laughed. It was a long-standing joke for was he not going to be the milkman himself?

'And the house?'

'All cleaned. I don't know how I would have managed without my sister. You must be worn out. How many journeys have you made today?'

'Four, I think and I forget how many yesterday. Perhaps I should have accepted your brother's offer of help. What I'd like more than anything is my bed, but these ladies will need milking, before long.'

'I don't think Martha will forgive you if you pass on supper. She has a treat lined up by all accounts; I should think it is one of her seed cakes.'

'Dear Martha. Someone will gain himself a good wife, perhaps I should have waited.' He ducked, laughing, as Ann swung her cloth at him.

'The Vicar and his wife came to call as well to see if we needed anything. They hope to see you in church on Sunday.' William nodded; he would be interested to hear Reverend Oliver's sermons. He was also headmaster of the newly built Grammar School in Grimsby and a renowned scholar. There were so few close neighbours in this tiny hamlet, just a few farm cottages and the owners of White House Farm, whose fields bordered his own. He hoped Ann would not be too lonely; she enjoyed the company of others and now her sisters would not be within easy visiting distance.

He led the cows into the field. They were far too skinny for the winter ahead, but the pasture here had not been touched all year and some goodness remained. It's an ill wind, he thought and one must be thankful for such mercies. He returned to the dairy to see if Ann needed any more help. She was as proud of her dairy as he was of the farm. The stone-flagged floor dipped in the middle to make it easier to wash out. Her butter churn was set up and deep shelves waited for her cheeses.

William often took Tom with him on his morning milk-round. They both loved the ride along the cliff overlooking the sea; everyday, come sun, rain or biting wind, the scene would change. The lad loved to watch the ships and fishing boats on the Humber, just as he had done. Sometimes they would buy a curd tart from the market. It brought back memories of his first visit to the town.

After much soul-searching, William named his second son, John. In naming the baby after his brother, he hoped that one day he might be able to forgive Joe. It helped that John looked more like his mother. John's eyes were blue and he had his mother's dimples and pale complexion.

It soothed William's heart whenever he dandled John on his knee or crooned his name as he rocked the cradle. Ann was amused that he took such delight in his children. Her own father had ignored his sons until they were ready to work on the farm with him. Of his daughters, he took little notice until they were ready to be walked down the aisle when he sighed in relief at another one off his hands.

'I grew up lonely without my brothers. Our two will always have each other and I will always be proud of them,' William told his wife as they stood by the crib, his face glowing with pleasure in the soft light of the candle. Every night before bed, they crept in to the boys' bedroom to tuck them in and plant kisses on the foreheads.

'Perhaps it's time you made it up with your brother,' Ann said when they had been at Old Clee for a couple of years. 'Do you never see him when you go to Grimsby?' Truthfully, he could tell her he did not.

It was not long after he had begun his milk round in Grimsby eighteen months after moving to Old Clee.

'Master William,' she'd called.

He looked at the woman, trying to recollect where he had seen her before. She looked sallow and thin, apart from the swelling he glimpsed beneath her shawl. A small boy stood by her side and she held a girl in her arms. He recognised the house they stood by more than her. It was the one his brother had lived in. Did he still live there? It slowly dawned on him that this woman was Madge.

'Are you married to Joe?

'Yes, for my sins."

'Where is he?"

'Fishing and when he's not, he's at the tavern.' Her contempt was evident.

William did not know how to react. Should he feel sorry for her? Her demeanour did not lend itself to pity.

'Can you spare a shilling to feed your niece and nephew?' It was hardly a question, more a demand.

He dug around in his pocket until he found a coin and tossed it to her. The little boy scrabbled amongst the gravel to pick it up. 'Just this once. It's my brother who should be taking care of you.'

'Don't I know it,' she said. 'But ale is his mistress, not me.'

The next time he saw her, she had a black eye.

'Did he do that?'

99

'Yes, wanted to know what I'd done to have money in my pocket,' she spat. 'Wished I'd never set eyes on the bugger. Your aunt was right all along. Shame I was daft enough not to see it.'

William's heart sank. What should he do; go and fight his brother again? What good would that do? He beckoned the boy to his cart and filled a tin cup of milk from a ladle attached to his churn. The boy drank the cup down and William did the same for his sister, all in silence. Madge glowered at him, little gratitude showing in her eyes. Her pert sullenness had changed to angry resentment over the course of the years. As a child, he had scattered farthings and halfpennies to the poor, but he didn't know them. These children were his own flesh and blood and a scratchy finger of discomfort crept up his spine whenever he thought about them.

He did not mention it to Ann, beyond saying that he had found out that John had married Madge. Her heart was too soft and he thought she would tell him not to be so proud. Instead he took to taking a heel of bread with him which he could hand to Madge, telling himself time was too short to stop and get into conversation with her. He avoided looking at the children. He never saw Joe and did not seek him out. He tried hard to put them out of his mind, but they were always there like a pin pricking his skin. Sometimes he got his farmhand, Alf, to do the Grimsby milk run. He was a trustworthy chap and could have done it more often but then Ann would have become suspicious.

How many twenty-six year olds are as fortunate as I, he thought. My own farm, a wonderful wife and two healthy sons and a baby daughter. It was the last day of October, three years since he had bought his own farm. The weather had been strange that day; sunny in the morning when he drove around the seaside villages but by the time he got home it had changed. As he unhitched the horse to lead it into the stable he looked up to see a blackening sky. Ann was in the dairy and came out to meet him.

'It looks like we are in for a change of weather.' She cast her eyes up and gasped. 'William, up there, I've never seen anything like that before, have you?'

100

She pointed to an enormous cloud, blue black on the outside but with all the colours of the rainbow in the centre. They stood entranced at the wonder of it.

'What do you think it means, William? Is it an omen?'

'An omen of what? Something good, I hope.' He took her arm in his and they gazed at it for several minutes in awe.

Not long after, he felt the first drop of rain on his face and they dashed indoors to escape the onslaught. The rain fell in sheets for two or three hours which made William's milk run to Grimsby later than usual. He was nearing the docks, where several inns had opened, as if there were not enough, already, he thought. Some offered accommodation to sailors and placed a regular order for milk during the winter months. A weak sun shone but not enough to lift his spirits or warm his damp clothes. At least his round was almost over and he could begin the journey home. He still had the cows to milk before supper and needed to check how much his farmhand had managed to do that day. The saturating rain had most likely delayed the turnip harvest. He hoped they could lift most of them by the middle of November, before any hard frosts damaged the crop.

Amidst the scrunch of the horse's hooves on the gravel, his ears pricked up. He caught a tune; it sounded ragged and mismatched. He strained his ears and as the cart came upon a patch of waste ground beyond the docks, he saw a group standing around a man perched on a box. They were singing a rousing hymn, which William recognised immediately, 'Let all the World in Every Corner Sing' but it was too early for Christmas and the song was no carol. A strange day for an outdoor service, he thought. William sat on his cart, listening, wondering what was happening. He found himself joining in the with the words. Singing hymns was one of life's pleasures. Alice had a good voice and they often sang hymns in the evenings with the children trying to join in as best they could. John could already hold a tune while Tom's voice sounded more like a squeaky cartwheel.

The man on the box turned towards him as he heard William's voice. He was about the same age, maybe a little older, clean shaven in plain, dark clothing with a white stock at his neck. He beckoned and William found himself dismounting from his cart, knowing the horse would stand patiently waiting. He walked towards the small group.

'Welcome brother, won't you join us?' said the man, in a gentle, unfamiliar accent, English but not from Lincolnshire.

They carried on singing until the last verse ended. All eyes were on the stranger. He stood looking at them and smiling. Seconds passed and his body appeared to tighten, the sinews in his face grew taut and at last he opened his mouth to let free a storm of fury, words thundering down on them. William's body shook as the words assaulted his brain with the power of a hammer striking an anvil. This preaching bore as little resemblance to the sermon William was used to in church as a crashing wave does to the ripple on a pond, a torrent as to a trickling brook. Every breath the preacher took, every word he spoke seemed to suck the air out of William's lungs until he was left gasping and groaning in pain at the wickedness of his life. Images flashed through his mind, his wagers on the horse races in June, the cock-fights, and the plays at the theatre behind the Golden Fleece, the pints of ale he drank in the Dolphin, all were a slippery-slope to damnation. He was a sinner and God knew it. He was looking deep in his heart, right this minute, and he saw the wickedness of his life. A woman in front of William fell to the ground, her hands outstretched, beseeching God's forgiveness.

And still the preacher ranted, his face shining with the glory of God. Joy began to isolate the pain, it flooded into William's heart, it sang to the preacher's cajoling, it danced through his blood. Fear, despair, hope and finally love cleansed William's soul and left him panting for more.

The voice ceased and he was bereft but he stayed put, his knees too weak to move. The preacher walked around the crowd talking quietly to each man and woman, his hand on their shoulder as they looked at him in amazement, tears of joy or repentance in their eyes.

As he came to William he asked, 'Brother, did you feel the Lord?' William shivered and could only nod at first but then asked.

'Who are you, where are you from, what happened here?' He was still shaking.

'My name is Silas King. I am from the Primitive Methodist Connexion. We have been sent out into the country to bring the message of God to his people.'

'Like John Wesley?'

'He always advocated preaching wherever you find yourself and where the people are. Too many now sit in their chapels and the message is not reaching the ordinary folk who don't know about the wondrous ways of our Lord. We want to get back to Brother John's early ways; to seek out our brethren in the fields and the factories, in the mines and on the docks.' His hands swept toward the Riverhead before he grasped William's hand. 'Will you join us, Brother?' His voice was low but the question came loaded with power and meaning.

William's heart wanted to say yes, but his head told him to be cautious. His heart burned with joy but in his head, there was a nagging doubt, which he could not dismiss.

'Do you have anywhere to stay for the night? I have a farm nearby and I would like you to meet my wife. There is so much I want to ask you.'

Silas King nodded and William pointed to the cart. How long his horse had stood there, William did not know but the sky was darkening again. He ushered Silas towards the cart.

'How did you come to Grimsby?' asked William, after urging the horse to walk on.

'I came into Lincolnshire to bring the word of God. In Market Rasen, I was told about Grimsby and how it was cut off from the world.'

'We are isolated here, that's true. We know little of the rest of the country and much passes us by. I've never heard of your Connexion although my wife was brought up a Wesleyan.'

'It was begun by Hugh Bourne in Staffordshire, a wonderful, devout man. He believes in holding Camp Meetings where we can reach crowds of people who thirst for knowledge of God. Have you heard of Mow Cop, where thousands join us for a whole weekend for prayer and hymn singing and sermons?' William shook his head. 'It is a remarkable sight, Brother. We know it works because we now have thousands of members who earnestly seek salvation by giving up the devil. Fathers, who no longer drink away their wages, men who have given up foul language and speak reverently of God, women who no longer lead a life of impropriety and take care to mind their children.'

'You must have been disappointed with the size of the crowd back on the dock then.'

'Not at all, we grow from small beginnings. A seed is all that is needed. We provide the earth and water and you, Sir, can provide the sunshine, if you will?'

William diverted the question with his own. 'How did you come to separate from the Wesleyans?'

'Unfortunately, these large outdoor meetings weren't approved of by the local Wesleyans and they cast out Brother Bourne. So, we started up our own circuits to get back to how it was when John and his brother, Charles, good Lincolnshire men, first began our Methodist meetings.'

Later in bed and unable to sleep, William knew that something profound had happened that day. Ann sensed it too. They had talked with Silas long into the night until their eyelids dropped from exhaustion. As tired as he was, William's mind was in turmoil. It was as though he had woken from a long sleep. His skin itched with nervous energy. What magic did Silas wield? Had he bewitched him? Up until this moment William had never thought there was anything missing in his life, but now he felt a hunger he could not explain. It was like a physical pain, an emptiness that needed filling. His soul felt hollowed out. In desperate need of sleep, he asked God for a sign, something that would help him to make up his mind.

Rising at six o'clock as usual, William found Silas was already up and about and marvelled at his energy.

'Let me help you in your chores brother, in return for your hospitality.'

That morning the dairy resounded to hymns being sung as the cows were milked, William's voice as loud as his new friend's. When William set out with the milk for Cleethorpes, Silas accompanied him, speaking to the people as William delivered his milk and later that Saturday afternoon they both returned to Cleethorpes Market Place for an outdoor service. The people were waiting, expectant, as the preacher stood on a wheelbarrow, with William by his side. The farmer had told them that morning to be ready for something special and that is what they got. Despite William hearing the message for a second time he felt no loss of fervour but was re-inspired and left shaking in dread of the power of The Lord, but it also fed something deep inside his soul, something he could never tire of. But still he doubted.

Many came up to shake him by the hand, tears glistening in the eyes of hardened fishermen, market traders, devout Methodists, and Anglicans alike. William encouraged them to come to his farm for a prayer meeting on the Sunday evening.

After supper, Mr King asked William what was troubling him? William delayed in answering, trying to find the right words. Both Ann and Silas looked at him expectantly. In the end, he decided to be honest.

'You say that people are changed by your open-air preaching and I have certainly felt its power.'

'You want proof?' Silas said, immediately understanding. 'We are always asked for proof and that takes time. Anyone can promise to reform, give up the drink, become an honest, God fearing, individual. How long will it take for you to believe that they have changed? A month? A year? We can bring them to the point where they commit to God and then we must help them to stay the distance. My mission here will not end once I have saved these hungry souls. No, that's when the hard work begins.'

Ann nodded her agreement, her eyes shining at William. Despite not hearing him preach, Ann was convinced of the man's veracity.

'Come with me again to Grimsby tomorrow, Brother. Pick a spot where the most hardened sinners go and we will begin the process of conversion.' William was surprised at the use of 'we'.

Silas insisted on walking into Grimsby with William's wheelbarrow on the following afternoon, 'We must be as humble as the men and women we want to help,' he said, when William protested. 'Brother Bourne walks up to forty miles a day in the hills of Staffordshire. Do you think he cannot afford a horse?'

William, duly admonished, chose a spot on one of the meanest of the new wharves. The tide was out, leaving only a narrow stream of water, the remaining thick mud stank of decay and fish. An inn stood on the corner and warehouses lay to the left. Silas chose to place his wheelbarrow facing the tavern. On their progress through the town they had picked up men and women who had either heard Silas King two days before, or who had been told about him. By the time, he stood on his platform a small crowd had already gathered. William stood to his right, facing the tavern, but masked by the gathering people.

They began with a rousing hymn, 'All People that on Earth Do Dwell'. Heads poked out of the inn door, to see what the noise was. Three men walked out and stood on the side of the wharf watching Silas. Then one bent down and picked up some dry horse dung and flung it at the preacher.

'Be gone, bleeding Ranters; leave us to drink in peace,' he shouted. His mate stooped to pick up more filth, but Silas did not try to avoid the muck thrown at him. He stood straight and tall, singing his heart out. William wanted to lash out at the men but Silas warned him against it with his eyes and a brief shake of his head. The men could not see William. The two who had shouted were not from Grimsby, their accent giving them away. The third was a scruffy, heavily bearded man, his eyes bloodshot with drink, his gait awkward and stumbling. Silas hopped down off the barrow and walked up to the men, which William thought a foolhardy thing to do. He envisioned his friend being punched and set upon by the drunkards, mentally going through which of them looked the easiest to fell. He balled his fists in readiness. Silas simply took hold of the bearded man and drew him into the crowd. He offered no resistance and his friends were too amazed to stop him.

'Brothers and Sisters, here we have a man in great need of salvation. Do you have children, Brother?' He asked of the man, who nodded, unable to speak, his eyes drawn to Silas's face.

'And are your children hungry, have you drunk away their food?'

'Leave him be,' shouted one of his mates, advancing towards Silas. The crowd moved around to stop them and the preacher launched into a sermon so powerful that all fight left the men. Silas held on to the hand of the bearded man, his grip vice-like.

William could not remember when he realised that the bearded man was Joe, his brother. Maybe it was not until he sank to the floor, sobbing and crying out for forgiveness. His eyes and voice gave him away. Things which his beer sodden body could not disguise. Once the sermon finished, William knelt to cradle his whimpering brother in his arms.

'How did you know?' he asked Silas, in awe.

'Know what?

'That this man is my brother.'

'We are all brothers, William. I saw a man whose soul was in torment, who was reaching out to be saved. He had no voice but God spoke to me through him.'

'You have given me the proof I was looking for.'

'No William, God does not offer such simple proof. If he's your brother, how is it that he is mired in such degradation whilst you are a God-fearing man?'

'Six years ago, he did a great wrong. I have not spoken to him since.'

'Do you not see, dear Brother, you have left him in the devil's clutches when you should have raised him from the gutter, as you do now. Look into your own heart. Are you not found wanting?'

If Silas had punched him in the stomach, it could not have hurt more than the pain William felt, deep in his gut.

'You know the parable of the Prodigal Son, William. Does it have meaning for you, now?'

William shuddered. Yes, he was to blame. He saw that with all the certainty of a lightning bolt striking him. Joe, his younger brother, needed help and he hadn't lifted a finger. On the contrary, he had left him and his family to suffer. He'd been too proud and vengeful. William lifted his eyes to look at Silas, saw the gentleness of his face contrasting with the fiery words of his sermon and thought, this is truly a man of God. All doubt receded from his mind.

Silas held out his hand and William caught it.

'The proof is that you are able to forgive. Are you ready to become one of us, William?'

'I am ready. Tell me what I need to do.'

Chapter 12

Ann uttered not a single word of complaint when William arrived unexpectedly with Joe that autumn afternoon. She might have, considering how William was turning their household upside down. She took it in her stride, her usual calm, unflappable self. The only proviso was that her husband must wash and re-clothe Joe; the stink of his trousers and shirt smelt worse than their midden.

William filled a tub with water and gently removed Joe's outer garments, resolving to burn them when he saw the lice crawling through the seams.

'Joe, what have you come to?' He asked his unresponsive brother. Could he see any trace of his childhood playmate? Not in his bloodshot eyes, which stared unseeing, as though dead. His flesh felt slack under William's fingers as he scraped away at the grime. He had to cut his matted hair and beard, the skin underneath blotched with insect bites. With his hair shorn he finally saw a glimpse of the Joe that he knew and tears sprang to his eyes. Joe retched suddenly, falling afterwards into his brother's arms, while William wiped his brother's mouth. He stroked Joe's head, recalling the good times when they played in the woods. Joe's shuddering gasps rendered him speechless but William soothed him by talking softly.

'With God's help, I will make you better Joe. You won't be alone again.' William continued to whisper as Joe lay unresponsive, save for an occasional shiver.

Ann had prepared a cot in the parlour and once clean, William lifted his brother and with Silas's help, walked him into the house.

'Sleep will do him good,' Ann said before she left to prepare supper.

'It will take more than that. He needs to rid his body of the poison. William, are you prepared to take charge of him?'

'Yes, Silas. I will never let him down again. Right now, I'm worried about his wife and children. I haven't seen them for a few weeks. It's only just struck me.'

'Tomorrow you must search them out.'

William nodded, guilt rolling over him in waves of dread at what he may discover. Shame at his neglect hammered in his head.

As dusk began to fall, Ann and William stood hand in hand and silent in the doorway of the dairy waiting for people to arrive. Silas, seemingly oblivious, prayed on his knees with his back to them. The sight of him made them humble and aware of their own shortcomings. How could they ever measure up to one so holy?

Everyone was there, including the children. Ann held their baby, Mary, while the older children sat in front. William insisted that Joe attend; he was not leaving to chance his brother's reformation. Friends, neighbours, both Anglicans and Wesleyans, all turned up until the dairy was heaving. They stood and sat wherever they could and no one complained, because they had come to witness the preacher who could change lives by the power of his words and the simplicity of his message.

William stood where he could see Ann's face; her reaction to Silas's preaching the best guage of the preacher's power he could think of, although he was now certain in his own mind. This sermon would be the fourth time he had heard Silas but it would be Ann's first. They began with a familiar hymn, filling the dairy with song. It acted like balm on William after the traumatic events of the day. Ann smiled lovingly at him as the hymn ended then turned her face towards Silas. An expectant hush descended as they waited for the preacher to begin.

'Today, dear brothers and sisters, we have witnessed a miracle.' His voice was soft but meaningful. William looked at him, surprised at the soft, low tone. 'I want you to bear witness to this, dear friends. Your neighbour, William Holtby, has experienced the power of God's love.' Silas's voice and tone rose to a crescendo. 'Come William, tell us how God has saved your brother and brought you to the glory of the Lord.'

All eyes fell on William. His mouth dried as he looked first at Silas, in shock at hearing his name, then at Ann. His wife nodded her encouragement and he found himself stepping forward. Silas made room for him on straw bale where he was standing. His hand rested on William's back, curbing the tremors he felt throughout his body.

'Today,' he began, licking his lips. 'Today, I found my brother after twenty years of separation. He was wretched and a sinner, but God singled him out to be saved.' William looked around, nervously, but saw everyone was with him. He raised his voice, 'God made me see the harm I have done by rejecting my brother. I too am a sinner; my sin was pride. Forgive me, Lord. I beg you.' He fell on his knees and a collective moan resonated around the stone walls of the dairy.

Silas gave William his hand to help him up, clapping him on the shoulder. 'Praise the Lord,' he shouted.

'Yes, praise the Lord,' Ann replied, walking towards William to embrace him.

As they turned to walk back to their places, Silas launched into his most powerful sermon yet.

After the visitors left for their homes. William helped Ann put their children to bed.

'What did you think?' he asked.

'Have you need to ask? I've never met anyone like him. He's the most wonderful preacher, I truly felt God move in me. I was so proud of you for standing up and admitting your fault.'

'I never thought I would have the courage to do that in front of all those people we know. But once I started to speak, God seemed to take over.' There was no other way to describe it. The burden of guilt he had carried for years was gone.

He and Silas sat with Joe until morning. While Joe slept a fitful, tormented sleep, Silas prayed with William and then they talked long into the night. He was all ready to join the Primitive Methodist Connexion, but William needed to know what he must do and was shocked when Silas told him he must prepare himself to be a lay preacher.

'But I haven't your knowledge, your fire nor your wisdom,' protested William. 'I'm simply a farmer.'

'I am not suggesting you begin right away,' Silas reassured him. 'First you must read your Bible and then re-read it and then once more again. You must know it as you know yourself. You must be able to conjure up the very essence of its teaching. Only then will God speak through you. Do not think of me preaching to you, no, it is God who speaks through me.' William regarded Silas with awe.

'Once we have our congregations in each village then we will need Sunday Schools so that men, women and children can be taught to read the words of the Lord. There is so much to do, William, if we are to lift our brethren out of the mire they have allowed themselves to be forced into.'

'Forced? Why do you say that, Silas?'

'When your life is not your own, when every working hour is at someone else's direction, when you have not enough food to feed your children, it's then that people lose hope and they fall into sin. We must force them to regain their hope and their self-respect. It is no good telling the poor that if they work hard and know their place that they will reap their reward in heaven, like the Anglicans preach. Rather they should obey God, work hard, and reap the rewards of his love in this life. If they save themselves from drink, gambling and other bad habits they can harness what resources they have to help their families.'

'Do you think it possible for people to raise themselves up when all about us there is greed and corruption,' said William, thinking of the Grimsby elections. Joseph Dewsbury, the agent for one of the candidates had commented that the reason his candidate had not won a seat was that he had not bribed them enough.

'It will take time; we must work for change, but only when we have brought the people to God. That is our primary duty. Pray with me again, William. Let God guide you.'

He managed a bare two hours of sleep before hearing Ann potter about the kitchen. His brother still slept as William made his way out to milk his

111

cows. He left Silas also sleeping; the man looked worn out with care. All that preaching must have left him drained. A Ranter; the nickname was apt, if dripping with sarcasm. Would he mind being described as a Ranter? If he could summon up half the passion displayed by Silas, he would be proud to be called one. His head felt heavy with responsibility and fear, but there was also joy that he had discovered something which would give his life meaning.

After milking he returned to the kitchen for breakfast to find Joe sitting at the table with Silas. His brother looked ashamed when he saw William, his eyes drifting down to the plate of oatmeal which Ann had placed in front of him. He mumbled something and William had to ask him to repeat it.

'I'm sorry,' he choked with tears in his eyes as he glanced up at William's face.

'Don't be,' said William, kneeling beside him. 'All guilt is in the past and I am as guilty as you. We are going to start again; you and I, brothers and friends.' Joe's shoulders heaved as sobs broke from his mouth. William hugged him, stroking the stubble on his head as Betsy had stroked his hair when he was upset. William vowed to forgive his brother. Anger was no longer going to play any part in their relationship.

Ann poured a mug of tea for William and sat down beside him, while he comforted his brother.

'Joe says his family are in the workhouse, William. He lost his job, his landlord put them out. They have been there these five weeks past.' She spoke softly. 'We have that old farm cottage; it needs a lot of work to make it habitable but ..'

William turned his head and nodded to her. Are you sure you don't mind?'

'No, they're your family. We must do everything we can to help.'

He felt ashamed of his own neglect, whereas his wife was full of Christian charity. 'You are the most wonderful woman, do you know that, Ann?' He took her face in his hands and kissed her. 'I'll go today to fetch them. They can stay in the parlour until we mend the thatch and replace the windows. Joe can stay in the cottage until he's fit to be with his family.

I'll do the morning milk delivery and then take the cart into Grimsby to collect them.'

Silas offered to go over to the cottage and make a start. 'Then I must be on my way, Brother. I need to find lodgings if we are to begin a Connexion in this town.'

'You know you are welcome to stay.'

Silas nodded his thanks. 'It will be easier for me if I have lodgings in town and I need to find a place for worship. The winter is coming and I guess those east winds will not make my job any easier continuing to preach outside. Don't worry, I'll be back as soon as I'm settled and we will make a start on your training. I have someone I want you to meet. Are you ready for a journey?' He smiled at William, without expecting an answer.

After his morning milk-round and a quick bite to eat, William re-hitched his horse to the cart to set off for Grimsby. He delivered to some customers on the way, intending to fit the rest in after he had collected his sister-in-law and her children. The House of Industry was only as old as the docks and imposing in size. He could not picture a larger building in town. The Freemen probably thought riches would flow into the town once the docks opened. It was a testament to confidence. But, like the docks and the new houses surrounding them, that confidence had been misplaced. William drew up his cart beside the stocks which had migrated at some point from the market square to the parish pound. He sat awhile staring at the building which now housed his relatives, along with scores of other poor souls from Grimsby and the surrounding parishes.

His head throbbed from lack of sleep and the drama of the last few days. Normally he was soothed by the horse's gentle walk and the motion of the cart. Today it was different. He felt on edge and his nerves thrummed with guilt. It all led to here. From the moment his mother died, there was an inexorable line stretching down the years to this place. Well this is where it stopped. Betsy would be mortified to think of her great nephews and niece trapped in the buildings ahead. He should never have allowed it to happen.

The place was not unfamiliar, but he was used to passing it by without much thought. It lay towards the end of his journey from Hatcliffe to Grimsby. He had always been eager to reach his destination, contemplating the week ahead. Nowadays he rarely passed this way; his customers were the shopkeepers around the Market Place or the docks.

He tried to imagine how his brother had descended so low that his wife and children were forced into such a predicament. Aunt Betsy always helped the poor with a few coins, even during the worst of times. What had he done for those in need? His brother's family were hungry and he all he given was a mug of milk and an occasional crust of bread.

His guilt gnawed at him and he was worried that Ann must think less of him for not stepping in before. Sliding down from his seat, he gave his horse a nosebag of food to keep it from wandering off and walked slowly to the entrance. How did his sister-in-law feel making this same walk, her children clinging to her hands, their faces gaunt with hunger? He shook his head to repel the image.

He lifted the big brass knocker and hammered on the door. He was about to knock again when the door opened and a sharp face peered out. William recognised him as one of Robert's school friends. He was now a man, but with same grey eyes, pointed nose and ears which stuck out from his face like tiny, misshapen wings.

'Yes?' the man said, with no glimmer of recognition and an impatient tone.

'I have come to remove Mrs Holtby and her children from this establishment. She is a relative and I will take responsibility for her.' William spat the words out, eager to be away from the place.

The door opened wider. The man said nothing but directed William to come through the door and pointed to a further door marked Matron in flaking red paint. William knocked and waited as heavy footsteps trudged towards the door.

'Yes?' the same impatient tone, the same features but bloated by time, her loose neck wobbling as she spoke. William repeated his explanation. She passed by him, uttering the instruction to 'wait there' while opening the door to a yard. Leaving it ajar, she walked through and turned towards her left. He followed her into the yard, in need of air, because the building smelt of boiled turnip and stale urine.

A group of men laboured in the yard to the right. They appeared to be breaking up heavy stones with hammers. They were grey with dust and emaciated, almost like walking skeletons. He felt ashamed to be watching them. The young man pushed past and beckoned him forward.

'Would you like to see the treadmill? It was built to my own measurements and instructions.'

William replied that he had been told to wait for the matron.

'Suit yourself but the old bat won't hurry herself for anyone.'

William found himself walking towards some outhouses at the far edge of the yard. In the first one four men were operating the treadmill. They were grinding, what he assumed were cattle bones, overseen by a lean, grim faced man who was admonishing the men to work faster. Although only their backs and legs were visible, William saw the tracks of their sweat in their smocks as it made runnels down their necks and soaked their skin.

'This is my father, the Governor.'

'Put your backs into it, you lazy scoundrels,' the only response to his son's introduction. One of the men turned to scowl at the Governor. William stepped back in shock. The man's face was hideous; one eye was missing all together, as was part of his nose. His left cheek was scarred, by what could only have been a sword or an axe slicing through his flesh.

An elderly man with arthritic hands and knees was shovelling the bone-meal into sacks, pain etched on his face.

'It makes damned fine fertiliser,' the son said, proud of his achievement. 'Are you a farmer? Would you like to buy a sack or two? I'll do you a good deal.'

A voice hollered from across the yard. William turned to look.

'Looks like she's found your relative.'

Glad to escape the macabre scene, William retraced his steps.

He found it difficult to recognise the truculent Madge. Her head hung low in shame. Despite the cold, she was dressed in a workhouse uniform dress of grey cotton. A grey cap covered her hair and half her face. Her feet were shod in oversized, scuffed boots, the soles parting from the leather uppers. She wore no stockings and was shivering in the easterly wind. William wished he had a shawl to give her.

'We had to burn her clothes. Did you think to bring any with you? If not, we'll have to make a charge for these.' William would not have given tuppence for them but he doubted that he would get away with less than a shilling. 'I'll go and find her children now.' The matron marched indoors and up some stairs.

'Thank you, Master William,' a tiny voice whispered, piercing his heart.

'Don't you worry now, Madge. I am taking you home with me. Joe's there and he is a changed man. I'll make sure of that.' She did not look up but he heard quiet sobs and her bony shoulders shook. He put a hand out to pat her and was shocked at how little flesh he felt under the thin material of her dress.

'Have they been feeding you properly?' he asked in concern.

'Turnip soup and bread, twice a day. The bread is full of chalk. I'm worried for my children. They were already starving when we entered.'

Steps sounded on the wooden stairs and Madge looked up, her sleeve wiping away her tears to show a face, aged ten years. What must she be twenty-three or maybe twenty-four? She looked older than his Ann. Lines of hunger scoured her face; her skin blotchy and marked by insect bites. A small strand of greyish, blond hair escaped her cap. All spirit had died from her eyes. William doubted that her own children would recognise her.

Matron pushed three waifs towards William. He had no way of knowing if these were Madge's but he hoped that she would know them. Their hair had been shorn from their heads, only stubble remained while open sores oozed on their faces. Madge gave a cry of horror and sank to the floor and put her arms out and they stumbled towards her; the youngest held by his older brother. Madge took the toddler in her arms.

'I told you to look after him,' she scolded his brother. The boy looked crestfallen and William's heart went out to the lad, no more than five or six himself. How could she have given him that responsibility?

The boy in her arms was too weak to move; his dull eyes appearing too large for his head and his head too large for his body. His lips were cracked and smeared with blood, the only sign of life an occasional shuddering cough. This was worse than William imagined. He doubted the boy would survive the journey home. Why had he not thought to bring blankets with him? He shook off his greatcoat to wrap up the child. The child's burning skin shocked him into admonishing the matron for the state of the children.

'We provide shelter, food and clothing. It's not my fault if they get sick. These children were lousy when they arrived.' The woman glared at him. 'You owe me ten shillings for their clothes.'

'They are not worth more than a shilling but I will give you two,' he replied, ushering Madge and her family to the front door as he saw the women's son walking across the yard towards them. He did not want to get in a fight, but he was determined not to give her ten shillings.

The matron had her back to the yard and as Madge reached the door, William thrust two shillings in her hand and turned smartly towards the exit, intending never to return. The Matron followed him, cursing him, her hand outstretched for more money, until William turned on her.

'If you think I owe you more, send an itemised account to my lawyer, Joseph Dewsbury.' He saw the look of uncertainty in her eyes and knew that he had won.

'She didn't burn my clothes, you know,' Madge said, within earshot, as he helped her onto the cart where she cradled her sick child. William draped his coat over them both. 'They were decent clothes, not a single patch on any of them. She sells 'em. I saw a man come for them. It weren't no rag and bone man, neither. One of our jobs was to launder clothes and I watched mine go in a sack for the man to take away.' She had found her voice and William was reassured to hear some of her complaining spirit return. 'I protested and forfeited my dinner as a reward.' Madge turned glaring towards the matron, who still hovered. Madge summoned up all her energy and spat at the woman.

William told his horse to walk and they moved slowly away. It was a quiet journey back to the farm. Every now and again William looked over his shoulder to see the children slumped against their mother, eyes hollow with weariness and hunger. He should have brought food as well as blankets. The sooner they got back the better. He geed up the horse to trot, a pace it was not used to and required much encouragement from his whip.

Ann had been looking out for him and met him in the farmyard. As the children and Madge were helped down from the cart, Ann's eyes widened in shock at the state of them. Ever practical, she ran back inside to fetch clean clothes and put water on to boil. William guided the family into the dairy. Once there he grabbed a ladle and a jug and spooned in buttermilk to give to the children.

'See if you can get the little one to take some first,' he advised Madge, before hurrying off to fetch blankets and bread. He knew Ann would not welcome them into the house before she was sure they carried no lice, nor did he want Joe to catch sight of them until they were cleaned up. He prayed that he and Silas were still in the cottage, where no windows faced the farmyard. However, he was out of luck as Joe stumbled out of the cottage and saw the cart. He ran into the house and not finding his family there, he made for the dairy, followed by Ann, shouting at him to wait.

But it was too late. Joe stood in the doorway, paralysed at first by horror and anger at the plight of his children. Madge had undressed them while William fetched the blankets and his two oldest children stood shivering, their ribs standing out from their emaciated bodies. The youngest, still wrapped in William's coat lay in his mother's arms, almost too weak to cough, a smear of blood at his mouth. Joe howled in shame as he turned to run from the barn but William caught him in his arms and held him fast.

Silas, hearing the commotion ran towards them and after peering into the dairy he walked over to William and taking Joe, he marched him back towards his family.

Silas bent his mouth to Joe's ear and began to whisper 'Right now, all you want is a drink to take away the pain. Am I right?' Joe nodded, tears of humiliation glistening on his cheeks. 'That is the devil talking to you. Do you understand?' Joe's eyes opened in shock as he carried on whispering. Silas did not intend to add to the children's misery. 'Your children need their father to show them the way to God. They should not see you in the grip of the devil. Come back to the cottage with me and we will pray for your salvation. When we return, the children will see a new father, one they can respect; one who cares and provides for them.' Silas gripped Joe's arm, turning him away from the dairy and led him back towards the cottage.

William shook with emotion as he threw blankets over the two children, who were sobbing with fright and cold. He gathered them both into his arms and promised them that they were safe and would never be hungry again. He realised he did not even know their names and asked them.

'Margaret,' said the girl, 'after my mother.'

'Billy, said the boy, 'after my uncle, my papa's best brother.' William held him tighter, unable to speak when all he wanted to do was howl out his sorrow. His papa's best brother had abandoned him to drink and poverty, but he had been given a second chance. He would not fail Joe a second time.

Madge screamed as the child in her arms gave a sigh and then lay still, his sightless eyes wide open, undigested buttermilk coating his lips. William gasped and buried his head in his hands. It was too late. He would have to bear his part of the guilt for not saving this innocent child for the remaining years of his life.

Chapter 13

Joe was in no condition to be seen or heard by the children. Silas advised that William stay with Joe in the cottage, as unprepared as it was. Within minutes of being with his brother, William was thankful for the advice, as Joe raved and screamed his grief and guilt. William tried to put his arms around Joe to hold comfort him but he threw him off, spitting at him in anger.

'Don't leave him or let him escape,' Silas said before returning to Grimsby. 'He has to work through his demons. He will crave drink but you must not give in to him.'

The two days that followed were a nightmare as William witnessed the disintegration of his brother. He held him tight, ignoring the stink of puke, as Joe's body shook against his. He knelt on the floor with him as Joe sobbed and begged for drink and banged his head against the earthen floor. He held Joe's hand as he gabbled, incoherent and rambling in torment, eyes wild and fixed until he screamed in terror and began to beat his fists against William's chest. Joe could not hear William's own choking sobs to see his brother brought so low. He cried out for ale and gin as William tried to make him sip water. He grabbed the mug and threw it at William, drenching him. Joe stank of piss and sweat and vomit. William held him as he would a child and stroked his head until he calmed before starting again to shake and scream and rave until William thought his heart would break. For three days and nights William devoted every minute to his brother until he too began to shake with tiredness. He wasn't sure how much more he could take.

Silas visited towards the end of the third day with a membership card for the infant group of Primitive Methodists.

'I have rented an old warehouse on the wharf so I hope you will all be there on Sunday Morning.' William shook his head, 'Joe is in no fit state and I dare not leave him. As it is, I have had to hire someone else to do my milk-round.'

'It will take time for the poison to leave his body, but it will leave and he will begin to recover. He should be calmer by Sunday.'

'Do you think? He's not eating and neither is his wife. They both seem bereft and Madge can hardly bear to look at Joe. She's carried food and drink here but never stayed to talk with him. She scurries off as fast as she can to Ann and the children. Their children are recovering, I'm pleased to say. Ann says it's a joy to see they are regaining their appetites and sprits.'

'Ann needs to give Madge work to do and not allow her to sit and brood. As for Joe, let him talk, once he's over the worst. When we prayed together I saw such pain in his heart. The devil has a real grip on him and you must find a way of loosening his hold. Bring him on Sunday, he needs to be there. We will save him, you and I, but he must let God take the place of Satan.'

Joe was incapable of talking before Friday evening but he did agree to swallow some broth, Ann had made from pork knuckles and vegetables.

'I could not have eaten without puking before.' His voice was ragged as he tore off a heel of bread. 'It makes me guilty to think of eating while my children starved. Did little Josh die of starvation?' His pleading eyes tore into William's heart.

'No, it was an infection. The place was infested,' Better that Joe did not know the truth. Hunger had brought the child so low he could not fight infection. William had sent for the doctor to attend the other children and he confirmed that all they needed was food. By that time, the children were deloused, in fresh clothes and sitting by the farmhouse fire. He remembered Ann's disgust as she washed the children and saw the filthy water, with its film of fleas and lice. They had been dunked in and scrubbed, despite protestations. Ann made William burn the clothes and blankets, but not his top coat. Instead she held a candle over every seam more than once and watched as the lice fell to the ground. Then she brushed the inside of his coat with a ferocity William had rarely seen and made him hang it out in the barn, before allowing it back in the house. She insisted on inspecting his skin for any tell-tale red marks. She would not put up with fleas in the house.

'Still it was the poor-house that killed him.' Joe said.

William could not deny it. But whose fault was it they were there? He poked at the fire, at least the chimney was now unblocked. On the first night, he almost set fire to the thatch. Joe appeared indifferent, while he ran to douse the fire. Just one more moment in the madness of the last few days.

He brought the conversation around to Joe himself. 'Why did it all go wrong for you? I remember you as a happy, carefree child.' Joe looked at him in surprise.

'Do you really not know?' William shook his head. 'On the day that Mother was buried, I lost the two people that I loved most, with no explanation; at least nothing that I could understand. You were there and then Betsy came and you were gone. I blamed her for everything, even my mother dying. It got twisted in my mind. Father forbade any of us from talking about you. In his own way, maybe he thought that was for the best, I suppose. All I remembered was that this crone, dressed in black, arrived from nowhere. In my mind, I made her into some kind of witch, with an evil stare, claws, and a crow's feather in her hat. She took both you and Mother away. For all I knew she may have killed you. Night after night I cried for you, until Father thrashed me for keeping everyone awake. After that I got angry. I refused to look after Uriah, refused to do my chores and each time I was beaten for disobedience, I saw Betsy's evil face laughing at me.'

William gathered his brother in his arms and held on tight, not wanting him to see his tears. He remembered that day. How could he not? It changed his life forever. Worse, he recalled taking his brother out to fight the evil witch who was threatening the princess. Maybe it was all his fault. Should he have let him see his mother in her coffin? He only ever wanted to protect his little brother.

'The sole thing I held on to, was rescuing you from Betsy. After Tom died in the wars, I was the elder son and I made Father tell me where you had gone. I stole enough money for a coach ride to Grimsby and bided my time. Tell me, William, did you miss me? Did you cry yourself to sleep? Did Betsy thrash you for crying at night, because you were lonely?' William saw the pain and hurt in his brother's eyes and forgave him everything.

'Your friend Silas says I have given myself up to the devil. If so, he has been with me since that day. Do you think that's possible, William?' His eyes accused his brother. 'No, the devil is not responsible for what I did, only me. I did it out of ignorance, out of pain, out of resentment, whatever. I wanted revenge on Betsy and when you turned on me, I had nothing left to live for. That's when I finally gave up on God, but the devil, he does not own me. In here,' Joe pointed to his heart 'is a void, a nothing, an emptiness that even my children could not fill. Madge trapped me into marriage, told me she was with child. Did you know that? Strange that Billy arrived nine months to the week after we married and not before.'

William shook his head, not approving of Joe blaming Madge. He is weak, he thought. Is that my fault too?
'You need to let God back in, Joe. Make your peace with Madge and regain your soul.'

'It's so easy, is it?' Joe laughed, mocking. 'Maybe for you, with your piety and money. But I am not you, never had your luck.'

'No, it will be hard, but I'll be with you, every step of the way.'

Joe shook his head, disbelieving. 'You have your own life and all I have done is bring you trouble. I know Betsy's seizure was my fault. I should have talked to you before I acted, but George Dawson fed my anger and made me believe Betsy had stolen Alice from her family too. He dropped me as soon as I gave him back the jewellery.' Joe laughed in bitterness. William watched conflicting emotion pass over Joe's face, ending in defeat.

'You told me then that I was jealous, but I wasn't, never jealous, just angry, always angry.' He sighed with weariness. 'Now I am tired of being angry. It's time I started to live for me, not for you. I need to clear up the mess I've made. From now I promise to put my children first. I didn't even get to watch Josh buried.'

William did not know whether to correct him. How could he have forgotten that scene? It was burnt into William's memory. The child was buried in haste because of the fever and William had to drag Joe to the graveside and hold him up to watch as his youngest, barely thirteen months old, was buried. He thought it may be the most pitiful moment of his life. Ann had stayed to comfort Madge in the farmhouse. There were no other mourners.

As William lay on his mattress that Friday, he decided it was time that Madge and the children moved into the cottage. It would give Joe a chance to think of something other than himself. He needed to find a few bits of furniture, but no doubt they had little enough before she entered the workhouse. He felt most for their children. What chance did they stand with parents who both felt so sorry for themselves and appeared actively to dislike each other? What behaviour had they witnessed? Drunken rages, fights? Anything seemed possible.

He missed Ann, missed her company. Since his brother arrived, he had not shared her bed, nor even had a moment's private conversation with her. He longed to put his arms around her and sink his face into her fragrant hair. He did not care that it was threaded with grey. She was troubled that her body had not regained its shape since Mary was born, but he loved its softness and curves, the milky smell of her breasts. He longed for her touch.

How would he cope without his soul-mate, Ann? He could not imagine a life without her and regretted that his brother did not have the same relationship with Madge. Ann was solace, comfort, love, happiness, laughter, and a wonderful mother. Everything he had ever wanted. They would get through these dark days together.

He had been brought to salvation just days ago, when he met Silas. He thought his life complete and then all this despair and trauma entered his life.' God is testing you,' Silas had said. 'Why,' he asked?' To see if you are strong enough for what lies before you,' Silas replied. I am strong enough, William thought. With Ann beside me, I will never weaken.

Chapter 14

William stood hunkered in his great coat on the deck of the steam packet to Hull one morning in December. Since the service began a year or so before, he had always meant to make this trip but had no reason to do so until Silas came along.

Everyone had come out to see the steam packet when it first arrived in Grimsby. There had been no bigger event in the town since the docks first opened seventeen years before. Somehow the wider world appeared nearer as visitors began to arrive, often for no better reason than to assuage their curiosity. Especially if it meant they could make the trip in less time than it took to eat a good dinner and be back in time for their bed. Some came to sample the delights of the villages which hugged the coast with their fine sandy beaches and bathing machines. More fishermen opened boarding houses and began to see a glimpse of prosperity.

As the boat steamed into the river, William's feet caught the roll of the waves beneath. He grabbed the wooden rail to steady himself, the giant paddles churning the muddy water. The metal funnel blew clouds of gritty smoke into the listless, murky air. The lack of sunshine did not do anything to dampen his enthusiasm for his trip over the river. He watched as Grimsby began to disappear, becoming no more than a smudge on the horizon.

Over the last few weeks, Joe had described why he loved to be out on the open sea. He told of the excitement of sailing a tiny boat against the elements and the salty sting of seawater as it smashed against his face. William wanted none of that and gave thanks to the Lord that the river today was flat calm, with scarcely a sigh of wind to disturb the dank air. His hands were becoming numb so he turned and walked unsteadily inside, joining Silas and the other passengers in the fug of the cabin, where the whoosh of the paddles reverberated, a constant backdrop to conversation.

'It's a good job we have steam to power us today. There's scarce any wind to fill the sails.' William was grateful that the boat had masts with sails, albeit not in use. He hated the thought that they could be stuck in the middle of the river should anything happen to the steam engine. Silas nodded to William but his eyes fell back to the book he was reading and William's thoughts returned to his family. Could it be only five weeks since the trauma with Joe and his family? It seemed longer. When Silas first suggested the trip to Hull, a week before, he had been unsure. Both Ann and Joe told him he should go.

'It's only two days. We can manage,' Ann said. She had been a rock beside him these last few weeks. He thought this year he would give her something more than the trinket he normally bought around Christmas. What it should be he did not know and time was running out.

'I can do your milk-round,' said Joe. 'Trust me, brother. I won't let you down.'

William wanted to trust Joe. Since Joe and his family had moved into the cottage, a sullen truce had been declared between Joe and Madge. He spent most of the day outside helping William with milking, his dairy round or working in the fields. How Madge spent the day, William wasn't sure. Her housekeeping was desultory, at best. Long strands of dusty, grey cobwebs still hung from the ceilings in her cottage, ashes were not swept from the grate and washing rarely graced the line. At first William hoped that Madge would relieve Ann of some of her work. Ann soon put paid to that thought.

'If only she would,' she said. 'If I lost a child, I would throw myself into work to ease the pain. But we are all different. Madge is the type who sits and mopes, believes she is hard done by and refuses to see God's blessings. I doubt she will ever change.'

'Remember how I was when Betsy died, my love.'

'Yes, I do. But you worked through it.'

'Only because I had you to comfort me and spur me on.'

William wondered if his dear wife fully understood what grief could do. She had lost a brother in the war, but a brother was not a child of your own flesh. Please God we never need to meet that trial, he prayed, silent in thought until Ann interrupted.

'If I give her a job, she takes twice as long over it and I then have to do it again when I see the mess she has made.' It was unlike Ann to be so critical. She must really dislike Madge.

'Poor Joe,' William replied, thinking that his brother had so many trials before him.

'Poor children,' sighed Ann. 'They're good children but I worry about what will become of them with Madge for a mother or if Joe begins to drink again.' Ann considered whether to tell William about Madge's bitterest complaint and decided she should. They had never kept secrets from one another.

'Madge thinks you should pay Joe for all his work,' she laid her hand on his arm as William's face showed a rare display of anger.

'It's not enough that I got her out of the workhouse, that I give them a free cottage, furnish it, clothe and feed them,' his voice was thunderous. 'Does she want me to lay off my loyal farmhand, throwing his family out of their home and his livelihood, so I can pay Joe instead?'

'No William, the problem is, she doesn't think before she speaks.'

He had it out with his brother when they were on the milk-round the day after. Joe looked mortified.

'No, I don't want wages. You and Ann have saved our lives. I couldn't be more grateful to you both. Let me get back on my feet and we will move back to Grimsby. I'm not cut out for a farmhand's job. I want to get back to fishing. I miss the sea.'

William began to feel queasy through lack of air and the motion of the ship. He decided to go back outside, in time to catch his first sight of Hull. For all his life, it had been the one place he aspired to visit. A rival to Grimsby, although way back in history, Betsy had told him, when they were ports of equal importance.

Even from the river he could tell that Hull had the upper hand, although there was little sign of the ships docked there. He glimpsed a sail in the river to the east of the town, but the packet steamed past the mouth of the river making for a pier at the edge of the town. The paddles slowed and as all the passengers gathered on the British Queen's deck, a sailor threw a rope to a man on the pier to secure the vessel.

Silas led William towards the old town. William's legs took a while to stop feeling the roll of the river rather than the firm, grimy cobbles they trod. They headed for an inn so that William could drop off his bag. He had insisted to Silas that he would prefer to stay the night in a respectable inn rather than putting any of the congregation to the trouble of finding him a bed.

'The man we are going to meet was almost press-ganged from that tavern,' Silas said, pointing to a building over the road. 'He escaped by a whisker and it probably saved his life. Your namesake, William Clowes, was a man like your brother Joe. He worshipped the tankard and lived a mean, sinful existence until that close shave forced him to re-examine his life.'

'Is he from Hull?'

'No, he heralds from Staffordshire, a friend of Hugh Bourne and a relative of Josiah Wedgewood. He trained as a potter.' William was impressed, everyone knew of the great Wedgewood pottery. His aunt had left him a blue and white jasperware pot. It had pride of place on Ann's dressing table.

'Why did he return to Hull?'

'We bring the word of the Lord to people most in need and Brother Clowes, remembering his own debauched youth, believes there are many souls here in need of saving.'

William observed a group of drunken sailors surrounding two women on the corner of the street ahead. He was concerned for the women's safety until he heard their raucous laughter. Silas hurried him on but not before one of the women took out a large, blue veined breast and waggled it at him, mocking his discomfort. William's face flamed, he quickly averted his eyes, almost tripping on a loose cobblestone. Shrieking laughter followed him up the street.

The George inn, situated in an oddly named street, looked far more salubrious than some they had passed. William asked the landlord where the name 'The Land of Green Ginger' had come from, but he merely shrugged, indifferent to a question he had been asked daily, but cared not enough to answer.

William asked to see the docks, before meeting William Clowes, so Silas escorted him up Parliament Street towards the quay side. They stood counting the masts but there were more than entered the docks in Grimsby in a year. William gazed at the scene as ships were loaded or unloaded. The bustle and noise from carts as they trundled through the docks entranced him, as did the voices shouting in strange accents and languages. Smells of fish and spices mingled with the dust of coal. His spine tingled. Betsy would have loved to see this. It was almost as if she stood next to him pointing out this and that, her excitement stirring the hairs on his neck beneath the muffler Ann had given him. He shivered, not in cold but in some vague recollection of a childish memory.

Brother Clowes lived with his wife in rented rooms, close by the docks. He met William with a firm handshake, a broad, powerful potter's grip. The pleasing sweep of his face welcomed him with intelligent, twinkling eyes. His fair hair was thinning at the temple and his nose, long and narrow, collided with his top lip where a confident smile put William at his ease.

'So, you have come for our Love-Feast, Brother Holtby. Silas wrote and told me that you are going to be a real asset to our Connexion.'

'I am very pleased to be here, Mr Clowes. I look forward to hearing your sermon.'

'As to that, we shall see. We expect a great many people and it's a chance for them to speak out too. Come, my wife has prepared dinner. Let me tell you about my travels in Yorkshire and the success we have had in spreading our message.'

As they talked William found himself astonished at the man's energy. It was apparent that in a few short months, Brother Clowes had walked all over Yorkshire, preaching in towns and villages, wherever he found himself, never knowing if he would find a bed for the night.

'I trust in the Lord to provide, and the Lord has never let me down.'

Hundreds were flocking to the call, not only those who led lives of sin and infamy but also pious individuals from other churches. William began to understand that he was part of a fast-growing movement, a groundswell of change, something to be proud of and his heart bubbled with emotion. Just to listen to this man was worth the trip and he lapped up his words like one of the feral cats which hung around his barn waiting for a saucer of milk.

'Don't you worry about the consequences of standing up in a strange place and preaching? How do you know that you won't be arrested or attacked by a mob?' William asked.

'I am sometimes afraid. The other day I was in York and I thought, who am I to address the people of this great city? I am but a humble man of no great station. The calming influence of the Lord fell upon me and I began to speak in the marketplace. Crowds soon drew nigh, but someone must have informed the authorities, and it was not long after that a troop of horse surrounded both me and the congregation.'

'Great heavens! What happened?' breathed William.

'I carried on. I deduced that they would either arrest me as a radical, disperse the crowd and tell me to go, or let me speak. Jesus instructed me to go to York and he protected me. The soldiers allowed me to exhort those sinners to flee from the wrath to come and many souls were saved that day. We now have a sizable Connexion in York.'

'I would not be that brave.'

'Jesus protects me and I trust him.' William was overawed by his calm manner and his faith in Jesus.

The feverish atmosphere hit William as soon as they walked through the door of a warehouse in Mill Street, where the congregation waited to begin their Love-feast. Upwards of five hundred folk, men, woman and children thronged the space and more were entering. He looked for the normal feast of dishes prepared by women such as his wife, but on a table to one side were loaves of bread and tankards of water. It was hardly a feast and he was pleased that he had eaten well for his midday meal. The warehouse echoed to the sound of chattering voices. Some were stamping their feet as the cold of the day outside permeated the vast space indoors.

He walked with Silas towards the front as Brother Clowes, wearing a double-breasted coat and a white hat, stood on a wooden box to face the crowd. People looked at him, expectant, their eyes alight with anticipation. He raised his arms for silence, hush descended, eyes closed as he began with a prayer. All sound apart from his strong, clear voice ceased. William felt a shiver run up his spine as the voice bored into his soul. He felt God speak to him through Brother Clowes. A calming certainty took over his body, insulating him from the surrounding chill. The prayer ended and William opened his eyes, looking around at faces filled with joy. Brother Clowes asked if any were willing to speak. A shout came from the middle of the warehouse, all eyes turning to see who it was.

'I, I will speak,' said a woman, short in stature but loud in voice. A passage was made for her and she stumbled her way to the front.

'I see that you are lame, Sister,' said Brother Clowes. 'Do you wish to sit?'

'Nay, nay thank ee, Sir.' She appeared overwhelmed at his kindness. 'I want to thank ee,' she said, grasping his hands. 'My husband was a fearful bad drunkard, but you 'as saved him, Sir. He no longer belts me and t' chillun of a night. Now we all kneel and pray t'Lord God, our saviour.'

'Is he here, your husband?'

'That he is, Sir. Over there,' she pointed to where she had come from. A shamefaced man stood, his cap clasped in his hands.

'Thank the Lord, for our brother is saved,' roared William Clowes. The warehouse rang with praise.

Another voice was heard, and then another. For hours, people clamoured to speak and Brother Clowes let them. Their words heartfelt, mostly uneducated, rang with pure sentiment. One elderly lady, who accepted the offer to sit, spoke the humblest of words.

'I ask the dear Lord to save my son,' she said to loud 'Amens'. 'He is hard now. Lord, make his soul as soft as,' she paused, searching wildly for a suitable word, 'soft as a boiled turnip.' She looked about her, but saw no laughter, only sympathy and 'Alleluias'.

As the Love-Feast ended, William felt drained from the emotion which had gripped him throughout the afternoon and evening. Although he was disappointed not to have heard a sermon from Brother Clowes, there would be time on the following day, before sailing back to Grimsby.

'What did you think of the meeting?' asked Silas as they walked towards their lodgings for the night.

'It was very powerful but it was not what I was expecting.'

'You have attended Wesleyan Love-Feasts?'

'No Ann has and she told me it followed a set path. This was more ....' William struggled for the words.

'An outpouring of love?'

'Yes, it was.' Simply put, that was indeed what it was.

'We threaten fire and brimstone but sometimes there is a time for love. One day, Praise the Lord, may we only have love.'

'Amen to that, Brother Silas.'

The murk and damp had blown away by the following noon. A strong gale took its place. William was making the return journey alone as Silas remained in Hull to discuss the planning for the first Primitive Methodist Conference. It was due to take place the following May in Hull. William ambled through the narrow streets of the old town with time to kill. He was hoping for some inspiration for Ann's gift. It came from a shop selling musical instruments and there it stood in the window, resplendent and alone. A second-hand harmonium. What could please her more? His darling wife sorely missed the one she grew up with and he entered the shop not caring if it cost more than he had put aside, because she deserved nothing less. The shopkeeper assured him it would be delivered in the week before Christmas. The family would sing carols accompanied by his wife on her harmonium. The eagerness to see her face when it was delivered consumed him all the way to the pier.

He stood waiting to board the packet as the water slapped at the edge of the pier. The coast of Lincolnshire stood out more clearly than the day before. Still far away, he picked out a church steeple in the distance, wondering which village it belonged to. He wrapped his coat around him as the freezing wind found its way through any gaps. The British Queen appeared to rock up and down as the passengers boarded and William felt the motion unsettle him immediately. He made for the cabin and found a seat but the seat appeared to sway, although fixed to the deck. He stayed put until the packet got underway, but then his stomach began to churn and he regretted the large breakfast he had consumed at the inn. He stood and made his way back to the outside deck, grasping at the rail as Hull began to fade away. He looked at the waves, choppier than the day before but not high. No one could say they were high. Joe had told him how waves could smash over boats and how the coble had to ride the waves in order not be overwhelmed with water. This was still the river, not the sea or the ocean but it mattered not to William. The queasiness came in waves through his stomach and up to his mouth. He swallowed it back and tried to think of the excitement he felt the day before when he realised that this new Connexion of the Primitive Methodists was what he had been waiting for.

He longed to take up the challenge of becoming a lay preacher. If only he could develop the same fire in his belly and the oratory of Silas and Brother Clowes. What men they were. Outstanding visionaries. He felt so blessed in knowing them. By dint of will, he clung to the ship and forced his mind to play though the events of the Love Feast. As they chugged into the dock at Grimsby, William thought that he had managed to overcome his sickness. By the time he had walked home, all would be well and he looked forward to sharing his adventure with Ann.

William departed the packet and began to walk the short distance to the dock exit, pausing to make way for a lumper unloading a ship. The man carried a sack hoisted across his shoulders intending to heave it onto a cart. Instead, his foot slid away on the wet dock and sent him crashing to the ground. William jumped back in horror as the sack split and spilled its contents beneath his feet. Toothless skulls with vacant eye sockets stared up at him; leg bones, bits of rib lay all around his boots. The seasickness he had been fighting spewed from his mouth and all over the bones, narrowly missing the docker, who lay aghast on the ground.

'What the fuck have you done?' exclaimed the man before picking himself up.' He glared at William, his mouth a sneer of contempt. William stared, helpless, at the stinking mess around him.

A sailor on the ship above threw a fresh sack down to the man, chortling at his discomfort. With his gloved hands the docker began to shovel the bones back into the new sack, wrinkling his nose at the smell of vomit.

'Where have all these bones come from?' Asked William, horrified.

'Soldiers' the man said without glancing up. 'We gets 'em from the battlefields of France, Belgium and Spain. It's good business.'

'They rob graves!' William was outraged.

'Nah, they're never buried. They're stripped of their clothes and their teeth within hours, then they're left to be picked clean by birds and wildlife. A year or so later they bundle them up and send them here. It'll keep the ship owners in business for a few years yet, they say.'

'What do they do with them?' William had more than a sneaking feeling that he knew the answer.

'Fertiliser. We sends 'em to the mill over there and they get ground up; sells like hot cakes.' He pointed to the quay opposite.

William thought of his brother, Tom. This was the stuff of nightmares; he could never share it with Ann, who had lost her own brother. Poor Tom, to be left for carrion. The irony of his brother's bones returned to his native country to be scattered onto fields, possibly even ploughed in by his own father, did not escape him. William shivered, as he wiped at the bile around his mouth with a handkerchief. A worse thought occurred to him, had those old soldiers in the workhouse been grinding up bones of fellow soldiers, rather than cattle? He dared not ask.

The man finished scooping the bones into the sack. As he tied, it he said. 'I heard tell of a soldier, injured like. He only woke up to find himself stark bollock naked and a cove yanking his teeth from his jaw. That soldier screamed so much that the bloke passed out in fright. So, this soldier grabs the thief's trousers, his jerkin and his sack and hobbles as fast he can from the battlefield. He sells the teeth and sets himself up us an innkeeper. Does good business from telling his story, I'm told.' He grinned a sardonic, toothless smile at William.

Shuddering William stepped around the cart with its loathsome cargo, eager to leave the man to his ghastly labour.

Chapter 15

1821

No one ever said it would be easy. Here he was running a dairy farm, delivering his milk, holding his brother's hand as Joe slowly turned from drunkenness to sobriety and walking miles out of town two Sundays a month, to preach in local villages. He was lucky to have a wife who supported him in his work, but she had three children to care for, a house to run as well as making the butter and cheese she sold at market. At least she now had some help around the house.

Six-year old Thomas, was beginning to help as well, but soon enough he would be at school during the day. A new, free grammar school was due to open in Humberstone the following year. It was two and a half miles away, not much further than Grimsby and would take boys at the age of seven. It had been more than a century since a bequest for a school had been made by Matthew Humberstone, but William often despaired of anything happening quickly in this corner of Lincolnshire. It still felt remote and neglected, while times were moving fast elsewhere. In many ways, he was grateful for the slow pace of change. He enjoyed the simple lifestyle and peace, but for the people without land or profession, times remained hard and hand to mouth. The poverty in the Wolds villages often shocked him. The message he brought fed their souls but not their bellies. He was unsure how else he could help them.

Joe had returned to fishing and lived with his family in Grimsby. William made a point of visiting them at least once a week, usually taking some milk or cheese. As far as he could tell, Joe was not drinking and attended the service in the warehouse most weeks. Madge received him with her normal disdain, but the children ran to him to be picked up and swung around, asking after their cousins. He missed Billy and Margaret and so did his children. Often, he suggested that they come and stay for a few days but Madge always turned him down flat. Her resentment of his perceived wealth remained an open sore, even though, given half a chance, he would have shared it with his brother. He realised that whatever he did, Madge would take offence. She enjoyed her beaker half empty because it fed her resentment. It suited her to bemoan her fate. How Joe must suffer, William sympathised with his brother, whilst admiring him for overcoming his troubles.

Ann's sister, Martha, had married in June the year before. On one of her many visits to their farm in the days before William had joined the Connexion, she had met a widower who attended Old Clee Church. Alfred Mountain lived in Cleethorpes with his two, motherless girls and William had been delighted to offer the farm as a venue for the wedding breakfast.

Martha, wore a dress of sprigged cotton as did her two step daughters, acting as bridesmaids. Ann had a moment of envy as she inspected her sister before they left for the church. She looked so young and beautiful in the pretty, summery dress, whereas she had worn a sensible dress of navy poplin for her own wedding in the autumn, seven years before.

William read Ann's expression and took her in his arms. 'You are always beautiful to me, my love. The day I married you, was the happiest of my life. I stood at the alter in Hatcliffe Church and couldn't believe how lovely you were walking down the aisle towards me.'

'I hope Martha is as happy with Alfred as I am with you, William.' Ann, raised her face to be kissed.

'And I wish our children find the same happiness when they marry.'

'Goodness! Let's get this wedding done first, before we plan our own children's.

They left Martha and walked the few steps from the farm, past the clipped yew hedge to the front door of the church, accompanied by Tom and John. Mary was left behind with the maid. William always liked stepping into the church. He had worshipped there quite happily until Silas appeared on the scene. Weddings and funerals now gave him the only opportunity to enter and walk beneath the ancient arches. They sat in one of the wooden pews towards the front, gazing at the stained-glass windows above the alter. William took Ann's hand in his, squeezing it gently, as the organist began to play. All eyes turned towards the bride as she walked with her ageing father up the aisle. Ann took a handkerchief from her pocket, dabbing at her eyes. Martha looked towards Alfred and as their eyes met, Ann emitted a soft mew of happiness to see their love. William felt a great peace descend on him. It was rare to feel peaceful in Chapel or drumming up a congregation in the villages. Here at least he could commune silently with God and nothing was expected of him, other than to sing hymns and kneel at the appropriate moment.

'We've missed you in church,' said the Reverend Oliver, shaking William's hand as they left after the service.

'God has called me in his own way,' replied William, smiling.

'And you must answer.' The priest bore no ill will towards his neighbour. 'Do come with your wife to the wedding breakfast.'

'I have another wedding in an hour, so thank you but no. Go in peace.'

'And you, Brother.' William answered automatically, then grinned at his slip up.

'Why are you smiling so much, William,' asked Ann, who'd run after the two boys, excited to be back out in the open air.

'Because I am the happiest man alive.' he said and kissed her on the lips in full view of everyone.

Silas, who was still based in and around North Lincolnshire, came to visit William at his farm one day in early April. William was driving the cows back to the fields from the dairy. He beamed to see the calves prancing in the new grass, although he was still supplementing the cattle feed with turnips. He had a mind to grow the new Swedish turnip which Ann's brother had begun to grow in Hatcliffe.

'Go into the house, Brother,' William shouted to Silas when he caught sight of him. 'I'll join you in a minute.'

When William walked in to the parlour, he found his son John fingering a tune on the harmonium, his little legs barely able to touch the pedals. Silas was encouraging him and singing along, as Mary sat on his knee. He must miss his family dreadfully, thought William. He knew that Silas had not been home for at least six months, maybe almost a year.

'I don't know where John gets it from,' said Ann, 'but he's entranced by music. He has a natural ear and picks up a tune as soon as he hears it. I've only given him a few lessons.'

'He gets it from you, my dear,' said William, as Ann called for her skivvy, Nell, to bring refreshment.

After some polite conversation, Silas brought up the reason for his visit.

'We are having another Conference next month and Brother Clowes suggested that you attend.' William saw pride sweep over Ann's face.

'Will it be in Hull again?' William asked, eagerly.

'No, this time it is to be in Tunstall, Staffordshire, where the Connexion began.' Disappointment seeped into William's heart.

'But that's miles away. I can't leave the farm for that long.'

'I thought you might say that, William. You must pray and Jesus will help you find a way.' Silas said.

'William, it is a great honour to be asked. You'll regret it most woefully, if you don't go,' said Ann.

'How long must I be away?'

'A little under three weeks, I should think. The conference lasts ten days and we have to get there and back. We 'll walk to the Trent, then follow the river to Nottingham and cross from there to the Potteries.'

'William, you could visit your father on the way.' Ann rose from her seat to put her arms around him.' I know you've been longing to do that.' He had written to his father via the vicar after Betsy's death but had received nothing in return. Maybe he was dead also. It would be good to find out for sure.

'But to walk all that way,' puzzled William. He was younger than Silas but he had never walked more than twelve miles in a day. That made him weary enough. 'Couldn't we travel by horse? It would be much quicker.'

Silas looked at him with a pained expression on his face. 'We'll preach every night on our journey and we preach to the poor. A Church of England vicar may ride a horse. We walk, you know that William.'

He felt suitably admonished. Yes, he did know that, but to walk over two hundred miles, there and back, he felt worn out already. However, something beyond tiredness was taking hold in his mind. Something fluttered in his stomach, was it excitement? Was it pride? Pride he should quell, no, it was excitement. He wanted to see what lay beyond his county. He knew life was changing elsewhere whilst leaving his villages behind. He could almost hear Betsy in his head, 'Do it, William' she would have said. 'Go. Take this opportunity. It may be the only chance you get.'

'Do you think I can be of use at this Conference? After all, I'm such a new member. I've only been a lay preacher for twelve months.'

'You're just the kind of man we want, sensible, down to earth, practical.'

Walking over to William, Ann placed her arms on his shoulders, her gentle face peering up at him. 'Go, William, we'll be fine. I'll ask one of my nephews to help. My brother has enough of them, not to miss one.'

The longer days of late April were perfect for walking. William rose before the sun, his stomach churning with anticipation. Ann waved him farewell, having packed sufficient food for a day or two in a pouch. They kissed, he embraced her, forlorn at the thought of leaving her.

'Don't worry,' she murmured. 'We'll manage. The cows have plenty of grass in the meadow. Alf will do your milk run and Tom's looking forward to helping me in the dairy.' Yes, Alf, his farmhand would manage; he was a good man and had two sons who were ready to shoulder some of the work. They had no real need of Ann's nephew, Jed, but he had come anyway. William was grateful to think a man would be in the house, while he was away, and he could always find work to do on the farm.

'It's you I'll miss, sweet Ann. I wish you were coming with me.'

'Write it all in the journal I gave you for your birthday; I long to hear all about your journey, and the Conference.'

He set off to meet Silas amidst the dawn chorus and the fragrance of the hedgerows where May blossom promised, and honeysuckle was about to open. The lane was empty at this early hour. He knew it as he knew himself, but this morning, he strolled along ready to see everything anew. All his senses felt alive. Past Weelsby Woods he walked, where the raucous squawk of crows drowned out the song of the blackbird and thrush. This glorious land, unaltered for centuries was his home. He expected to see the modern world on this journey, but he had this bounteous land to come home to and he sang his praises to the Lord for that.

William was singing a hymn as he approached Nun's Corner and he heard Silas's singing before he saw him. He was sitting beside one of the stones of the old nunnery. To spend three weeks in the company of this man was some recompense for the loss of Ann. His admiration of Silas knew no bounds. He was guide, teacher, and friend, but one day he would be called to mission elsewhere and William already dreaded that inevitability. Silas made no secret that as soon as North Lincolnshire was secured and able to run under the direction of lay preachers, Silas would be on the move His work would continue wherever his conscience called him. They turned west at Laceby onto the Brigg road and William began to remember that day when Betsy rescued him. It's strange to think of it in that way, but he did. The time before Betsy was hazy. He told Silas about his childhood memories.

'I wished I could have met Betsy,' Silas said.

'You and she would have liked each other, I have no doubt. She taught me so much. Ann is like her in many ways, hard-working, practical and, above all, kind to everyone she meets. Goodness shone out of Betsy, although not everyone appreciated it.' He told Silas about the deal made between Joe and Alice's brother. 'I have you to thank for allowing me to forgive Joe for his treachery.'

'No, I may have been the spur, but you forgave Joe as soon as you recognised his need. Anyway, tonight, we will meet your youngest brother, and your father, God willing.'

William's anticipation grew as they walked. He had put aside thoughts of his family for so many years. It had been easier that way. Now he tried hard to remember them, but the images lay locked in his mind. What was he expecting from the visit? The only way he could picture it, was if his family arrived unannounced on his doorstep. What a welcome he would give them. It would not matter if they were strangers. Ann would hurry into the kitchen to rustle up food and drink. He would find the most comfortable chair by the fire for his father to sit in, and take pride in introducing his children to him.

They stopped in Brigg for some food and a beaker of cold tea. It was Market Day and the town was every bit as busy as William remembered. It had an air of prosperity which in Grimsby remained lacking.

Silas looked about him with different eyes. This was a town which deserved his attention, maybe not this year, but next; another town to be opened-up to the Connexion. He sensed the poverty behind the new brick buildings and town hall. Since he began his missionary life, the souls of sinners spoke to him of their misery, like ghosts whispering inside his head. He toyed with the idea of delivering a sermon here in the market place, but reluctantly decided it could wait, William was impatient to leave.

They stopped at Broughton, William looking for places he recognised. Granny Leaning's cottage, as he remembered it, was nought but the meanest hovel. An elderly woman sat outside chopping onions. She looked up as he approached, her rheumy eyes clouded with anxiety by the stranger's proximity.

'Granny Leaning?' William asked.

'Nay son, the old lady died ten years back. Her daughter still lives by the church,' there was warmth in her toothless smile.

The Aunt Lizzy who opened the door on his knock, was no longer the younger version of his mother, she had turned into her own mother. He shook his head; the likeness to his granny was uncanny. He had no need to introduce himself.

'William?' her shock was palpable.

'How did you know?' He asked once he was inside. Silas had excused himself to walk around the small village, while William welcomed the privacy.

'You are your father, a more prosperous version, a happier version too.'

'He's still alive then?'

'As far as I know. I haven't seen him these three years past.'

'Why unhappy?'

'Your mother dying and you leaving, well he was never the same after that. My mother couldn't forgive him for letting you go. She told him straight, on the day of the funeral, that even when she was on the parish she would never have given up one of her children, not for all the money

141

in the world. She refused to visit after that. I was worried for your brothers and sisters so I did go, at least once a year. Your father changed and it was an unhappy house. Tom left for the army as soon as he could, your sisters married and Joe ran off, who knows where.'

'Joe's in Grimsby, he's a fisherman and has two children. He's sorted himself out.'

'Thank goodness. I think there was some trouble when he left. Are you going to see your father? William nodded. 'Expect a bitter man. He never mentioned you after you left, but I think he has regretted it every day of his life.'

William sat, stunned and saddened. 'I don't know what to think. I feel guilty now but Betsy was so good to me, like a mother. I've never regretted moving to live with her.'

'I'm glad about that. None of it was your doing, so don't feel guilty. I suppose Betsy had her reasons for taking you, but many's the day your Granny and I cursed her for the way she took you. You didn't hear the bawling and wailing when your father told us you had left for good. I remember his fist crashing down on the table and demanding that we never speak your name again, but I saw the anguish in his eyes. I dread to think what your poor mother would have thought.' A tear escaped from her eye and ran down her crinkled cheek.

All this was over twenty years ago, but for Lizzy it remained raw. He had assumed it was just Joe who had been affected. This deep emotion was difficult to digest. He scarcely remembered his homesickness and only knew his aunt as a woman he admired, not some scheming, cold-hearted tyrant, which is what Lizzy appeared to be suggesting. Were his memories at fault? Did he have to reassess his relationship with his guardian?

As William left the cottage, Silas noted his grey and troubled face. It was not tiredness, despite the miles they had trodden. He waited for William to speak and he did, pouring out his feelings as they continued westwards out of the village. When they arrived at the woods, Silas stopped and turned towards William, placing his hands on his shoulders, staring into his eyes. Strength and certainty shone in his blue, penetrating gaze.

'Do you doubt God's plan, Brother? If you had remained in that humble cottage, would you now be a preacher? You who are a man of great heart and resourceful enough to do the job which God has given you? Betsy was his instrument, are you denying that?'

The simple power of Silas's argument overwhelmed William. He sank to his knees and Silas joined him in prayer. Would he ever be clever enough to understand God's will? For Silas, it was straightforward. He saw God's hand in everything, had an answer for all questions. William could only watch and listen in awe.

'Can I ever reach salvation, Silas? I fear I doubt too much.'

'Pray, William. Learn to listen to that inner voice.'

They stood up and Silas embraced him before they set off on the final stage of their day's journey. As they strode along the track, William stopped dead, his eyes scanning his surroundings.

'I know where we are,' he said. 'Let's take this path to the right. It's a shortcut through the woods.'

'You see, Brother, you are learning to use your eyes,' Silas laughed and they stepped on to the path, through the bluebell scented woods, their spirits high and with renewed spring in their step.

The village of Frodingham was meaner than William remembered. Even the church had seen better days. His footsteps drew him unerringly to the door of his father's cottage, some deep recessed memory guiding him. He knocked at the ancient plank door as Silas stood behind him. Seconds later he was staring into the face of a young man, swarthy from the fields, whose black hair and brown eyes spoke of the mother Uriah had hardly known and could never remember.

'Uriah?'

'Yes, I don't know you.'

'I'm your brother, William.' Uriah showed no recognition, only disbelief. 'I remember you as a baby. Has father never told you about me?'

The door was pushed further aside and an older man appeared. His head sprouting a few grey hairs, his eyes unmistakable, set in a heavily lined face.

'Father, it's William. I have walked from Grimsby to visit you. This is my friend, Silas. May we come in?'

Without a word, William's father ushered them through the door as Uriah stood open-mouthed and suspicious. Silas attempted to shake Mr Holtby's hand and thank him for his hospitality, but was brushed aside.

'What do you want, William? I have nothing to give you as you can see.'

If anything, the cottage was more spartan than it had been twenty years before. That no woman had lived here for many years was evident in the lack of any homely touch. William shivered, unsure whether to feel guilty that he had some responsibility in this or thankfulness that he had escaped it.

'Shelter for the night, that's all. Silas and I are walking to Tunstall in Staffordshire for a conference and so I thought we might call and stay here for the night.' To say that he was dismayed by the chilly reception, was an understatement.

'We have no spare food.'

'I have some my wife packed for us in my bag.'

'So, you have a wife.'

'And children, Father. I have my own dairy farm.'

Uriah had still not stopped gawping. 'Who is this, Father?'

'Your brother, William. His aunt brought him up. I gave him away so he could be a gentleman. You don't look like no gentleman to me. Was it all for nought?'

'We are preachers, Father. We wear plain, simple clothes and the dust you see is of the road.'

'Your son, Mr Holtby, is a man of consequence in Grimsby and a pious man to boot,' Silas interrupted, attempting to mollify the situation.

Doubt crept into his father's eyes. 'Preachers you say.'

'This man,' William touched his friend's arm, 'saved Joe from the drinking himself to death.'

At last some interest. 'Joe, our Joe. He's in Grimsby?'

'Yes, a fisherman and with a family too. Silas is a powerful preacher, Father. Listen for yourself; Silas will preach on the green this evening.'

144

'If you have saved Joe from his thieving ways, then I thank you, Sir. But as to preaching here, I warn you, the new vicar is a man not to be crossed. Are you one of those Methodists?'

'Primitive Methodist.'

'Never heard of 'em. I don't want you causing trouble, William. We have to live here.'

'Come and listen, Father, Uriah too. You won't be disappointed.' Both father and brother looked doubtful.

Expectant people sprinkled the village green as dusk began to fall. Silas had been around the village drumming up interest, while William attempted to engage his father in his life and family. The fine evening encouraged a good turnout. There was little enough excitement on a weekday for such a tiny village as this. Most would be working in their gardens until night fell. The smell of wood-smoke mingled with the first flowering lilies of the valley, their tiny white bells glistening on the edge of the green.

William stood beside Saul searching the crowd for any faces he might recognise, but the only ones were those of his reluctant father and brother, who stood near the back. Even the villagers appeared to disregard them, as though they were of no consequence. No girl fluttered her eyelashes at Uriah, let alone attempted to engage him in conversation. Instead there was a discernible space around them. He began to understand why Joe had escaped and why he had treated Betsy so badly. There was something very wrong in his family, something that had not been present before he left. The reunion with his father had not been successful, much worse than he had ever envisaged. His brother appeared to resent him without any reason he could deduce. His father was a puzzle. William was no prodigal son returning cap in hand; he was a landowner of good status so why was his father so unwelcoming? If he regretted sending his son away, why did he not show pleasure on his return?

William guided the crowd to an area of the green which he hoped would be unobserved by anyone standing by the brooding windows of the Ivy-covered parsonage. Once the crowd had settled, William expected the usual hymn but Silas surprised him by launching immediately into his sermon.

'Put to death, therefore, whatever belongs to your earthly nature: sexual immorality, impurity, lust, evil desires and greed, which is all idolatry. Because of these, the wrath of God is coming.' Silas was on fire, he lectured and cajoled, castigated and harangued, burning with passion. The villagers stood quaking in fear until one sank to the ground, crying 'Father, save me, for I have sinned.' Then another and another joined the first. It was like listening to Silas for the first time. William's body tingled with emotion as he passed amongst the crowd helping the sinners to rise and be delivered into God's love. The sermon had been going for no more than ten minutes when a booming voice was heard from the edge of the green.

'Begone you Ranters! I have sent for the Magistrate. You people get back to your cottages now. Don't listen to these false prophets.'

'Join us in our prayers, Vicar,' said Silas calming his tone. 'We do no wrong here, the people thirst for God's forgiveness.'

'Begone, I say. We do not want your type here.' He had a riding crop in his hand and began to lay about the congregation.

William, incensed by the vicar's violence towards his flock, charged towards him and wrestled the crop away from his hands. The priest may have been young but he was no match for the solid farmer.

'How dare you come into my village and try to steal these people away from my church,' he hissed, spittle spraying William's face.' He hit out at and delivered a glancing blow to William's face. William was about to return the punch when he heard Silas above the fray.

'Don't do it.'

William remembered Silas's instructions that if ever he met with resistance, he should not rise to it, but turn the other cheek. He resisted his natural inclination and took a deep breath.

'Control your flock while you can, Father, but we will be back and we will save them from God's wrath, be sure of it.' He snapped the riding crop in two and threw it at his feet. 'Do not harm these good people. They are God's children.' Silas walked towards him and took his arm.

'Well done, my friend,' he murmured. 'It looks like our meeting is at an end.'

The crowd had begun to drift away, cowed by authority and the threat of the Magistrate. Many depended on the local squire for their living.

'I told you,' William's father caught his sleeve. 'Go, you are not welcome in my house.' His father hurried away back to his cottage with Uriah in tow.

Silas and William stood watching every one leave. They were alone apart from a youngish woman who approached once the vicar had departed in triumph.

'Come William, don't wait for the Magistrate, you can stay with me, and you too Sir,' her wandering eye did not look at Silas but away to the left.

'Hannah?'

'Yes Brother.' She hurried them towards her house.

'How did you know it was me?' Asked William.

'Haven't I looked for you every day since you left? I knew you would return one day. You're the spit of Father, in any case.'

She almost pushed them through the door, keen to avoid trouble but knowing none of the villagers would give them away.

She was married to the village blacksmith, Ephraim, a powerfully built man, of plain face and demeanour. He greeted them with a firm handshake.

'You are welcome here, Sirs,' he said. 'Hannah mentions you in her prayers every night, Mr William,' his smile showed crooked teeth but his words were genuine. 'Will you take a mug of ale?'

Silas and William both declined but were happy to be offered water from the village well.

'It's a long time since I drank this water,' said William, grinning at his sister. 'I am pleased to find you so settled. Are these your children?' He pointed at the boys of around ten and eight who stood shyly in the doorway.

'That's our Billy and George,' Hannah said proudly. Another namesake, thought William ruefully.

'They're fine boys. Come here both of you. I'm your Uncle William.' He ruffled their hair and gave each of them a silver threepenny bit. Then

147

looking at Hannah said. 'I saw Aunt Lizzy in Broughton today. She told me that Father regretted sending me away with Betsy, but he was so cold to me just now. I thought he would be pleased to see me.'

'Aunt Lizzy has it wrong. It's what she would like to think, but she's being too kind to him. He changed after Mam died, that's true. He drove his remaining sons too hard, was never satisfied with them. So, Tom left and then Joe escaped and now he's left with Uriah. In his twisted mind his sons have deserted him and you were the first to do so, never mind that he let you go for money. I feel most sorry for Uriah, he's a lost soul and is not as unfeeling as he first appears. I'm determined to find him a good wife. If the magistrate turns up tomorrow, however, I wouldn't put it past Father to inform on you. You had best be gone before first light.'

'That's what we intend, Hannah. We have a long journey ahead.'

'That was a mighty, fine sermon, Mr King,' said Ephraim. 'I remember my grandparents telling me they heard John Wesley preach in Lincoln. They converted to Methodism on the spot. I was born a Methodist and I'd like to remain one. Will you come back and preach in my forge, if needs be?'

'Thank you, Ephraim, for the invitation. Next year I will come for certain, to here and to Brigg.'

'We'll be waiting and in the meantime, I'll talk to some of the villagers who might also like to join. There's plenty of folk who dislike this new vicar. He's a distant cousin of the local Lord, so he likes to play the fine gent, but the Baron himself is not so bad. I think this vicar tries to conjure up more authority than he has. His sermons are as dull as a rusty nail; we could do with some fire and brimstone.'

Silas and William left Frodingham before dawn. Hannah added to their food supplies and kissed William, asking him to return some day. She told him that their eldest sister, Sarah, lived in Scotter and to call, if they were ever that way. As they strode out of the village westwards towards the Trent, William asked Silas why he had not begun with a hymn the day before and immediately delivered such a fiery sermon.

'Ah, you noticed, my Friend. That vicar was always going to be my enemy. I needed to get to the people as quickly as possible. We would have had our first converts if he hadn't interrupted. When I return, they will be waiting, thirsting for salvation. We will have our Connexion in all these villages within the twelve months. You'll see. Those poor villagers will still have to attend the church in the morning, no doubt, but in the afternoon, they'll be ours. Your brother-in-law will make a fine lay preacher.'

It began to drizzle; the dawning sky hid the sun as threatening rain clouds gathered high above them. William hunkered down into his oil skin cape and leather cap. There was so much to think about. Normally, he might have expected to mull it over before sleep, but exhaustion had hit him and he was grateful to be offered his nephew's bed for the night. At least meeting Hannah and Aunt Lizzy made up for the disappointment of the reunion with his father. Families are more complicated than I realised, he thought. There was Lizzy blaming Betsy, Hannah blaming her father and Father blaming his sons for the break-up of the family. Where was love and forgiveness in all this? He trudged along the track, without noticing the countryside around him, weary from this new burden of guilt. Silas, sensing his mood, began to sing a gentle hymn and within seconds William joined in. A hymn never failed to lift his spirits.

'It's not far to Gunness, William. We should be there within the hour and tomorrow evening we will stay with my wife and children. I can't wait to see them again. Are we not blessed with our children, William?' Silas broke out into a rousing 'Now Thank We All Our God,' and William wondered if Silas ever suffered from loneliness or doubt.

The sky was beginning to clear by the time they reached Gunness, where the broad Trent lay, a greenish brown ribbon dissecting the landscape. Over the river lay the wharves at Keadby, a low, flat barge was tied up alongside the dock, its decks laden with black, dusty coal. Beyond the barge to the north lay the entrance to a smaller waterway.

'Is that another river?' asked William.

'No, it's a canal. We'll pass many on our journey; they cut across country to the centres of industry, our best recruiting grounds. We turn left here and this river takes us all the way south to Nottingham.'

It was at this point that William left behind all that was familiar and comfortable. He felt it in his gut as they turned south to walk into a new world.

Chapter 16

William's Journal

Friday April 27th

My darling Ann, how to describe the first two days of our journey? You knew I would find the walking hard and I have. My feet are sprouting such a crop of blisters that each step today proved painful, as though walking on burning cinders. My calves are so sore that I long for a tub of hot water to jump into and for you to rub my aching back.

In the thirty odd-miles we have walked, nothing was strange and I wondered what I would write in this journal. How disappointing for you, sweet Ann, to read that we passed new-sown barley fields and lush meadows full of grazing black cattle. The blackbirds continue to sing sweetly and the cuckoo's call is the same here as it is at home.

The truth is that once we got to the Trent I began to see glimpses of another world. Wide barges were sailing down, catching the tide. Several passed us as we plodded south towards Gainsborough, their decks piled high under tarpaulins. Silas says they take coal, earthenware, and all manner of goods from the midland cities, each carrying many times the load of a wagon. We had been walking, maybe two hours, before we saw the Gainsborough to Hull Steam Packet, smaller than the one I caught to Hull. I asked Silas if we may catch it on our return but he looked at me and said, 'Don't you want to visit your sister, Sarah, in Scotter?' By that I gather he wants to see if he can mission Scotter next year. The man has too much energy and puts us all to shame.

We stopped for a break in Gainsborough, which is a fair-sized town. Along the river, wharves and warehouses abound; it's a veritable inland port, with a handsome new stone bridge. I hoped we would linger but Silas said 'No, we must press on if we are to make Nottingham by tomorrow'.

Beyond Gainsborough the river begins to meander amongst wide flood plains and we began to see horse-drawn narrow boats which navigate both river and canals.

We rested for the night at an inn and I talked to one of the bargees, after he stabled his horse. A good horse, he told me is worth its weight in gold, and can judge what's required almost as quickly as his master. The bargees earn decent money for their labour but only see their families for one day in seven or so. I should not like that, dear Ann. I miss you dearly. I cannot think how Silas manages to see his wife but for a day or two every few months. He is so looking forward to his visit home tomorrow.

He, of course, preached a sermon this evening. There were few listeners but they were respectful and shook his hand before returning to their barges.

Saturday April 28th

Today, with my blistered feet covered in goose fat, and bound in rags beneath my boots, we crossed the river by ferry and left it behind. We made our way through Sherwood Forest. I confess my interest in Robin Hood waned after mile upon mile of trees. Only the pretty village of Edwinstowe, where Maid Marion is supposed to have wed Robin, broke the monotony.

As we drew near to Nottingham we could see the castle on the hill, surrounded by the town and both of our spirits rose to think of the end of our day's journey.

The streets of Nottingham are a warren; they run hither and thither, meandering like the river. Washing hangs from rails outside rickety dwellings, never glimpsing the sun. I wonder the laundry is any cleaner after the mud and the filth of the lanes. My heart bleeds for the children running ragged and barefoot amongst it all. I held my nose as we walked through, wondering why the town is in such a bad state.

We were greeted with delight by Silas's wife and children. Mrs King is older by far than her husband and quite grey under her cap. She has a cheerful face and twinkling blue eyes which put me at my ease at once, bidding me sit in the most comfortable chair and rest my poor feet.

Silas tells me that we have broken the back of our journey and can take a day of rest tomorrow. For that I truly praise the Lord. I found my bed just after supper and was grateful to retire, leaving Silas to talk with his wife.

Sunday April 29th

After morning service at a chapel close by, Silas arranged an outing for me with a neighbour, Nathan Miller. Mrs King accompanied me, knowing that I would get lost as soon as I stepped from the house. Imagine my concern when we stopped in one of the poorest alleys at a crumbling dwelling with a worm-eaten plank for a door. She tapped on a tiny window to the left of the door and a few seconds later a woman welcomed us in. Mrs King refused, saying she must get home but gave the woman a loaf of bread.

Mrs Miller bid me follow her down a short, dark hallway, to a room on the left. It is easy enough to describe, a room around ten-feet square, with that single window to the front, before which sat two stools cut from wooden barrels, one with a spinning wheel beside it. An upturned box served as the only table. A small girl sat on the plank floor playing listlessly with a peg doll. Briefly her eyes met mine. All I saw was hunger in her tiny thin face. Oh, Ann, I was back in that House of Industry in an instant.

Adjusting my eyes to the gloom, I glimpsed movement and a male voice greeting me. I hadn't noticed him with his back toward me but my eyes were immediately drawn to his crippled right leg, as he hobbled towards me. His face, despite the pain evident in the creases around his eyes, was intelligent and welcoming. He held out his hand and I grasped it, feeling the strength in his calloused fingers.

'You see me down on my luck, Sir,' he said. 'A year ago, I rented three rooms and had employment as a frame knitter. Today we survive on my wife's spinning and the Connexion's hand-outs.' I was struck by the lack of bitterness in his tone.

It seems that he slipped in the mud and fell under a wagon. They saved his leg, although his ankle is badly damaged and painful. This was the man who was to show me the sights of Nottingham, Ann. He saw the doubt in my face and his expression softened as he assured me he was up to the task.

'You must let me pay you for your labour', I told him and I dug in my pockets for some coins.

'A florin will be enough Sir,' said he, taking a coin. 'I will not be able to walk a whole day, only a half,' he said in explanation. Immediately I felt humbled by his fortitude and his lack of self-pity.

His wife handed him his cap and his crutch. I was surprised when she tied the crutch to his wrist with twine and then noticed that he had lost all but his thumb on the right hand. He swung his right leg forward, using the crutch to balance and we walked slowly up the hill towards the castle. If you've never been to Nottingham, he said, the castle is a good place to start.

As we walked he told me of his life. He is still a young man and had knitted stockings since he was twelve years old. Lately, his wife has spun the wool and he used his machine to knit the hosiery. I commented that it must pay well, but he looked at me quizzically.

'Until we lost half our trade.' Seeing my bemused expression, he pointed at my trousers and grimaced and then it struck me. When did I last wear stockings, Ann? A simple change in fashion and a whole industry under threat and we none the wiser. I tried to stammer an apology but he shook his head. 'We cannot resurrect the past' he said, 'although the Luddites tried their best.'

Apparently, they were a big force in Nottingham. But, he explained, they did not smash up machines for the sake of it, but as a complaint about wages being lowered when demand dried up. Too many machines meant the factory owners undercut the frame knitters.

He told me he would rather be his own master than work in a factory, but that is what is happening. The masters are enriching themselves and the labourers becoming poorer. We see that for ourselves in the Wolds villages, I told him.

He asked me then about my family and I told him about you and the children and about our little farm.

'Will your sons become farmers?' he asked, not waiting for an answer. 'If I had a son I would not let him become a frame knitter, nor a lacemaker. Do you know what I would do, Mr Holtby?' I shook my head. 'I would send him to school,' said he. 'If you have education then you have a chance to make something of yourself.'

I was lucky, I told him. I had an aunt who also believed that education was the answer. But how are the poor to pay for schooling, I asked him? How could they afford for the children not to work?

'There's the rub,' he said. 'I suppose you have to start small and teach one child who can then teach others. There's a school in Nottingham trying to do that. It keeps down the cost. Perhaps for the poorest, you teach them on Sundays.' But they must learn to write mind, reading's not enough.'

Ann, it was like a firework going off in my head. I suddenly saw what we must do. This man, who has lost everything, realises what I have failed to understand. Being able to read and write is the only way we can safeguard people's lives. Reading is not enough, it must be writing too. To read the word of God is only half the battle. Writing offers a way out of destitution and hopelessness.

I remember little of Nottingham, although he did his best to show me the sights, the castle; the caves; where they hold the lace market and the goose fair. None of that registered with me. My head was buzzing with ideas about how we should begin a proper Sunday School. Don't you think that would be a wonderful thing, Ann?

Later I asked Silas what he thought about my idea. Ann, he looked at me with that amused smile he has and chuckled slightly.

'William,' he said, 'soon I will be leaving Grimsby. It will be up to you and the other preachers to take our movement forward. When you meet Brother Bourne in Tunstall, tell him of your plans to educate the labourers' children. I think you will find him very open to your idea.'

'Silas, you planned my meeting with Nathan. You knew what he would tell me and how I would react, didn't you?' I said.

'It's always best you find things out for yourself,' said he, chuckling again at my pretended outrage.

Oh, I shall miss him when he leaves us, as I know you will too. He has been the best of friends and an inspiration.

Tonight, we attended a service at Broadmarsh Chapel. Everybody was eager to hear Silas preach. As soon as we stepped out of the house we were swept up into an army of folk thronging towards the chapel, their clogs sounding the drumbeat of our movement. It stirred my blood and made my heart beat with pride. There was little chance of getting lost, although I admit I panicked when I lost sight of Silas for a moment. I need not have worried. So many people stopped to welcome him home. A tide of people surrounded them and Mrs King grabbed a hold of my arm and asked me to carry her youngest boy, who was in danger of being swallowed by the crowd.

The chapel is a disused factory, three storeys high but big enough inside to hold a thousand souls. When we arrived, there were already hundreds of them, eagerly anticipating Silas's arrival. Mrs King made her way to the front and I followed in her wake. No one seemed to mind as I pushed my way forward.

I could hardly believe the size of the congregation. Mrs King told me it was only five years since Sarah Kirkland first preached here and converted Silas. You remember Sarah, don't you Ann? We heard her preach with her husband, John Harrison, that time they came to Grimsby. You were amazed that a woman, especially one so young as she, could stand up and preach to men with such fervour and resolution.

I asked Mrs King if she regrets that Silas is away from home so much. But she smiled sweetly at me and shook her head saying 'He is doing the Lord's work and I can be patient, and with such people as you to take his mission further, he will leave it in safe hands when the time is right'. Flustered, I replied that I prayed that their trust in me would prove well founded.

When Silas arrived, room was made for him to progress to the small stage that had been set up for him. The factory resounded to his welcome, the noise bouncing off the ceiling and the flagged floor in such waves of greeting that my ears rang with the clamour.

Silas held his hands up for quiet. 'Thank you, Brothers and Sisters,' he said.' I have long looked forward to seeing you all again, but I have been busy bringing the word of the Lord to our cousins across the river in Lincolnshire. My work is going well and I want you to greet our friend here, Mr William Holtby who is helping to bring the people of Grimsby to salvation.' The crowd shouted their welcome and my face flushed with embarrassment as I was invited to go to the front. I was thankful when Silas announced a hymn, releasing me to creep back to Mrs King.

What an evening it proved to be, Ann. I knew myself to be in the company of a master. Silas worked that enormous crowd to fever pitch and several folks were saved that night. The sheer power and delivery of his words, I can only aspire to, never match, and I am glad of it. I'm happy with our simple life. But if I had the power of Silas to bring people to such joy, I know I would have to leave my farm and set out on the path of a missionary.

One thing Silas showed me on the way back from chapel left me dumbstruck, and I hope it will come to Grimsby within my lifetime. It's gaslight. You will ask 'whatever is that, William?' Silas explained that they make gas from burning coal, which is then pumped through pipes around the street and up to lanterns which are lit by a taper and behold the streets are bright with light, even though the sun has fled. The oil lamps in Grimsby Market Place are nothing to these lamps.

Monday April 30th

Today we set off in the rain; my boots sliding on the slippery cobbles. I was thinking of poor Nathan and his accident and asked Silas how he could survive with so little money coming in.

'Did he not tell you? Nathan is both a humble and a resourceful man,' he said. 'He is learning to read and write. My wife is teaching him. He will then teach others at Sunday School and be paid to read and write letters for people.'

'How can he write?' I asked. 'He has no fingers on his right hand.'

'Did you not notice?' Silas asked in mock amazement. 'He is left handed. He will learn to write as well as you or I.'

157

Ann, I began to think myself stupid not to have noticed. But then I thought, how could I have known and I looked at Silas, to find him laughing with delight to have fooled me. I never knew he had such humour in him. I am seeing such a light-hearted side of him when I have only known him to be serious. We both fell about laughing at how he had duped me, and it lightened our path as we left Nottingham behind for Derby.

The road to Derby was pleasant enough and being a toll road was in good condition. Wagons and coaches passed us by, splashing us from head to toe with mud, but I have learned not to complain about walking all the way. The rain petered out by the time we passed through a village where most of the houses have windows across the top floor, letting in a great deal of light. Silas told me they were the homes belonging to frame knitters who worked upstairs as families. 'Poor light tires their eyes,' he said.

'Do they not suffer lower wages now too?' I asked.

'You are learning, William. Families who toil as weavers, lace makers and knitters are all being driven into the factories. But the factories, mills and mines are our best breeding grounds. The dreadful conditions drive the people to us and we give them hope of a better life.'

Derby is a pleasant market town, much smaller than Nottingham, but even here they are installing gas lamps. I must talk to some of the Freemen when I get back home to see if it is feasible in Grimsby. It would save some from falling over in the dark and lessen crime, I'm sure.

Talking of crime, I was a witness to one today. I watched a thief being arrested and rather than feel outraged at her behaviour, which I know was wrong, I felt an overwhelming sadness. Do you think badly of me? Let me write down what happened.

It was In Derby, where we stopped to eat the bread and cheese packed for us by Mrs King. A barefoot, ragged girl, of maybe sixteen years of age, ran into a shop near to where I was sitting. She then darted out, a pair of clogs in her hand, chased by the shopkeeper, who shouted 'Stop thief'. A passing man tripped her up and she fell, sprawling on to the cobbles, not far from where I sat. The man who tripped her, hauled her to her feet, holding her fast. A constable was called and before he came I observed the girl. She was scarcely more than skin and bones. The dress she wore was in tatters, her feet grimy and her face streaked with dirt. But she had most unusual hair, the colour of horse chestnuts with glints of red, although all in tangles from lack of combing. She appeared to be looking at something in the distance, shaking her head as a kind of warning. I turned and saw a younger girl unmistakably a sister, with the same hair. Her hands were over her mouth as though in shock. Just then the Constable arrived and put the older girls' hands into irons. Her face was impassive, defiant almost. She was led away. Someone spat at her and the spittle dripped down her face, but with her hands bound she could not wipe it away.

'What will happen to her'?' I asked the man who had tripped her up.

'Gaol or maybe transportation if she's done owt like this before.'

The thing that struck me was that she did not shrink or beg and crave forgiveness for her crime. No, she stood proud and her unrepentant demeanour was a sight that will stay with me. I thought I ought to be shocked by her actions, should be ready to condemn her, but I wasn't. All I felt was pity and guilty that I had not done anything to help her.

So, in that guilt, I beckoned to the younger girl. She tried to ignore me, so I smiled and held out a hunk of bread. She could not resist it and came towards me, snatched the bread and ran off back into the crowd of shoppers. What if the girl has no other family, I thought? Who will look out for her? She was no more than thirteen. I felt helpless, moved by what must be a frequent occurrence, for no one else appeared distressed. Should I be bringing down God's wrath on the older girl for her sins? It troubles me and I crave your opinion.

Silas had been on an errand to one of his many acquaintances and had seen nothing of all this, so I recounted the tale to him when he returned. He looked at me with compassion and told me that there was nothing I could do but pray for the girls.

'Pray that God will lead them both to the path of righteousness. There are many paupers in the land. You cannot take all their burdens on your shoulders. Do what you can. It is all God expects.'

I know he is right, Ann, but I cannot help imagining my own children without sustenance, shelter or protection. My heart bleeds for those girls and you, with your soft heart would do so as well.

We rest tonight in a cottage near a village called Sudbury. Silas has no compunction about knocking on doors to find accommodation. Eventually we found a Methodist household who agreed to put us up for the night.

I fear I have been poor company, only wanting to write in my journal because it brings me closer to you, my love. I left Silas to discuss the finer points of the scriptures with our hosts and they do not appear to have taken offence at my absence. As I write, it is growing dusk and I sit on the bough of an old apple tree, about to burst into bud. It will be a pretty sight in a week or so. The countryside around here is lush and green. To the north are hills which Silas tells me stretch all the way to Scotland. If I remember my geography, they are called the Pennines. I have a fancy to see them.

The light is fading too much for me to write more. I wish you goodnight, my love.

Tuesday May 1st

Well we have arrived in Tunstall and yet another county, Staffordshire. The walk today was much more up and down. I felt so weary as we climbed the last hill and looked down on to strange shaped chimneys, pouring out smoke. Silas tells me they are bottle kilns for the making of pots and that is exactly what they look like, huge bottles made from sooty, red bricks with open tops, each pumping out so much smoke that it created a vision of hell.

I told Silas how tired I felt but he laughed and said that he would not mind if he had to walk all of it again. How does he have so much energy? He never flags either in spirit or in body. He puts me to shame and I four years younger. It must be God who drives him forward.

Everything was arranged for us on our arrival. Our accommodation is spread around the village and I am staying with a potter and his wife, whose children are now all flown the nest and consequently, need the little money I will pay them for their hospitality. Their cottage is as humble as my childhood home, but their hearts are warm and their Faith strong.

The conference begins tomorrow and I am in a great lather tonight. Who am I to presume to work with these great men? I feel a fraud because I know so little of the world. Silas has tried to reassure me, as he always does.

I know that you will be praying for me, my love. It is a great comfort to feel myself wrapped in your prayers.

Wednesday May 2nd

How shall I explain today's happenings? It did not start off well, nor Godly, but with a great argument.

Silas called for me and took me into Tunstall. The new chapel where we are meeting looks more like a pair of stone cottages. Silas told me that Hugh Bourne paid to have it built, but with thrift in mind, he had the forethought to have the building designed so it could be changed into housing, if our Connexion failed to thrive. I looked forward to meeting the great man.

With enormous trepidation, I entered after Silas. You know me as confident, but I was suddenly shy and tongue-tied; my mouth as dry as dust. I need not have worried for who should greet me but Brother Clowes and he took time to introduce me to the other gentlemen. I asked which of the men standing there was Hugh Bourne but imagine my surprise and disappointment when told he was not amongst the delegates.

We began with a prayer and then took our places at table. Each man had to introduce himself and say which circuit he was representing. We were almost finished when the door opened with a crash and a man stood there, glaring at us. Silas whispered to me that it was Hugh Bourne. William Clowes stood up to greet him but he barely acknowledged him. Instead he looked around the table and his eyes fastened on one man. He strode over to him and manhandled him out of his seat. You could have heard a pin drop. Everyone was open-mouthed with shock.

'Get you gone, Joseph,' said Brother Bourne. 'I must take your place. It's not right that I am excluded from this conference. I have more right than you. Have I not paid for this chapel?' With that he sat down, daring anyone to complain. Joseph, I do not know his last name, stood there shocked and hurt, expecting someone to complain at his treatment. When no one did, he turned and slammed the door shut on his way out. You could hear a collective sigh as everyone breathed at last, but I can tell you, Ann, it was

not the way I expected to meet the man I have admired these last two years. I fear everyone around that table will not dare to cross him, in case of similar treatment. He is used to getting his own way. And by the end of the day's proceedings, I detected a measure of jealousy towards William Clowes, who is held in very high regard by everyone, but maybe not by Hugh Bourne.

The rest of the day was peaceful enough as the agenda for discussion began to be settled. We finished as we started with a prayer to God.

You know me, Ann, I'm not used to sitting for a day. I may have joked with Silas that I was ready for a rest from walking, but my bones so ached more from lack of movement that, by the end of the day, I could have walked up Mow Cop. Silas promises he will take me there to show me the place where the Connexion really began.

Friday May 4th

I was too exhausted to write last night. For two days, we have sat at table and done nothing but talk until my head began to spin.

I told you that William Clowes was popular. A measure of his popularity can be detected by the pleas that he mission in Manchester, leaving Hull behind to others. But the laymen of Hull have different ideas and begged him to stay. Hull won, I have a feeling that Hugh Bourne thought the greater distance between them was an advantage, because he means to wrest some of the power back to Staffordshire. I will write about that later.

Saturday May 5th

Silas told me it was an easy walk to Mow Cop, no more than four or five miles each way but uphill. Let me tell you, Ann, the Pennines are not like our gentle Wolds. Our hills are tiny, nay puny, in comparison, while the Pennines are steep and windswept. Wind from the west blows so hard that what few trees there are, bend and bow in supplication. It was such a day today, although Silas tells me that the warm winds of May cannot compare to the bitter, driving winds of winter. I detected little warmth for it was unseasonably cold and bleak.

The land around this place is barren and unproductive and I pity anyone trying to make a living from it. Silas told me that the people here were as uncultivated and godless as their land and, if not for Hugh Bourne, would have remained so. We sang as we walked. He showed me Harrishead, where our founder was born and later saved.

I asked Silas about the man who was so easily discarded on Wednesday. He told me he was a local blacksmith, a good and pious man, and an early covert to the Connexion, but with more radical views than Hugh Bourne. He is well thought of in Tunstall, by all accounts. I expressed the opinion that he seemed like a man I would like to know and we left it there.

We soon came within sight of Mow Cop and began the climb to the top where a strange ruin perched upon the bleak and gloomy summit. I wondered who had wanted to live up there, but Silas told me it was a rich man's folly, nothing but a place for a summer picnic. Can you imagine having naught better to spend your money on than a fanciful ruin on a windswept hill? How profligate!

Silas bade me turn around when we reached the top. It took me a few moments to get my breath back but I did as he asked and was overawed at the sight. You could see all the way to the great mountains of Wales. I tried to imagine the hordes of people who came to Mow Cop to listen to the preachers.

Sunday May 6th

The chapel at Tunstall is already too small for the congregation. Today, in a nearby field, they held a fund-raising meeting for a new and bigger chapel. It seemed that all of Tunstall came to pray and gave me an idea of what the camp meetings must be like. I decided to lose myself amongst them, to feel what they felt, as if listening to William Clowes for the first time. A young couple welcomed me to share their bread before the meeting began: good, honest, hard-working folk, their faces alive with expectation. They were both potters, you could see it in her fingers when she broke a *hunk of bread off for me. The grey clay, not completely scrubbed from her hands and a sprinkling of grey dust in her husband's hair.*

As Brother Clowes began his sermon, the hubbub stilled and only his voice resounded around the field. The power of his words made my spine tingle. Just as in Hull, the crowd began to bear witness and speak of their own experience of God. I wonder if he ever manages to finish a sermon, Ann. Having directed them to this tumult of emotion he stood back, only encouraging and praising where needed.

Between sermons there was a break and noticing the tall blacksmith, who had been so unceremoniously thrown out of the conference, I made my way through the throng to greet him. I had to introduce myself, although he told me he recognised me. With some trepidation, I asked him how he felt about his ejection from the conference and was surprised when he laughed. His wife, he said, was a sensible woman and soon calmed him down. To have built up the movement from nothing, Hugh Bourne can be allowed his occasional overbearing ways, she told him.

He invited me to drop by after Silas King's sermon and I agreed. Twilight was upon us before we left the field and I was becoming cold. I followed the crowd back towards the market place and found the house of Joseph Capper.

As well as blacksmith, he is a travelling preacher on Sundays, like myself. He told me he had been converted with his parents at the first camp meeting on Mow Cop. I was so excited to hear that and begged him to describe the scene, which surpassed even my wildest imaginings. He told me that Hugh Bourne had no idea how many would turn up but trusted to God to spread the word. Flags were placed along the route to Mow Cop so the people could follow and they did in their hundreds, some walking for hours to get there, and all by word of mouth. The preachers stood on mounded stones to sermonise, while others held prayer meetings and yet more told of their adventures and how they came to God. Hugh Bourne lacked no further encouragement; the thirst for God's glory shone that day and has been gleaming ever since. I thanked my new friend for telling the story and we said a little prayer of thanks.

Joseph Capper has no real education and the only book he has read is the Bible but I have rarely met a man who has such a simple, devout goodness about him. He is as big-hearted in soul as he is in body and the love he holds for his fellow-man, shines from him.

He told me much more than I knew of the conditions in the factories and mines around here and I saw how it troubled him. But, I countered, at least there's plenty of work and it pays better than an agricultural labourer's wage.

'That is true,' he said, 'but the factory and mine owners will not improve the workplaces unless they are forced to.'

'Who will force them,' I asked?

(And this is where I could not agree with him) 'The people,' he said. 'Every man should have the vote for how else will things change?'

I fear my mouth hung open in surprise. He laughed and then told me to think about it at my leisure and I would come to see the sense in it.

I left soon after but his parting words keep coming back to me.

'I will devote my life to helping my neighbour. Did not the good Lord give us that as one of his commandments? I will fight for mankind, not with weapons but with the truthfulness of God's words and intent.'

I shook his hand as I left and felt the power of the man. I cannot doubt his good intentions but I believe he is misguided if he thinks the poor would use their vote wisely. I don't doubt some reform is necessary, when a great city like Manchester has no representative in parliament and yet Grimsby sends two members to London, and those votes bought by strong ale and coins. It will give me much to think of on the long journey home.

Wednesday May 10th

Well it's all over. These last three days of the conference have decided much but all I desire now is to be back on our farm with you and the children. It has been a long two weeks since I left. The thought of our walk back leaves me with both dread and elation. I must tell myself that every step is a step closer to you. I'll not be sad to leave this smoky atmosphere for the clean air of Lincolnshire but I will be sad to say goodbye to my new friends.

165

I should not admit to pride, but it is a collective pride in what we have accomplished. The Connexion has grown so much that we are to print all our own hymn books and establish a book room. Brother Bourne believes that only by educating our children can we rid the devil from gaining a hold on them and on this, I agree. But, he is to wrest the printing back to Staffordshire, away from Hull, so he and his brother will have charge of it and not William Clowes,

I have decided that my purpose in life, along with growing our Connexion in Grimsby, shall be the establishment of Sunday Schools for the children. For without education how is the ordinary man to progress?

I have been thinking about Aunt Betsy a great deal, these last few days. I see her guiding me to this point. She believed so much in education that I believe I will be following in her small steps. We shall bring hope and learning to the poor children of Grimsby and our nearby villages.

Part Three

John

1829-1848

Chapter 17

1831

John snapped his father's journal shut. He should try to sleep. Instead he sat in bed, with the journal in his lap, thinking. The candle stuttered beside him. He turned to look, it was almost finished. Goodness knows what time it was. He had never meant to read for so long.

It was sheer chance that he had pulled the old journal from the shelf. John had read almost everything else from his father's bookshelf and the latest volume of the Primitive Methodist Magazine held no attraction for him. He was almost sixteen and reading obituaries and worthy articles on religion or even the odd article on science would only serve to send him to a quick sleep. When he first pulled the journal from the shelf, it looked uninteresting, mostly notes on his father's preaching in local villages and texts from the Bible. He had flicked through before placing it back on the shelf and then came across an account of his journey to Staffordshire. He vaguely remembered his absence but his parents never talked about it.

The candle finally died. John replaced the book on the cupboard between the beds. He would read about the journey home another time. Tom, in the bed next to his, had been asleep for hours, but that was often the case. The physical effort of working the farm left his brother exhausted and he had no trouble in sleeping, whereas John idled the day away in the lawyer's office, often berated for his day-dreaming by both Mr Dewsbury and his father, when he got to hear about it.

John settled under the covers and closed his eyes, but sleep refused to come. He could not stop thinking about the journal. Reading it gave John a whole new insight into his father. Up to this point he had taken his father's love for granted and tried to obey his wishes, although he sometimes questioned them, receiving a stern reprimand in exchange. But John respected his father, he just did not want to be like him; he wanted more than Grimsby. It felt too constraining to live in this tiny corner of Lincolnshire and see nothing else of the world. There was one big problem with thinking he could escape and that was Emily. He spent his day-time hours dreaming of her, sweet Emily, whom he had loved for years. He had not doubted they would marry since he was seven and she five. The only problem was that she would never leave her family or Chapel to live with him elsewhere.

Chapel, that was another concern. Being brought up in a household which revered God, strict Chapel ways often irked him but he would be hard pressed to explain why. Of course, he believed in God, but sometimes Chapel felt like being in a straitjacket.

These thoughts flitted around his head, scarcely settling on one subject before veering off in another direction until at last his mind gave up the battle and blessed sleep arrived.

His tiredness the following day led to a further telling off from Mr Dewsbury.

'If only you would apply yourself John, you could go far in the legal profession. I know you have a brain in there, but if you carry on this way I can see us parting our ways.'

The blood drained from John's face and his heart raced. He did not want to be sent back to work on the farm, knowing that his brother would inherit it. He liked the law and thought it suited him.

'Do you understand that this is the last warning I am giving you, John? I will write to your father to tell him.'

His mouth too dry for speech, John nodded in shame. He had not been thinking about Emily this time but about the journal and how he wanted to discuss it with his father. He no longer saw him as just a preacher and a farmer, but a man he wanted to get to know; a man of tenderness, compassion, and determination. He knew his father to be straightforward, honest, a man of simple needs but had never seen beyond that. Instead of trying to butt against his father's wishes, he realised now he wanted to make him proud. Yet here he was being threatened with dismissal.

Perched still on his clerk's stool, he raised his face to Mr Dewsbury. 'I give you my promise, Sir, from this moment on, I will not give you cause to complain. Write to my father by all means, but I swear I'll work harder.'

Mr Dewsbury held out his hand for John to shake. 'That is a deal you will not break, son?' John shook his head.

'Never, Sir.' John was almost as surprised as Mr Dewsbury to hear the determination in his voice. Something had changed him. He heard a tiny voice in his head 'When I was a child, I thought as a child, but when I was a man, I put away childish things'. The words from Corinthians hit him with a force he could not resist. He sat on his stool almost unable to breathe. He cast his eyes down to the papers in front of him, the copperplate writing appeared to jump out at him, demanding he take notice. He did not need to clear his head to start working and began to write with renewed diligence.

With it being Saturday he finished work at one o'clock and walked over to the offices where his cousin, Billy, worked. The two boys were more like brothers. Although Billy was the same age as Tom, he could not have been more unlike his older cousin. Billy was sharp and interested in everything whereas Tom spoke rarely unless it was about the farm. It was natural that Billy gravitated towards John and they teased each other mercilessly.

Billy tended to lodge with the corn merchant during the week but always spent Saturday night and Sunday with his uncle and his family. Since Billy's father had died in a fishing accident and his mother left Grimsby, he looked upon William as his guardian. His aunt and uncle loved him and he was more than happy with the arrangement.

'You look serious, John.' Billy clapped him on the shoulder, 'It's Saturday, we have the afternoon free. What shall we do with it?'

'Mother has asked us to go brambling. She wants to make jam. We could walk out to Weelsby Woods after dinner. I'll be pleased to get out into the countryside after a week penned up in that office.'

'Can we get some young ladies to walk that way with us, do you think?'

'Well if we ask my sister, Mary to come, Emily may be allowed to accompany us. Who are you thinking of?'

'Well it's not Ada and Mabel, that's for sure.' John laughed. Emily's spinster sisters shunned light-heartedness. They wore their religion as a badge of sanctity, but unfortunately nobody else matched up to their ideals. 'You know those two make my flesh creep. If you marry Emily I hope you know what you're getting into.'

John brushed away his concerns. 'Emily's not like them, she's more like her mother. She has a sweet and loving disposition.'

'Love is blind, as they say. No, I wondered whether we might invite Sally White.' Sally also lived in Old Clee and was friendly with Mary. John smiled to himself. He liked Sally, a pert sixteen-year old with a wit to match Billy's. With two girls joining them there was a chance Emily would be allowed out.

It was Mabel who answered the door to John's knock. Her stiff expression told John all he needed to know. Emily would not be joining them. Emily was required to help pack up the house. John's plea that the move from the cottage in Clee was not for another two weeks cut no ice. The door closed in his face. Billy's expression of amused 'I told you so' did not help.

'I don't understand why her sisters show their disapproval so much,' he grumbled as he closed the front gate.

'They disapprove of men, even the most well behaved ones and you're not exactly without fault. Do you remember last Christmas?'

John flushed. He had written Emily a song comparing her lips to a rosebud. It was a poor effort but he made the mistake of writing it down and offering it to her. Mabel found it and raised such a fuss that his father had to admonish him. But we're practically engaged, he'd cried. In the end, he was forced to apologise to Emily's father. The embarrassment still rankled.

As they walked back to the farmhouse John told his cousin about his father's journal.

'I remember him going away for a few weeks, but where he went I'd no idea. How amazing to think of old, stick in the mud Uncle William walking all that way.' John cuffed his cousin. 'I'm never going to stay here all my life. When I'm eighteen I'll be off.'

John's heart sank. Billy was his best friend, the only fun countering the seriousness of Chapel.

'When you're a bit older you should join me, John. I can't wait to see the world.'

'Emily won't leave her family.'

'Then put Emily aside. There's more than one golden haired beauty out there. Find yourself a woman, not a child. Those sisters will never let her grow up, you know.'

John sighed. His heart was set on Emily and he could never think of leaving her to marry someone else.

'I'd like to read the journal,' Billy, unusually tactful, changed the subject.

'I'm in enough trouble with my father,' said John, fingering the letter from Mr Dewsbury, which sat in his pocket. 'Don't tell him I have let you read it, until I have his permission.'

After morning service on Sunday John gave his father the letter.

'Before you get angry with me, Father, let me say I have changed my ways.'

William looked at his son, saying nothing and then read the letter. 'It says here that you worked diligently all morning, having been given a harsh reprimand and that he believes you mean what you have promised him. What did you promise?'

'I read your journal, Father. It made realise that I need to find my purpose in life and that I won't find it unless I work hard at becoming a lawyer. Then I might be able to make a difference to people's lives, as you have done with your Sunday Schools.'

William had not picked up his journal in years and he could scarce remember what he had written ten years before, but his memories of the journey remained fresh in his mind. They had guided him over the years, as had his friendship with Silas. They wrote to each other but he missed his presence.

'I'd like to read it with you, Son. If I had known, it would have that effect on you, I would have given it to you to read years ago.'

'You're not angry about me taking it without your permission?'

'No.'

'I've lent it to Billy. Is that alright?'

'Fetch Billy and we'll look at it together.'

John, Billy and William spent hours over the next few weeks looking at the journal, discussing the sights William had seen and talking about issues as they cropped up. With the Reform Act present in everyone's thoughts, because it would give William a vote for the first time, there was much to discuss. Billy and his uncle took opposite viewpoints about the extension of the vote to those owning land over worth ten pounds.

'It doesn't go far enough, Uncle. How long will it take me to accumulate that sum?'

'I believe you can do it, Billy. You're only seventeen and if you work hard and are sober in your habits...'

Billy interrupted, 'How many working men will ever earn enough with a wife and family to provide for? My father, if he'd lived, would still not have the vote and yet his views were carefully considered.'

'You're young and hot-headed but even you can't expect the vote to be given to all men?'

'Why not?'

'Because they lack the knowledge to vote. I believe they have to earn the right to vote.'

'And the Freemen of Grimsby exercise their knowledge wisely?' Billy laughed in scorn. 'Of the men you met in your travels, how many will now have the vote?'

'Very few.'

'And yet, you write of them with respect for their views.'

'Some may be fit, but there are thousands, nay hundreds of thousands who think no further than their belly and their hearth and quite rightly so. Let us have education before the vote.'

John took little part in those lively discussions. He preferred to listen as they sallied back and forth. He admired Billy for standing up to his father but was more inclined to trust his father's judgement. After all, what had Billy seen of the world? He might change his views if he ever left town.

One day, when John was replacing the journal on the book shelf he noticed something covered in brown paper wedged behind another book. He eased it out. The slim volume sat in the palm of his hand, innocuous yet oddly enticing. He opened it up and began to flick through, noticing spidery handwriting in the margins and occasional passages underlined. He turned to the front and read the title, The Rights of Man, by Thomas Paine, a book John had never heard of. There was an inscription in shaky handwriting to his father.

'Dear William, I had hoped to read this with you one day. My time is running out. Read it with your own sons, Betsy.'

He wondered why it had been covered up, as though to hide it. Starting to read, he grew bored very quickly. He put it down on the table, meaning to find something else.

'What's that you've got there, John?' Billy had entered the room.

'It's nothing. I've not seen it before but it doesn't look to be of much interest.' Billy walked over to the table and picked it up. 'I've heard of this. Can I borrow it?'

'Help yourself.'

The following Sunday, Billy produced the book with a flourish.

'Listen to this. 'The duty of man is to God, which every man must feel and with respect to his neighbour, to do as he would be done by'.' He raised his eyes to look at John and his uncle, who both nodded in agreement. 'Now we come to the important bit, 'If those to whom power is designated do well, they will be respected: if not, they will be despised; and, with regard to those whom no power is delegated, but who assume it, the rational world can know nothing of them'.'

'What is this?' William took the book from Billy's hands. 'Where did you get this?'

'From your bookshelf, Uncle.'

William flicked through. 'That's Aunty Betsy's handwriting.'

'She underlined various passages. Look here.' Billy took the book back. 'This she has underlined twice. 'When it can be said by any country in the world, my poor are happy, neither ignorance or distress is to be found amongst them, my jails are empty of prisoners, my streets of beggars, the aged are not in want, the taxes are not oppressive, the rational word is my friend.' And it finishes, 'Independence is my happiness, the world is my country and my religion is to do good.' What do you think of that?'

'That book was written in defence of the French Revolution, and we know how that turned out. It's poppycock because it can never happen. Has never happened. The poor will always be amongst us.'

'Why does it have to be so, Uncle? Why should we not aim to be better?'

'I fear you will be forever disappointed, Billy. Those who are rich and powerful, will always find a way to be so. It is their nature. The only hope for the poor is to turn to the Lord and renounce the Devil.'

'How does that put food in their mouths?'

'Frugality, spending what they have wisely. Look, I agree it seems unfair, but what would you have, bloody revolution?'

'No Uncle, I would have the vote.' Billy slammed his fist on to the table, his voice raised.

A vein throbbed in William's forehead, while sweat glistened on Billy's pale brow. The tension between them was palpable and John was grateful when his mother came into the room asking if anyone would like a cup of tea. She almost stepped back after viewing the way her husband and nephew were glaring at each other. William stomped out of the room, pushing past his wife.

'I've never seen William look so annoyed,' she said. 'What's been going on?'

'A difference of opinion, Mother. Nothing more. It will blow over soon enough.'

Billy walked over to his aunt and put his arms around her. 'I'd better go. Thank you for looking after me all these years.'

As he left, Ann looked shocked. 'He's coming back, isn't he? What did he mean?'

But the difference of opinion remained and was not repaired. When Billy announced a few weeks later that he was moving to Hull, William did not seek to keep him from going, but appeared relieved. John asked him why, because he was upset to lose his friend.

'I love Billy, but he must find his own way in the world. If he stays I worry about the influence he will hold over you.'

'But all he was doing was speaking his mind. Should we not at least consider his views and talk about them rationally, Father? It sounds as though you have closed your mind.'

'If he falls in with troublemakers, he could earn himself a spell in prison. The authorities do not take kindly to such talk.'

'It's only talk, not action. When has he ever suggested doing something against the law?'

'Stay away from such talk, John. It will do you no good. If Billy contacts you and tries to draw you in, be of firm mind. I wish I had known that book was there so I could have burnt it.'

John was shocked. He had never thought his father intemperate. If his aunt had deemed the book suitable and worthy of consideration, why should he not read it? He wished he had not dismissed it so easily and that Billy had left it for him to read, but he assumed Billy still had it.

John stood on the dock where the steam packet to Hull was boarding. He had tears in his eyes as he grasped his cousin's hands, blaming them on the bitter January winds.

'You realise it was here on Ranter's Wharf where Silas King and your father saved mine from drink and destitution.'

John looked puzzled. 'I never knew Uncle Joe had a drink problem.'

'Well he did. He would have died if your father and Silas had not stepped in. So, I shall always remember your father with gratitude and you with love, John. If you stay and marry Emily, I wish you a long and contented life. One day I might come back to see you but I need to find my own direction. You understand, don't you? This place is too small, too narrow. We are on the cusp of change and the world grows smaller. The railways are going to bring prosperity, but the workers need to share in that new wealth. I want to see that happen.'

Wordless, John stood as Billy strode up the gangplank and stood on the deck to wave, his face muffled in a woollen scarf his aunt had pressed upon him. John hated to see him go. He was the one person he could talk to about anything that worried him or interested him. As the ship moved from its berth, John stamped his frozen feet, but no warmth crept into his bones. Loneliness gripped his body and his soul, icy fingers creeping through his blood.

As the ship receded into the distance John's mind flew back to the day three years before. It was the day John first saw death but found the friendship of the cousin he was now losing.

Chapter18

1829

John was getting ready for school, thankful that it was his final year. He was never going to be the kind of pupil the master wanted, unlike his older brother. Tom worked diligently and plodded his way through the lessons, neither a star nor a dunce. Like his father, Tom wanted to farm; school had to be endured until he was old enough to leave. John, on the other hand, could have been the star pupil. By the time, he entered school, he read with an accuracy and fluency which put his elder brother to shame. It was much to John's disgust that he was held back by a reluctant schoolmaster who required all boys to work at a similar pace. John responded by questioning his authority, for which he was soundly beaten. William had to plead several times for the school to keep John. It was only because he was man of such good standing that he persuaded them to let John stay.

In some ways, John was a trial which William had to bear. In naming him after his brother, he wondered sometimes if God was testing him or playing with him. How many times had he raised his eyes heavenward as he heard about his younger son's misdemeanours? The boy always tried to argue that what he had done was reasonable. Why did he have to attend regular Anglican services as well as Chapel? Because it is a school rule, was not good enough for John. Why did he have to learn this subject when all he wanted to learn was another subject? It was all why, why, why with this son.

William should have been exasperated with the boy, but he held a sneaking admiration for him too. His musical ability astounded Ann, as John overtook her teaching by the time he was ten. If not on the harmonium, his head was always in one of Betsy's books. William recognised that John had far surpassed what the school had to offer him. Most of the students were farmers' sons like Tom, who aspired to no more than working alongside their fathers. But what John needed was discipline and William was determined to make him stay at school, however much the boy moaned.

As John was tying up his boot laces there was a hammering at the door. He opened it to find his cousin, Billy, his face flushed from having run from Grimsby.

'Is your father here?' he cried.

'He's in the dairy,' John answered.

Billy turned and ran across the yard to where the horse stood with his head in a bag of hay. Tom appeared, struggling with another iron churn to add to the load in the cart. John stumbled after Billy into the remains of the heavy sea mist from the evening before.

'Uncle William,' Billy shouted, before John had stepped a yard; there was desperation in his voice. William's face appeared around the dairy door, annoyed at the interruption.

'It's Father, he hasn't returned from fishing. Mother's beside herself,' cried Billy. 'Will you go look for him?'

William sought to calm Billy, asking questions, while Billy stamped both feet in impatience.

'He's been gone since late yesterday afternoon. Mother's been at the dock since sun up. All the other boats have returned and the men say the fog was so thick you couldn't see a finger in front of your face. But it cleared two hours ago, and there's still no sign of them.'

'It's too early to panic, Billy. Your mother's fretting for nothing.' William inwardly sighed. Madge continued to be a trial. 'Why don't you go home; your father will most likely have returned by now.'

But Billy persisted, 'You don't understand. Two of the fishermen told us they heard something strange, you know how noise carries across the water when there's fog. They heard a grinding, snapping noise, followed by cries and shouts for help.'

William's heart sank. 'Boys, take all the churns off the cart, I'll go and get blankets.' He ran to the house, calling for Ann.

A few minutes later, all the Holtby men were heading for the sea to search, John included. William's heart was heavy with foreboding. The sun had shone bright the previous afternoon, and they expected a grand harvest moon, but by suppertime a thick, cold mist had rolled in.

There were no rocky cliffs to smash up boats. The currents and shifting sand banks were a danger to shipping, but not a fishing coble when oars could be used to push off from a sandbar. The biggest danger to the smaller boats, were rough seas, but last night had been calm. If there had been some freak accident there was a large section of coastline to search, William knew he needed more people.

As soon as they reached the Market Place in Cleethorpes, he set the boys to gather a search party, while he spoke to some of the fishermen. They confirmed that they had heard distant cries but with the fog they had been unable to determine the direction of the shouting.

'It didn't last for more than a few seconds, Mr Holtby. We thought it must have been one crew calling out to another, nothing untoward.'

Leaving the horse and cart at the Dolphin, William directed some of the men who had gathered to search east along the beach towards Humberstone. He, with Billy and his sons, set off west towards the Grimsby marshes.

William kept Billy by him. If they found anything he wanted to protect his nephew. At fourteen, the boy respected his father, although he was not close enough to follow Joe into fishing. William had found Billy a good job with a corn merchant, which suited his lively, quick intelligence. The boy was a credit to his father, but William felt sorry for him because Madge continuously nagged at her son. William did not understand her. Billy remained her only boy but she always brought up the loss of her other son as justification for why Billy should do better. He'd had words with his brother; could he not control his wife? Joe had looked at him with sadness and guilt. 'I caused the death of our youngest', he'd said, 'she will not forgive any of us for that'.

'Joe, Joe,' their cries mingling with the shriek of seagulls. The pockets of swirling mist had receded, leaving a day of autumnal promise. Gulls swooped above the seashore and rippling water. On any other day, it would be pleasant to stroll along the beach, thought William, his heart heavy in his chest. The tide was on the turn, wet sand stuck to their boots as they crunched along the shell strewn beach.

The search party arrived at the marsh where the Grimsby horse racing was held. Someone shouted out. William broke into a run. Billy's legs were twenty years younger than William's and he arrived at the body first. The corpse was lying on his front, his face smothered by the sand. He wore no boots but his fisherman's clothing was unmistakable. As someone turned him over, William offered thanks to the Lord, it was not his brother, but Billy broke into sobs.

'It's Benjamin, Father's partner.' William gathered Billy in his arms, as he wailed the last of his hope into his uncle's shoulder. John looked embarrassed by his cousin's open show of distress. Pray God, William thought, that John does not have to go through such agony. He has not yet learnt what this loss can feel like.

'Tom,' he spoke calmly to his oldest son. 'Fetch the wagon and horse from the Dolphin.'

As his son ran back to Cleethorpes, he held his fourteen-year old nephew at arms' length, looking directly into his eyes. 'I think it best if you stay here with your cousin, John, while we continue the search.'

Billy was about to protest but stopped and nodded his head in acceptance.

'John, stay close to Billy and comfort him. Pray boys, pray for my brother.' His voice was kind but stern and John looked up at his father and felt ashamed of his earlier embarrassment. What if he were to lose his father? He had never considered the possibility. His father was like a rock, unyielding, strong and permanent. The very idea of his dying took John's breath away. He gulped and took his cousin's hand, squeezing it and breaking into prayer, with Billy raggedly joining in.

William nodded approval to his son then took off his coat, laying it tenderly over the body and re-joined the rest of the men in their quest. A hundred yards further on, they found a youth clinging to a plank of wood, not dead, barely alive. Someone else threw a coat over him and pressed warmth into his body. The boy's face was blue with cold but William feeling a pulse in the boy's wrist, found it faint but present. Someone else threw a coat over him and pressed warmth into his body. As soon as Tom arrived with cart they lifted him on board into the waiting arms of another rescuer.

"Drive him as fast as you can to the doctor, Tom," his father said.

William continued the search for his brother all day and into the dusk, but found no sign of him. Aching with tiredness and dejection, he and the boys arrived back at the farmhouse in time for a late supper.

'I have to go and see Madge,' he told his wife, as she pressed him to rest his legs. 'We'll keep Billy here tonight, but I can't delay. She deserves to know what we have found.'

'She'll know already. You know how news travels around here,' said Ann, her hand stroking his arm.

'Yes, but she has to hear it from me. Keep supper warm, my love.'

His voice sounded so weary and dispirited that she worried for him. If she knew Madge, she would display such helplessness that William would feel obliged to stay with her, but he needed sleep if he was to continue searching the following day.

They gave up the search a day later with no sign of any more bodies, but a message that Joe had been found came three days later. He had washed up on the Grimsby marshes. William, prepared for this eventuality, loaded a coffin he had acquired in readiness, onto his cart. He set off alone, not wanting Billy or Tom to see his brother's remains. John had been sent back to school the day after the initial search. William found himself reciting prayers and hymns on his lonely journey, anything to stop the dark thoughts in his head.

He could smell the body before he reached the spot where a stranger stood guard. The man held a handkerchief to his face, while he shook William's hand and mumbled his condolences. William managed a wan smile before walking towards the remains. A tangle of rope revealed little of the body, save for the colour of his hair. A hand lay outstretched, as though trying to grasp onto something, the fingers bitten to the bone. He forced himself to say prayers over the body, while attempting not to gag. William did not want to remember his brother like this but no doubt his dreams would remind him.

The man had lifted the coffin off the cart in readiness and the two men grasped the limbs and laid the body in the box. There would be no laying out, the sea had washed his brother enough and he wanted to spare the widow any further distress. Taking nails and a hammer, he did as his father had done for his mother and closed the coffin. His thoughts turned towards his mother and the missing years of his brother's companionship. He was relieved they had made peace and enjoyed the last ten years of brotherhood.

He offered the man a lift home, calling at Billy's workplace to collect his nephew on the way and then took the coffin back to Madge. With any other sister-in-law, he would have taken her in his arms to comfort her, but she stood at her door, her ice blue eyes, accusing her son and William. Billy was distraught but she had no comfort to offer him.

'If you had been with him, you might have saved him,' she spat at her son. William drew back at her spiteful words.

'And what could Billy have done, exactly?' he asked. 'It's more likely you would have had a dead son as well as a dead husband.'

'Billy can swim; he should have been with his father.'

'You're the most unreasonable woman I've ever met. Don't you realise that Billy here is now your only support. What are you going to do for money? You should be thankful to have a son who has a job.' Far from mollifying her, it just seemed to make her worse. William did not want to leave Billy with her but he told his uncle he would be alright and to go home.

'I'll let your sister know what's happened, Billy.' William said, as he took his leave. Margaret had gone into service earlier in the year and was living in Waltham. 'Do you want me to arrange the funeral?' He half expected Madge to start shouting again, but she did not. He took that as acceptance. Yes, she'll be happy for me to bear the cost, he sighed. He could not begrudge his brother a decent funeral.

Before setting off for home, he visited the boy who had survived and was pleased to find him well enough to talk. His mother bustled around making tea for her guest, effusive in her thanks for saving her son.

'It was not me but God, who saved your son. We only found him, but please thank God, Himself. Come to Chapel on Sunday and we will say a special prayer of thanksgiving for your son's deliverance.' Flustered, the woman bobbed a curtsey, and made herself scarce so they could talk.

The boy told his tale haltingly but in detail and when he had finished, William left a sovereign by his bed.

On his return to the farm, Ann saw from his face how difficult this had been for William. He sank his face into her bosom, his chest heaving in sadness.

'Come', she said. 'Take yourself to bed. You've not slept these last few nights. I will bring you a posset to help you sleep.'

He did as he was told, grateful as ever for her care. He climbed the stairs, his body shuddering with the effort and could barely manage to take off his coat before sinking into the softness of the feather mattress.

She sat on the bed while he drank, listening as he repeated what he knew.

'It seems that they sailed out of Grimsby that afternoon in bright sunshine, but as they made for the entrance to the sea, they saw a wall of dense fog heading towards them. They turned back, hoping to beat it back to the dock, but were enveloped within minutes. There was only one thing to do and that was to wait it out. They took down their sail and stowed their oars, knowing it was hopeless to try and find the shore. They might easily row around in circles or worse, they could just as easily find themselves in the middle of the ocean, or on Spurn. It was better to bide their time. The current was more likely to take them to the southern shore of the estuary. I know Joe was sensible and not prone to panic. They were not afraid; the sea was calm. Before they slept, they sang hymns and trusted in God to save them. I am relieved to think that Joe's last thoughts were of God, aren't you Ann?' She nodded, holding his hand in comfort.

'They settled for the night, one keeping watch. The boy was on watch when it happened. He did not see the ship until it was driving into them, over them. It had not set anchor. Most captains coming across such fog in that dangerous channel would set anchor, wouldn't they? Although it may have been one of those drunken river pilots convincing the captain he could guide them into Hull.' He cried out in indignation, tears of anger forming at his eyes. 'But if the Captain had been doing his job properly, this should not have happened. I'll be taking it up with the harbourmaster, tomorrow.'

'Shush, William. Don't think about that now,' his wife tried to pacify him.

'My brother was heard crying out to the Lord in his final moments,' William gave in to his grief, but grateful to the boy for giving him this nugget of consolation. It would make his sermon more meaningful at the funeral. He was determined that he would officiate. It was the last thing he could do for his brother. He closed his eyes, as Ann stole from the room, and fell into a deep, thankfully dreamless sleep, safe in the knowledge that Joe had as good as death as possible.

Chapter 19

1842

Billy stood underneath the gas lamp, calling to John as he left his place of work. His voice was unmistakable as was his appearance. He may not like it said, but Billy resembled his mother more than his father. Now, more than ten years since he had last seen him, the likeness was even more apparent. The two cousins embraced, the years apart swiftly receding.

'What brings you back here, Billy?'

'To see you of course, Cousin. I have been waiting for you, hoping that you were still working for old man, Dewsbury.'

'His son, Billy. Joseph Dewsbury died these five years back. Have you been to see Father yet?'

'No, I don't want Uncle to know I am here.'

'Why ever not? He'll be delighted to see you.'

'I am here for a reason he may not like. Will you step into a tavern to talk with me?'

'Billy, I have signed the pledge. I am well known here and word would get back to my family and the Chapel.'

Billy sighed, 'I thought you might still be entwined with the Chapel. I have a room in a lodging house near the Riverhead, we can talk there, if that is more to your liking?'

'I can't stay long; my wife is expecting me for supper.' John stiffened at Billy's derogatory comment about his Chapel attendance. They set off to walk the short distance.

'I suppose you married the delectable Miss Plumtree.'

'Yes, on my twenty first birthday. We have a daughter now. Are you married, Billy?'

'Me? No. I don't have time for such domesticity.' John thought that an odd statement but was intrigued. His cousin seemed on edge, more like John himself before he settled down to his life of work, home and chapel.

Billy's room was tucked away at the back of one of the newish houses around the docks. It was clean, but bare of fripperies. A bed, a chair, a chest of drawers, where a plain earthenware jug and bowl stood, were its sole contents.

'How long are you staying here?' The lack of belongings surprised John.

'I'll be back in Yorkshire in two days. I have only come to see you. Sit on the chair. I'll make do with the bed.' Billy sank onto the mattress, which creaked and sagged, despite his wiry form.

'I really can't stay. I'm always home by seven. I like to see my daughter, Dorothea, before she goes to bed.'

'Tell me, John, what did you think of the Reform Act and the Poor Law?' John's eyes widened in surprise, where on earth was this conversation going? He struggled to gather his thoughts.

'Well, Father was pleased, of course, he got the vote. The Freemen were outraged because Grimsby lost an MP...'

Billy interrupted in frustration. 'You, John, you. I can guess what Uncle and the Freemen thought.

John considered for a moment. He had buried all his rebellious ideas years ago, refusing to air them for love of his family. Since he married, he scarcely read the newspapers but he knew of the Charter which had failed so dismally three, maybe four years before. No one in Chapel bothered themselves with politics, other than campaigning for the abolition of slavery, but that argument was won.

'I suppose I hoped the Reform Bill would go further, but I was only seventeen when it passed and since then I have given it little thought. The Poor Law, I take the lead from my father, he was against it from the start, although he was glad to see the back of the House of Industry. It was so badly run. I only hope the Caistor Poor House looks after the inmates better.'

'John, I'm disappointed. This insular town appears to have enveloped you in its blanket of chapel respectability. Have the Prims here become like the Wesleyans, middle class and staid? Have you lost your ..'

John stood up, 'I don't know what you want, Billy, but I don't have to listen to this...'

'What, John, the truth? Come on, just listen for a moment. I want to open your eyes. We are living in the moment; I truly believe that. Good things can happen if we make them happen.'

John sat down. 'I have no idea what you are talking about, Billy. I can't stay more than five minutes longer.'

He left the lodging house carrying a sheaf of newspapers and pamphlets which Billy had urged him to read. So, there was to be another petition to parliament, and Billy wanted John to garner support in the town. Against his better judgement, he had arranged to meet his cousin the following evening, once John had had time to read and consider what was asked of him. A part of him wanted to discard the papers right then, throw them away and forget about Billy. He had not liked the zeal and passion in his eyes. Should Billy not be using all that emotion to gather sinners to the Chapel?

As he walked home, he started thinking of his father and that journal. He was not far off his father's age when he had taken a risk by becoming one of the first Primitive Methodists in Grimsby. No one could deny the good they had done. The evidence lay in the size of the congregation in the Loft Street Chapel on Sundays and beyond that were the Sunday Schools. He wondered how many children had been taught to read and write, solely because of the Sunday Schools. He was proud of his father. What had *he* to be proud of? Would he go through this life, short or long, without making a similar mark on the town? As he stepped through the doorway of his house and greeted his wife, John decided that he would read the papers Billy had given him. What harm could it do?

'Whatever's the matter, my dear?' Emily said, bringing him the warm milk he liked before bedtime. 'You look troubled.'

188

John looked up, anger clouded his eyes. 'I've been reading about our brethren in Yorkshire and how the poor are being forced into workhouses.'

Emily, clicked her tongue, 'That's not the kind of thing you should read before bedtime. We normally read something from the Bible.' She sat down in her chair, settling into the comforting crewelwork cushions she had spent so many hours embroidering.

'Listen to this, Emily. Labouring families are trying to live on seven shillings a week, a shilling for rent and with the price of corn so high they have money for only two loaves of bread a week. Their poor children live on potatoes and barley cakes with no money for clothes, bedding, soap and these are working men, not the unemployed. Children are dying for want of food and warmth, Emily.'

'Please don't talk of such things, John. It will upset me so. Can we not have a verse from the Bible?'

John looked at her with concern. The last thing he wanted was to upset his wife in her condition. She was just beginning to show and, as yet, they had not announced the good news.

'Very well my love, I'll not trouble you with such tales again. What verse would you like?' He stroked her heart-shaped face and leant over to pick up the Bible which sat on the table next to his armchair, a constant companion to their neat, ordered lives.

He could not sleep that night. The stories he had read in the paper, like that of the family whose children had died one by one of fever from having to sleep on a bare brick floor. Or those families torn apart on entering the workhouse, with little likelihood of ever leaving. He had no idea conditions in the country were as bad. Imagining his own dear family in such a position, tore him apart. He lived in a protected bubble, where nothing untoward had happened since his uncle's drowning thirteen years before.

Back in Billy's room the following evening, John wasted no time in chit chat.

'You have to realise, Billy, this is one of the least radical towns in the country. Since the Municipal Reform Act, the only argument that goes on here is the bitter rivalry between the Freeman and the new Corporation.

The Freemen are not about to relinquish what remains of their power by petitioning for more men to get the vote.'

'So, the Freemen won't support the petition, they're still a minority in town.'

'I doubt those who were given the vote ten years ago, will urge suffrage to be extended. They regard their vote highly; highly enough to be unwilling to share it.'

'You will get nowhere with that attitude, Cousin. We have to persuade through the force of our arguments.'

'Is it the moral force argument you support, or physical force? I can't have any truck with riots and rebellion. Who is it in Leeds that you work with? I hear Feargus O'Connell is a madman.'

'Oh, so from knowing nothing yesterday, you are now expert enough to have a view on Feargus. He's a fine man, let me tell you.'

This discussion was going nowhere. Despite his reservations, John agreed to try and get signatures for the petition. The stories he had read the evening before, pricking sufficiently at his conscience.

'When will you return, Billy?'

'By the middle of April.'

'That's only eight weeks!'

'Just think how much Silas King achieved in eight weeks.'

John knew Billy was adding sarcasm to the mix. He would not rise to it. Why had he agreed at all to do this? It was the mental image he had of Dorothea dying of starvation in his arms, which caused him to say yes. Without extending the vote, working men could not hope to repeal iniquitous laws such as the Poor Law, he understood that. Billy might not want to approach his father, but John was reluctant to begin collecting signatures without first speaking to him.

'I'll make a start on it this Sunday,' he said to mollify his cousin.

'Good man,' Billy clapped him on the back.

On Saturday afternoon, after he had finished work at midday, John called on his parents, with Emily and Dorothea in tow. His mother idolised her grandchildren and threw her arms around Emily when told the news of another grandchild arriving in June. John asked his father if he could speak to him on a matter of urgency.

'Why don't we go for a walk and let the womenfolk chat about babies? Goodness knows there are enough of them around with Tom's two and they have a third on the way, did you know that?'

John nodded as his father gathered together his coat and hat and bent down to put on his boots. He showed no sign of ageing, although nearing fifty, he was as agile and strong as he had been at thirty. John doubted he would be the same at his age; hours of office work made his muscles cramp and his eyes ache, he said as much to his father.

'What you need boy is more fresh air. Let's walk for an hour or two and blow all those cobwebs away.'

They talked companionably about the family as they set off towards Weelsby Woods. The biting easterly wind made a countryside walk seem more welcome than the seashore. John was grateful for the warm scarf and gloves his wife had knitted for him. His father did not appear to feel the cold. At last John screwed up his courage to say what he had mulled over in his mind.

'I saw Billy this week, Father.'

'Billy was in Grimsby, and he didn't come to visit?' His father looked hurt, as John knew he would.

'I think he didn't want to see your disapproval. He's finished going to Chapel.' Silence followed this statement. 'He's become involved with workers' rights and Chartism.' More silence. John looked at his father's face and saw more puzzlement than disapproval. 'He lives in Leeds,' John ended lamely, as though it explained Billy's choice.

'And he wants you to do what?' His father stopped walking and turned towards John, seeking an answer, his tone expectant rather than grim, which encouraged John to continue.

'They, the Chartists, are presenting a new petition and are gathering signatures. I have agreed to get some from Grimsby workers.' His father pursed his lips while he digested this information.

'First, let me say I am disappointed that Billy did not come and talk to me. I think that says something about him and you should be wary. Second, although I don't agree with extending the vote, I am not against you attempting to get men to sign but you need to be aware of where this may lead. If all you do is get signatures and leave it at that, you should have no problem.'

'That's all I mean to do, Father.'

'Very well, I would be concerned if you began to get more heavily involved. I have never said this before but when I married your mother it was for many reasons, but not for love. That came later. We fit together and she has supported all that I do and all that I am. I care for her beyond words.'

'What are you trying to say, Father?'

'Your wife, John, I know that you love her, but her older sisters seek always to control her and she lets them. Is it not time you put paid to that? She should look to you for guidance. You and God.'

'You want me to stop her from seeing Ada and Mabel? But they only live around the corner.'

'No, John. All I am saying is, be careful. Her family hold such strict views. In a battle between you and her family, who would win? The older girls remember their father before he found God. He was too fond of the ale house and once you have experienced a life of hunger and uncertainty as the children of a sinner, you never want to return to it. Life became much better for them after they started to attend chapel. Their fear colours their attitude. But Emily should accept that her life is with you and not them.' He paused to let the warning sink in. 'She is, I think, unduly influenced by her sisters and they will reject Chartism out of hand.'

'I never knew that about Mr Plumtree.'

'I only told you so you would understand why Emily's sisters are so strict. Changing the subject, what made you decide to help Billy?'

As they resumed their walk along the muddy track through the woods, John told his father of the newspaper reports he had read and his reaction to them.

'So, it's not just about men gaining the vote and the secret ballot? It's the Poor Law too. If you want to know about rural poverty just visit the Wolds. Perhaps this is against my better judgement after what I have said

192

about being careful, but I think you need to open your eyes about what's going on around you. I'll take you with me to some of the small villages starting next Sunday. It will do me good to do some missioning again. It must be ten years since I gave way to younger legs. Will you join me? Maybe we can get some more signatures too.'

John's attempt to gain support for the petition in Chapel was not successful. He stood and faced the congregation explaining the reasons why they should support the latest petition but had been rebuffed.

One of the rewards of being a Freeman had been to get paid for their vote, although they would never admit to it in Chapel. The Reform Act diffused their power and resentment still rankled. For some it was the riots in Newport after the first petition failed which swayed them. For others, a disinclination to get involved in politics at all. One or two came up to him privately and told him they would sign, but his paper was worryingly bare at the end of his first week.

Before he stood up in Chapel, he asked Emily what she thought about the petition. Her lukewarm response disappointed John. she was, however, delighted that John was to accompany his father to the surrounding villages on a missioning expedition. He mulled over the conversation with his father many times that week, recalling little incidents which had not bothered him before. There was the time when Ada, the oldest sister, criticised Emily for washing some dishes on a Sunday when it was the maid's afternoon off. Or the time, Mabel, the middle sister, told Emily, when she was seven months pregnant with Dorothea, that she would not be welcome at Christmas supper in her condition. Emily had been upset, but he was quite glad of the reprieve. The atmosphere in the Plumtree house was stultifying and he disliked going there. He realized now that he should have objected and supported Emily. If he had not supported her, why should she do the same for him? He must set the example.

It was as if he was visiting the Wolds for the first time. As a boy, if he had no chores, he had roamed the hills and seashore during his school holidays. Sometimes he had been accompanied by his brother, Tom, but mostly a school friend. They had been a playground for fishing, climbing, making dens, everything a boy with time on his hands enjoyed. This was the first time he had accompanied his father and he took the opportunity to pump him for information about what it was like to be a labourer in the Wolds.

'As little as fifty years ago, the Wolds were fit only for sheep. It was covered in furze and gorse, but during the French Wars, with the price of grain so high, they began to plough it up for wheat and barley. It took time to get it into condition. One of my first jobs was to spread bone meal on the fields. I did everything that the labourers do now and believe me it's hard work. Just be thankful that you have not had to do it. There is dignity in the work too. Don't look down on these people, John.'

'I never would, Father. Is there enough work for everyone who needs it?'

'One of the problems with the Wolds is not lack of work, but housing. Our first village, Laceby, is an open village with no large landowner to block housing and it's growing year by year. But the inhabitants must travel for work or sink into further poverty. Ask questions, find out for yourself.'

A society had existed in Laceby for almost four years. Welcomed as an old friend to the chapel, William accepted the invitation to preach. John always loved to listen to him and judging by the attention he was given, so did the congregation of around sixty souls. After the service, William called John up to tell them about the petition.

As he stood in the chapel talking about the Charter, John watched eyes glaze over, then feet begin to shuffle and within two or three minutes the words began to dry in his mouth. In desperation, he wafted the paper about his head and cried, 'Who will be the first to sign?'

No one made a move. Not a single hand rose in the air, until a small girl put her hand up and asked if it was time to eat. Several people chuckled and with the tension broken, began to drift away.

'What did I do wrong, Father?' he asked as they left the village walking east up into the Wolds. 'If I can't get a signature in Laceby, what chance do I have in the smaller villages?'

'You talked only about the Charter. What do equal constituencies and annual parliaments mean to these people? They don't write for the most part, read only the Bible, if at all. They have no expectation of being able to vote and what it means for them. They are scared of their masters and their only hope is that they can feed their families at the end of the week.'

John sighed, 'I should never have agreed to help Billy.'

'The question you should be asking is what are they most afraid of?'

'You said, they were scared of their masters.'

'Yes, John, but why?'

'Their jobs, if they lose those, they lose everything.'

'And what happens then?'

'The workhouse! Of course, I need to start with why they should demand the vote to overturn the Poor Law.'

'That's why you are doing this. Don't give up, John. I think it unlikely you will get many to sign, but you will learn more by listening.'

They came into East Ravendale, scarcely more than a handful of tumbledown, ancient cottages. His father began to sing a hymn loudly, walking up and down the street until heads poked around doors.

'Why it's Mr Holtby, have you come to preach today?' asked an old lady, with a toddler in her arms.

'I have. Mrs Fisher, isn't it? How are you dear lady?'

'It's been a long time since you wus here; we've missed your ranting.'

'Well I've brought along my son to help today.' The old woman gave John a gummy smile.

'I remember when your father and that Mr King came the first time; they didn't half shake us up. I've never been so well saved.' John took her by the hand, feeling the calloused fingers clutch at his. 'I live with my daughter now that my husband's gone. I don't know what I'd a done if she hadn't teken me in.'

The anxiety in her watery eyes hit John like a punch to his stomach. The justness of the petition coursed through his blood.

'Do you think we might step in for a drink before we begin? We've walked a long way,' said his father.

The old lady clucked and said, 'Where are my manners, Mr Holtby? We've only water, but it's fresh from the well.'

John followed his father into the single storey thatched cottage, grazing his head on the low beam. As his eyes adjusted, he caught sight of a baby lying in what looked like a box, close by the dying embers of a fire. A pan on three legs stood in the cinders, the remains of a thin soup, simmering gently. A single wooden chair stood by the fire and a wooden bench sat by a small table, which was crammed with all the plates, pans and dishes owned by the family. Through an open door, John could see a bundle of mattresses and covers strewn on the dirt floor.

The old lady scooped a ladle of water from a pail into an earthenware jug and handed it to William; he drank deeply before handing it to John.

'How many children does your daughter have?' asked John.

'Six, Sir, one for each year of marriage.'

'And you all live here?' As soon as the words left his mouth, John regretted them. His mind could not comprehend nine people living in this tiny cottage, no bigger than his own parlour, and with so little comfort.

'Where are your family today?' asked his father.

'Out gathering wood; it's been such a cold month and my rheumatics are playing up somethin' shocking.'

'Well give them all my best.'

'I will, Mr Holtby. They'll be sorry to have missed you.'

It was a small congregation, half a dozen men, their wives and a few children, but they listened attentively to William's sermon. John appreciated how his father spoke their language, moulding his prayers to their needs. If nothing else, John was learning how to speak to a different audience from the one he was used to. When his father called on John to talk about the petition, he chose his words carefully.

'Dear Friends, I feel I already know you through my father,' he began, and looking around the small group, he noted their expectant smiles. 'I am much troubled, and I believe you are too,' he paused, knowing that their smiles would fade as he progressed. 'As a Christian, who believes in the teachings of the Bible, I think of the words 'Do unto others as you wish they would do to you', and they trouble me. Not because I think them wrong, oh no, dear brothers and sisters, I think them right.' Heads were nodding. 'However,' another pause, 'I fear our blessed Queen's parliament has forgotten this teaching when they passed the Poor Law Act.' After a momentary intake of breath from the congregation, heads began to nod vigorously. 'The question is, Brothers and Sisters, what can we do about it?' The atmosphere had changed from joy to anger in an instant.

'Tear it up,' cried an elderly man.

'Go back to outdoor relief,' cried a woman.

'I wish it were that simple,' said John. 'I believe the only possible answer is to let all working men have the vote, and let your voice be heard in the seat of our great parliament. For that reason, I come to ask you today, to sign a petition that will go to London; a petition so large that it cannot be ignored. Which of you men, will sign first?' Silence and shuffling of feet, just as at Laceby. John's spirits sank; he really thought he had won them around this time.

'I live in a tied cottage, Sir. If my master heard that I signed, I would be out. It's not that we don't want to sign, it's that we're feared to sign.' Other heads nodded at the young man who was brave enough to speak.

'How would he know?' asked John.

'You say this petition is going up to parliament, so people there'll see it?'

'Yes, of course.'

'Well, the Earl's in the House of Lords and he dines with Mr Parkinson at the hall.' John had no answer. He supposed theoretically it was possible, but would an earl check millions of signatures? It was most unlikely. He could see how they would not want to risk it.

Mrs Fisher came up to John as he prepared to leave empty handed. 'Thank you for trying, Sir. It's just that we're terrified of ending up in the Poor House. If any of us loses our employment or home, then there's nowhere else for us. I know we're a disappointment to you.'

'Indeed, you are not. I understand.' He attempted a reassuring smile.

'Do you see what you're up against, now? His father said, as they walked out of the village.

'You knew it would be like this, didn't you?'

'Of course, but I'm proud of the way you handled yourself there. We'll make a preacher of you yet. Why not stick to preaching, son?'

'The conditions they live in, Father, it makes my blood boil.'

'Let me tell you, my grandmother lived like that, but after her husband died, she got relief from the parish. If it were today the whole family would have ended up in the workhouse. I find the Act as despicable as you do, but you're facing an impossible task. All we can bring them is hope for a better future in the next life, as hard as that sounds. We don't have the people who can educate them out here, the villages are too small.'

As they made their way to Waltham, the last village before returning to Grimsby, John almost gave up. His father talked sense and yet, and yet, something inside him kept gnawing at him.

In Waltham John fared better; being a larger village nearer to Grimsby, there were some skilled men in the congregation. By the time, he got home he had four signatures for his trouble, a baker, a blacksmith, a thatcher and a shopkeeper.

'I don't suppose you want to go out again next Sunday?' asked his father as they reached the farmhouse.

'Yes, I do,' he said, 'I want to see more villages. I want to learn about their lives. No matter if we get no marks on my paper. I cannot turn away from these people.'

'You take after your Aunt Betsy. She hated to see the poor and was always giving them money, but she knew where to draw the line. Don't be drawn into fighting their battles, it will do you no good.' William grabbed John, by the shoulders and stared into his eyes. 'Do the Lord's work, son, not Billy's, not these Chartists. No good will come of you fighting the landowners.'

The more John saw of the plight of the families in the villages, the more his father wished he had never begun taking him. The day they took the cart to Swallow and Rothwell was the worst. It was too far to walk there and back and preach, with rain clouds threatening a soggy tramp through isolated countryside.

John had not been to the villages in Cherry Valley before. Both hamlets were hidden from view off the main road to Caistor. They left the horse and cart to be cared for at an inn. The tiny village of Rothwell appeared to cling to the sides of the hill, almost swallowed up in the mire of poverty.

John had stopped asking for signatures after his father's sermon. He told them about the petition to give them some hope that things could change, and in return he listened as they described their lives. He heard how the children tramped miles each day to work on the land for gang-masters, earning seven pence for an eight-hour day for pulling couch grass, picking stones or planting potatoes.

He looked at the children in front of him, tousled hair, ragged clothes, unshod and dirty; all of them skinny, apart from one, whose belly, showed she was with child, yet no more than a child herself.

'Both boys and girls work for these men?' he asked.

'Aye Sir, we know it's not right. The girls can be led into wicked ways, but we have no choice. We need the money.'

'What age do they begin this work?'

The mother who answered looked ashamed, 'Seven or eight, Sir. Sometimes I goes with 'em, if there's enough work.' Like Mrs Fisher, the woman looked two decades older than her years. John had been astounded when his father had given Mrs Fisher's age as forty-five or so. John had thought she approached seventy.

'So, is there not enough work at hand, close to the village?'

'No, Sir. We would move closer to the work, but there's no cottages for us.'

Why, he had asked his father on the return journey, do the farmers not build cottages on their land?

'Before the Poor Law they were afraid to. The inhabitants might qualify for poor relief once they became infirm. Now it suits them to have gangs of workers, whenever they have need, and forget about them in between. That way they save money.'

At night, after Emily had retired for the night, he sat with his head in his hands. Because she was with child, he did not want to trouble her with the images and tales which stopped him from sleeping. The petition had to work, conditions would not change unless it did. He was pinning his hopes onto that, however much his father told him that he was living in a dream world.

What did he have to show for all the hours spent in the previous six weeks trying to twist hands to sign? Less than a dozen names. He imagined Billy's scorn when he arrived to collect the petition, but John cared nothing for that. He cared only for the people he had met; God-fearing men, women and children, who scraped a pittance from their labours, with only heaven to look forward to, and a real dread of entering the workhouse to die. Many of them had told him they thought it inevitable. What other option was there?

How can I live with myself if I do not get more names? The only answer he could see was to go into the town taverns and gather signatures. It was the only way.

'I will stand up on Sunday in Chapel and beg for forgiveness. It's not as if I am going to drink or sin,' he said to himself. The decision allowed him to sleep fitfully; his dreams peppered with the poor and the hungry.

The news of the petition's failure, which came in summer, made John fall into a fit of depression. It was not long after his second daughter was born. He should have been delighted. Emily thought he was disappointed that Edith, was not a son. He tried to reassure her, but each time he looked at his girls, he saw the haunting faces of the children in Rothwell. His children had food in their stomachs, a roof over their heads and warm clothes, and he felt guilty. A guilt which drained the joy from his life and was fed by the newspaper reports he now so avidly read. Parliament had refused to accept a petition signed by over three million people. It seemed to John that they cared not a whit for the conditions in the country, nor the millions of hard-working, sober people who slaved for others on starvation wages.

He knew it was unreasonable, but he blamed himself for not having obtained more signatures. In the end, he managed a hundred or so by visiting the taverns in Grimsby and Cleethorpes, much to Emily's family's disgust. He was beyond caring about that. He tried talking to them about the conditions in the villages, but they closed their ears. Ada informed him that nothing was worth putting his soul into such jeopardy for, no matter that he had not drunk the ale. His father understood and ameliorated the Chapel elders' condemnation as best he could. He tried to put the blame on himself by taking his son to the villages, which set him on this desperate path. The condition put upon John was that he was to renew his pledge and avoid setting foot in any tavern. At the time, John thought that was acceptable and agreed. The petition had only just been submitted to parliament and hope clouded his judgement.

Emily tried to understand at first. He hated to upset her by revealing the degradation he had witnessed and kept the worst from her. Consequently, she did not condone his visiting the taverns and was shamed by his begging forgiveness in Chapel. He detected a withdrawal of trust from her, which added to his depression. All those years of loving and trusting each other, destroyed. Did she have so little faith in him?

He understood now what his father had been warning him about, but he was helpless. His eyes had been opened and forever more would not close. His ears had heard the suffering of his fellow man and the noise deafened him. He had smelt and tasted the poverty of the rural villages and tables groaning with delectable food, now sickened him. Some days he thought he was going mad.

When the petition was rejected he felt in honour bound to revisit all the villages and tell them the news. The people saw the hurt in his eyes and despite their own deprivations and worries did their best to thank him for his efforts. He vowed not to forsake them, but had no idea how he would achieve that. The men shook his hand and the women patted him on his arm. On his lonely walks home, he took no pleasure in the warm, summer sun, the ripening grain, the song of the birds or the fragrance of flowers. He felt as though he had forgotten how to speak to God.

On visits to his parents they saw only a husk of their son, his spirit damaged and hurting. William took to praying for his recovery, while his mother baked all his favourite foods and tried to tempt him. He derived some comfort from her gentle ministrations and wished he could lay himself in her arms and sob out his grief for the plight of those villagers. He feared a week's constant tears would not be enough. The hole in the centre of his being would be never satisfied. He did not know how to fill it.

Throughout August he read of strikes and unrest in the North and the Midlands and his heart was with them. He willed them to succeed, his head knowing they would fail, and that failure defeated him again. At work, he went through the motions, in Chapel he mouthed the words, grateful that he was still able to take pleasure in playing the music for the hymns. He prayed but found no comfort or answers in prayer. In his home, he felt lonely. His wife was overtired herself. The new baby had colic so he pressed Emily to sleep in the evenings, knowing she might be up half the night. Only Dorothea gave him comfort, her sweet, innocent face always welcomed him home and before she went to bed he took the chance to forget his troubles by sitting her on his lap to tell her a story. To an outsider his home would appear to be a haven of simple domesticity. All was as it had been, and yet to John, everything had changed.

One day he read in the Chartist newspaper that a Joseph Capper of Tunstall had been jailed for inciting people to riot. The name rang a bell and he took the paper to his father.

'You met him, didn't you?' His father read the brief article and his eyes looked troubled.

'This is what happens, John. You stir things up and then you end up at odds with the law.'

'You thought him a good man, a lay-preacher, like yourself.'

'I did. He must have gone too far. The authorities don't lack for excuses to jail people. I will write to his wife. But be warned, John, Billy may well end up in trouble too. I worry for you both.'

As the months progressed, he wearied of his black mood. At Christmas, he smiled as Dorothea played with her new rag doll and Edith tasted her first bite of mashed up roast chicken. He even agreed to attend his in-law's party where they played twenty questions, an acceptably educational parlour game. Later he wondered what kind of Christmas the Fisher family were having, or the Capper's. Mrs Capper's son had written to William saying that his father had been maliciously prosecuted and false witness was to blame for his imprisonment. 'See', his father had said, 'this is what happens when you stand up against authority'.

Realising that no one around him was going to change and that it was up to him to compromise, John swore some New Year's resolutions. He decided to try to be happy with his situation and accept his lot. He was twenty-five years old, in the prime of his life and had much to be grateful for. If he could not help change things politically, at least he could offer spiritual and practical help to the communities of which he had become so fond.

'Emily,' he said, on New Year's Day, 'Forgive my low spirits these past few months. I promise this year will be better.'

His wife took his hands in hers. 'Oh, John, I feared you had gone for good. I've been in despair to see your suffering. We have been praying for you.'

'You have?' John was astounded. 'I thought you had stopped caring about me.'

'Never, John. I will always love you, though I may not understand you.'

'What did you mean by we have been praying? Who has been praying?'

'My sisters and I,' Emily looked puzzled as she saw a frown sweep across his face. 'I was disappointed in you at first and now I realise I should not have doubted you. I feel it is my fault that you have been so distant. I have let you down. But our prayers have been answered. God has brought you back to me, hasn't he?'

John was not sure that God had anything to do with it but as he felt Emily's hands go around his neck and her lips touch his, a huge weight lifted from his shoulders and he buried himself in his wife's love once more. He had been drowning and now, at last, he swam to the surface, took a huge breath and allowed his despair to float away.

Chapter 20

1847

The town buzzed with new found optimism. Since the Grimsby Railway act passed in 1845, everyone was in a state of anticipation. No one in John's family, apart from his father, had ever set foot beyond North Lincolnshire and here was Emily asking if they might go to London for a visit. Whatever next? John thought, will she ask to go to Paris? He smiled with indulgence as she dandled their new son on her knee. London used to sound as far away as the moon but in a year or two it would be within a few hours' journey. He could hardly believe it himself.

His life felt truly blessed. He had his own law practice, a loving family, and his occasional visits to the villages of the Wolds offered the opportunity to ease his conscience. He rarely preached but was happy to be of service in writing letters, interceding in disputes between landlord and tenant and offering advice. Wages had risen after the terrible depression earlier in the decade, although no one could call them sufficient. At last, following the dreadful famine in Ireland, the corn laws had been repealed and the price of bread was falling. He had witnessed the effect of the potato blight in Lincolnshire too, the stink of the rotting vegetable was hard to miss, but at least the poor in England had bread and turnips or swedes to eat.

He heard a knock at the door and a few seconds later the maid announced his father. It was always a pleasure to have a visit from his father but it was a rare occurrence. They normally visited the farm. The girls loved going to the see the chickens and pigs, as much as they loved the beach at Cleethorpes.

'What brings you here, Father?' asked John, after William had greeted his daughter-in-law and tickled Walter, much to his delight.

'I received a letter addressed to you.' William passed it to his son, who eased it open.

'It's from Billy,' he said after scanning the contents. 'He's getting married and wants me to be best man. It's a small affair, apparently, so the invitation is just for me and Emily.'

'Oh, when is it?' asked Emily, her face lit with surprise.

'Next Saturday, in Leeds.'

Emily's face dropped in dismay. 'Then I can't go, what with Walter not weaned. Shall you go, John?'

John looked at his father. 'What do you think?'

'I don't know, Son. Someone from the family should be there but I worry that he is going to draw you into his schemes again.' His father's face looked troubled and then cleared as he looked at Emily. 'I am pleased that he is marrying. Nothing settles a man like a good wife.'

'It's only a wedding, after all. I think I will go. Billy says I should come on Thursday to meet his bride; they are having supper with her parents. I can take two or three days off work, there's nothing vital that can't wait.' He was excited by the prospect.

'I remember my first visit to Hull,' said his father, now reconciled to his son going. 'It will do you good to see something of the country. At least you won't have to walk all the way. I wonder what it will be like to take the train. You'll have to tell us all about it, when you get back.'

The steam packet to Hull took scarcely any time at all. When he arrived, John felt as though he had left one life and entered another. He had never seen such bustle. Is this what it is going to be like when the new docks are built, he wondered? Work had already begun on reclaiming the land from the east marshes. His father told him how his Aunt Betsy would have been thrilled. John was pleased because it offered new job opportunities for labourers from the villages. He had encouraged several to leave and find work and lodgings in Grimsby. It may only be temporary work, he told them, but other jobs are bound to arise from increasing prosperity.

He stood in admiration on the railway platform in Kingston Street Station. The drawings he had seen in magazines could never do the train justice. He found his heart swelling with pride to think of such British ingenuity, so simple and so elegant. To be connected to the rest of the country was bound to change lives for the better, he thought, as he clambered into a carriage that would take him to Selby and on to Leeds. A quiet anticipation gripped him as the train chugged from the station. Clattering wheels on iron tracks, the piercing whistle and gritty smoke from its great engine, he took it all in as his excitement mounted. It must have shone from his face because a passenger opposite asked him if it was the first time he had been on a train. He nodded and the man proceeded to tell him at length about all the engineering that went into the railway. John was content to let the man ramble on, occasionally nodding his head, as though giving him his full attention. His eyes kept slipping, however, to the countryside flying past.

John was happy to see the man get up to leave the train at Goole. They shook hands and John thanked him for his company and commentary. If asked to repeat any of it, he would have been hard-pressed. For the remainder of the journey his eyes never left the window. Everything mesmerised him, it was all new and yet oddly familiar. Churches with spires or steeples, small towns, villages, people working on the land, or on wharves, all of it normal English life, but more prosperous than he had seen before. The scene changed as they began to approach their destination. Here was a city with back to back housing, dirty, big, but wealth and poverty oozed through the smoke from its chimneys.

Billy met him at the station. They shook hands and then Billy threw his arms around John and hugged him.

'I have longed for you to see this city, John. Great things lie ahead for us. Don't you feel it?' He laughed at John's bemused expression.

'What? You think I just brought you here for a wedding?'

John's heart sank. 'You are getting married on Saturday? That's why I've come.'

'Yes, yes, of course. Would I lie? You'll be able to tell Uncle William and Aunt Ann all about it, and about my bride.' His eyes twinkled in merriment.

John was relieved but unsure. Something was going on. What was it? 'Who are you marrying?'

'Her name is Jeanie and that's all I am going to tell you. Come, I'll take you to my lodgings.'

He took John's bag from him and walked swiftly towards the street, leaving John no time to admire the station. As they exited they were caught up in a crowd, more people than John had ever seen in one place. It was a maelstrom of people, horses, carts and carriages. His head began to spin and he had to call out weakly to Billy, 'Don't rush. If I lose you, I'll never find you.'

Billy's lodgings lay in Holbeck, just south of the city centre. In Grimsby, there had been a recent flurry of housebuilding, mostly substandard it had to be said. The Freemen were always ready to turn a profit and if that meant cramming in several families to a house, without so much as a staircase or a privy, then they would. In summer the stench permeated the streets around. This was similar but on a scale John could scarce believe.

'How can you live amongst this, Billy?' John suddenly longed for the clean air the Wolds, as he felt the grit and the grime settling on his face. His eyes smarted and taking a clean handkerchief from his pocket, he wiped his face. It came away smeared and grey.

'I live here because I work here. These buildings and the people in them are my work.'

'You speak in riddles, Billy.'

'All, will become clear.'

Billy's lodgings were in a house as grimy as any other in the district. It stood at the end of a terrace of brick buildings.

'These are mostly lodging houses, one family to a room and it doesn't matter how large the family is. I, however, am lucky and you'll see why soon enough.'

John looked up the street; soot blackened bricks, some with cracked glass in the windows, stuffed with paper or rags to keep out the draughts, no trees or greenery anywhere. He could never imagine himself living in such a depressing place. How could his cousin abide it?

Billy let himself in with a key and beckoned John to climb the stairs after him. He had two rooms a tiny bedroom and a sitting room, both as spartan as the room he took Billy to in Grimsby, except for one thing. On every surface, he could see there were pamphlets, books and posters. John picked up a poster to read.

Peace, Law and Order is our motto
Public Meeting
October 20th

'So, you're still involved in Chartism? I thought it had all gone quiet after the riots and imprisonments.'

'The struggle for suffrage will never cease until all men and women get the vote.'

'Women! That will never happen, surely.'

'We'll win the vote for men and then you watch, the women will rise up and demand it too.'

'And how long do you think this all going to take?'

'It may not happen in our lifetime. I hope it does. This struggle will never be over, John. If we don't win next time, it will be up to our sons and their sons.'

'Oh, dear God, I should not have come. After the failure of the last petition, I thought I would go mad. I can't put myself through that again, nor Emily. She wouldn't forgive me.'

Billy looked at him with concern. 'I had no idea, John. I'm sorry. I should have returned for a visit after we lost the vote, but it was a hectic time with Feargus and the others on trial.'

'I blamed myself for raising their hopes, you know.'

'Who?'

'The farm workers in the Wolds. Their poverty and fear of the workhouse shook my soul. Father took me there to see the conditions for myself.'

Billy placed his hands on John's shoulders and looked him in the eye. 'In this work, there's no time for blame or guilt or sentiment of any kind. You must stamp on all those feelings. Only build anger, anger that feeds on anger. It makes you strong.'

John shook his head. 'Then I am not your man. Anger's not in my nature.'

'Not anger against any person in particular. Against the system, that's what it needs to be. And not hot-headed but cold and iron-hard.'

John shook himself free, desperate to change the subject. 'Tell me you're not bringing your wife to live in these rooms.'

Billy laughed. 'Freshen yourself up John, there's water in the jug and a towel. Then come and meet Jeanie.'

Five minutes later saw them walking downstairs. John expected them to leave the house and was surprised when he tapped at the door to the right of the stairs and then walked in. John followed into a room where a coal fire blazed making the room stuffy and hot. A woman stood with her back to the window chopping vegetables.

'Hello Mrs M, this is my cousin, John.' The woman turned, wiped her hands on her apron and came forward to greet John.'

'Ye are mair than welcome, Maister John.' Her dark brown eyes and broad smile put John at his ease, although he was still confused.

'It's a pleasure to meet you, Mrs M?'

'Macdonald. But I'm happy with Mrs M.'

'And you're Billy's landlady. Is that right?'

'And soon to be maither-in-law,' she laughed. 'Did he nae tell ye? Ach he's a one.'

A hooter sounded somewhere outside. Its long, high pitched noise unfamiliar to John and he looked up startled.

'My man and Jeannie'll be back any minute. I'd best get on if supper is to be ready.' She turned back to her vegetables which she quickly despatched to a blackened pan, hanging from a hook above the fire.

'We'll go and meet Jeanie then.' Billy led John to the door and out of the house. As they walked, crowds of women and girls flowed towards them, their heads covered by shawls. Some walked arm in arm, chattering as they passed, boots and clogs hammering on the cobbled street. John had never seen anything like it.

'They work up at Marshall's flax mill,' Billy had to shout to make himself heard. All at once a woman peeled herself away from her friends and came towards Billy, pecking him on the cheek.

Jeanie was not what John expected. He only had his wife and her sisters to compare her with. She might as well have belonged to a different species. When she took his hand after being introduced he felt the ridges in her fingers from physical work. Her hands were as hard as Emily's were soft. Her face was lively under her shawl, stray strands of reddish, blond hair escaping to frame an oval face. She linked her arms to both men in a very forward fashion and marched them back to her house.

John was thankful that Emily had decided not to come with him. He could not imagine what his wife would have made of Jeannie and her family, and she would have thrown her hands up in horror at the thought of staying in this area of Leeds.

Once in the house, Jeannie threw off her shawl, ran to hug her mother and then quite unashamedly threw water over her face, hands and arms, from a bowl on a sideboard, drying herself with a clean rag. The front door opened and closed with a bang and a man entered the room. Suddenly it felt overcrowded. This great hulking man must be Mr Macdonald, thought John. His arms, oily with grease and dirt, rippled with muscles. His hands, flat and broad, with long straight fingers were caked in grease. He made straight for the water and scrubbed at his face and hands before greeting anyone. His wife stood by to inspect his face for any marks he may have missed. Satisfied at last he wiped himself with the rag, while his wife went to the back door and tipped the water outside.

At last, after carving some bread for his wife, he greeted John. 'Come sit opposite me, John. I want to hear all about ye and your family. Billy tells us vera little.' His accent was mild, tempered by his daily work amongst Yorkshire folk. John did as he was told, shy amongst all these strangers.

'What work is it that you do, Mr Macdonald?' he asked, as he sat on the bench. An oilcloth lay on the table, which Jeanie was setting out with knives and forks.

'I'm a mechanic at the mill; I keep all the machinery going, so that Jeannie here can produce her cloth.'

'That must be a very skilled profession Mr...'

'Call me Robbie, John. All my friends call me Robbie. Aye 'tis skilled.' Jeannie set a plate of steaming vegetables with a thick slice of boiled beef in front of him. He took up some bread and dipped it into the broth and sucked at it. 'Mother,' he said, looking at his wife, 'you have outdone yersel. This is guid, isn't it?' He looked at John who now had a similar plate in front of him.

John nodded and smiled. He was warming to this family: straightforward, good folk, with no pretentions or guile. He wished Ada or Mabel could see him. They would have a fit.

But that was nothing. The talk over the supper table ranged freely and comfortably. It was obvious that the whole family were more knowledgeable about politics and the mood of the times than John himself. He was at first dumbfounded to hear Jeannie butting into the conversation with her views, which were as well thought out as any man's.

In bed that night, he realised that Jeanie and her parents impressed him. He could not remember an evening which he had enjoyed so much; no pretence, no simpering inanities and no rebuke for an unapproved word. Meals with his sisters-in-law were mostly silent after grace was spoken, and Emily had brought that tradition into her own house, as much as he tried to engage her in conversation. She tended to give short answers and never asked him anything about his day, let alone 'what did he think of the Factory Act or the new Whig Government and wasn't it marvellous that Feargus had won a Nottingham seat, the first Chartist MP.' His head was reeling from it all and he was thankful to have an early night. He had already been warned that the hooter would go at six a.m. for the start of work. He wondered that Jeannie was so lively after a twelve-hour working day.

'So, what do you think of my betrothed?' Billy asked after they had left the house the next morning.

'She's wonderful, the whole family is.'

Billy smiled. 'Yes, I think so too. With her by my side I think I could conquer the world, let alone any government, Tory or Whig.'

211

'What is it that you do, Billy? You don't work in a factory, so how do you live? Who pays you?'

'I'm paid by the ordinary people. How was Silas King paid?'

'By the Connexion subscriptions.'

'Yes, and that's how I am paid. We learnt our lessons from our Wesleyan and Primitive Brotherhood. How do you think we got our first supporters and how do we hold on to them? Yes, we have our own camp meetings and love feasts. Don't look so horrified, John. At least we elect our leaders.'

But John was not horrified. It made sense, perfect sense. Yes, he was shocked, but shocked by the audacity and the simplicity. He trailed after Billy during the morning as he put up posters for a meeting, gave out pamphlets from a leather satchel and stopped to talk with acquaintances, who all treated John with friendliness and respect, as Billy's cousin. As they walked, Billy pointed out the mill where Jeanie and her father worked. It was enormous, built like a temple, with six sturdy columns soaring skywards. John had never seen anything like it. It dwarfed the largest building in Grimsby, the relatively recent Rope Works.

'There's a room in there that's a full two acres, John, the biggest room in the world. Jeannie says the noise from the machinery is enough to wake the dead.'

'Is it designed to look like a Greek temple?'

'Egyptian, I think. But what would I know? Just think of the power and the money that goes into such a building. There's work in Holbeck for thousands with the foundries and the mills but there's still dreadful poverty and sickness caused by overcrowding. We must have change, cousin.'

John could see that. He could not fail to miss the dirt which clung to every surface and the smoky, greasy air tasted sharp and bitter in his throat. Some of the people in the streets were well shod and dressed while others were in rags and many of the children ran around barefoot. They came upon a family begging in one street. Father, mother, five children all of them looked hollow-eyed and weary. John could not resist giving them some money.

'Bless ye, Sir.' The father said.

'Where are you from, have you shelter?'

'Ireland, Sir. There's no food at all. I am looking for work, so. Do ye know of any?'

John shook his head and gave them man another florin. 'Buy some food for the children.'

Billy took John's arm to move him on. 'This is a rich country, John. Look how they treat our citizens. Everyone should have the right to housing, work, education and enough food in their bellies. We will only get that if each man can vote.' They came to an abrupt halt. 'Now John, you are going to have to give up one of your principles,' he said, as the clock in a church tower pointed to twelve.

'What do you mean?

'I have some colleagues I want you to meet, but it's in here.' Billy pointed to an ale house.

'No, I promised.'

'Promised what?

'Promised the elders I would never set foot in another one.'

'Well, who's going to tell if you don't?'

'You know it doesn't work like that, Billy. I would have to stand up in Chapel and beg forgiveness for breaking my promise. I can't do that to Emily.'

'You don't have to drink the ale.'

'I know that.'

'Look, we meet in a back room. It's not part of the tavern, really. There's even a separate door.'

John dithered, undecided, until a man clapped Billy on the shoulder and shook John by the hand and said, 'Well what are standing out here for?' It was as simple as that, John entered and risked damnation.

When John thought back on that meeting, he wondered at the similarities with his father's description of conference. There was the obvious difference, no hours spent in prayer for sure. But he listened fascinated to the discussions on how things had gone since the last meeting; planning the next big rally; the number of new members; what could go in the newspaper; study groups and classes, the list went on. His wanted to re-read his father's journal to make sense of it all. How could anyone think I was damning myself by being there, he mused. He did not feel guilty. The meeting had stirred something up in him again. It must be wonderful to have such friends all working to a common purpose. With a shock, he realised he envied Billy; envied his work, his commitment, even his wife and her family. Not that he didn't love Emily, he adored her, and always would. But how could one not envy a relationship based on such equality of intellect?

He had been staggered when Billy told him that Jeanie would continue to work at the mill after they were married and that if there were children her mother would look after them while she worked.

'Do you need some money? I can give you some if you're short,' he'd offered.

'No', Billy said. 'She wants to continue working. It's a good job, pays well, Jeanie enjoys the companionship and it's useful for making contacts. She talks to the women in her dinner break about the things we're interested in.'

On the morning of the wedding, Billy and he had gone for a walk so as not to be in the house while Jeanie got herself ready and John asked if he ever heard from his mother.

'I know she lives in Hull. When I went to live there, I saw her from time to time. She has another son; he must be sixteen or so now.'

'Why did she...' John did not know how to ask.

'Dislike me? I don't think she would ever admit that and certainly after her son was born she acted quite friendly. It was my father she was angry with.'

'Why?'

'Because he would never give her another child after the baby died. I heard them arguing, well you couldn't help but hear. 'I'll not watch another of my children die,' he told her. I don't think he ever went near her again.'

'But it wasn't her fault. Father said he died of a fever.'

'No, it was his fault because of his drinking and he punished himself for it. The trouble was he punished her too. Why do you think I do the work I do?' John looked blankly at him. 'It's because of those few weeks I spent in the House of Industry. The very name makes me want to spit. It was nothing more than a place to kill off the poor, both in spirit and reality. That matron was a jealous bitch. Did you hear about the time she tied up a woman and flogged her, then left her all night with barely a stitch, just because her insufferable husband had laid his filthy eyes on her?'

John had not even remembered that Billy and his family had been in the workhouse. He knew Billy's brother had died, but not the circumstances. It all became clear. The work Billy was doing was personal to him and because of that he would never give up. That anger inside him had been growing since he was five years old. No wonder he felt as he did.

How could he describe the wedding to Emily? The wedding itself was simple enough. They had walked to Chapel at about ten o'clock. There were a few people there, but most of Jeanie's friends were working. When Jeannie arrived with her father, she looked radiant in a plain green woollen dress and her hair caught up beneath a pretty lace bonnet, which allowed a few strands to tumble around her face, setting off her grey-green eyes. He saw Billy catch his breath as he caught sight of his bride and John's heart swelled with pride to see the two of them so in love.

The wedding breakfast was held in a nearby hall after the hooter had sounded the end of the working week. Everybody brought food, whatever they could spare; bread and cheese, rhubarb pies, even haggis. It was a gloriously happy affair.

'Ada, Mabel, I wish you could be here,' thought John, as he was caught up by some young woman and twirled around in delight to the music of fiddles and pipes. The party went on for hours until they waved goodbye to the bridal couple, who were going home to Billy's rooms. No wonder he laughed that first evening, thought John. It's hardly a bridal suite. What he did not know was after they had left that morning, Billy's bedroom had been decorated with paper flowers and bunting prepared by Jeanie's friends.

John's train left early the next morning. He spent a peaceful, contented last night on a mattress on the floor, near the glowing embers of the kitchen fire. Before he left, Jeanie's parents thanked him for coming and assured him of a welcome any time. Their hospitality touched him. He told them that the visit was one of the happiest times of his life.

Billy walked him to the station. 'You know where I live. Stay in touch, cousin. We should not be strangers.'

'Thank you so much for asking me to act as your best man. I don't know why you did that. You have so many friends.'

'Uncle William rescued me, saved my father from himself. If ever you need rescuing, John, Jeanie and I will be here for you. You are always welcome. Remember that.'

John did not answer; Billy's words had thrown him. Why on earth would he ever need rescuing? Instead, he shook his cousin's hand heartily, took his bag, which Billy had insisted on carrying and climbed on to the train.

It was only when Emily was unpacking his bag that John saw what Billy had put in it.

'What are these?' she asked; a note of accusation in her voice.

'Pamphlets. I had no idea Billy put them there.'

'I'll throw them out then, shall I?'

'No, leave them. I'll deal with them.' He saw a slight tic appear under her eye. She did not want to hand them over, that much was apparent. He held his hand out, waiting. Eventually she thrust them at him. He smiled and thanked her, at which point she turned on her heel and walked through the door. He sighed and wished he might talk with her as Billy and Jeanie discussed things.

He gave little detail in his description of the wedding, beyond saying that the bride and her family were hard working decent people, the wedding had been well attended and he had enjoyed himself. They were more interested in his description of the train ride, knowing that within a year or two they would have that opportunity themselves. He kept the ale house visit to himself. After all there was no likelihood of a reoccurrence.

Chapter 21

After his visit to Leeds, John settled back into his normal life. On the outside, everything appeared the same. On the inside, his views had undertaken a subtle shift but he had difficulty processing them into anything meaningful. It felt as though he was waiting for something to happen, something that would force him into deciding the future direction of his life.

He was in Aylesby, a village to the west of Laceby. To justify his walks into the Wolds he had to preach from time to time and this was one of those occasions. The autumn rain had churned up the roads but this Sunday the sky was blue and cloudless. He was in full flow when he heard a high- pitched scream coming from a barn beside the patch of ground where the small crowd had gathered to listen.

A child ran from the barn crying to his father, 'It's Mary Jane, she fell on the ploughshare and she's bleeding.' The father and mother ran into the barn, John followed to see if he could help. Immediately he saw it was serious. The ploughshare had punctured the child's back and dark red blood was oozing out.

'She needs a doctor,' said John.

'We have no money for a doctor.' The mother cradled her child, anguish written across her face.

'I'll pay, but we cannot wait for one to come here, we must get her too one soon. Who has a carriage?'

'That will be Miss Black, Sir; her up at the big house.'

'Show me.'

John and the father, whose name was Jim Watson, ran up the long drive to the house and John banged on the door. A manservant opened, looking askance at Jim's hands which were sticky and red with blood.

'We must speak to Miss Black urgently.'

'She may not be at home, Sir.'

John pushed the man aside and made for the nearest door, which he opened but finding no one, raced across the hall to another door which opened from the inside.

'Benson, what is the meaning of all this noise and who are you, Sir, to come barging in to my house?' An imperious, elderly woman stood barring his way.

'There's been a dreadful accident, Ma'am,' said John. 'We need to get a child to a doctor if her life is to be saved.'

'Is that you, Jim Watson? Is it your child?' she looked at his hands.

'Very well, you may take the horse and cart. Tell the coachman.'

As Jim left the house to go the stables, John asked, 'Do you not have a gig, Ma'am? She needs urgent attention and a gig would be much faster, or a brougham maybe.'

'The brougham is new. I don't want blood on the seats, nor do I want my carriage horse breaking a leg in all this mud.'

John looked at her askance. 'It's the life of a child, Ma'am. I think she may die if she does not get attention soon.'

'Mr..' she looked at him enquiringly.

'Holtby, Ma'am, John Holtby.'

'Mr Holtby, I do not know who you are, but I know Jim Watson and his family. Believe me they would not miss one child, they have already more than they can feed and it's far better if they do not have a crippled child to contend with. I wish you good day, Sir.' She closed the door to her drawing room in his face. John stood there, fuming. He had never felt such rage, his fists clenched by his side and his mouth working up some retort that he wanted to yell through the door.

'I think you should leave, Sir.' Benson the manservant, stood by his side. He at least looked ashamed. John turned, knowing there was nothing more to be done.

He accompanied the child and his parents in the cart, the Shire horse walking at his own steady pace. Rags had been stuffed into the wound on her back but John could tell from her greying face that she was sinking. He urged the coachman on.

'It's no good, Sir,' he said. 'He's been trained to walk and with this heavy wagon he could not keep up any speed.'

John sat in frustration, his thoughts seething with hatred. How can God ask me to forgive such a woman? How is it Christian to turn her back on an innocent child?

He knew it was too late before they arrived at the doctor's house. The mother began to wail. Jim Watson thanked him for trying to help. The poor was man stricken with grief. As soon as the doctor confirmed what they all thought, John left them and walked home, having first told Jim that he would pay for the girl's funeral. They wouldn't hear of it, they said. John refused to listen; his conscience would not let him do otherwise.

All the way home he thought about the accusatory words he would like to put on her grave stone. It would not happen, he knew. The vicar would not allow it, and there would be no gravestone. None of the farmhands had money for one. The poor are as hidden in death as they are in life, he sighed.

As soon as opened the door to his house his daughters ran to meet him and he gathered them up in his arms and put his face into their clean hair, smelling their youth, their vitality, and their playfulness. That little girl would never play another game. She had most likely been up in the hayloft, squealing in delight as her brother threw straw over her until she lost her footing and toppled over the edge. Poor boy, he would always blame himself for the death of Mary Jane. But John knew who was really to blame and there was nothing he could do about it.

Emily walked towards him, a questioning look on her face, telling the children to get down, their father was tired. He hugged them tighter, he never wanted to let go. Eventually they squirmed and he had to relinquish them. As they left to read a religious book, the only entertainment Emily allowed them on a Sunday, he sat on the stair, put his head in his hands and sobbed.

'Whatever is it, John?' Emily knelt beside him. He told her what had happened. This time he told her the brutal truth, unable to dress it up in platitudes.

Her hand rose to her mouth. 'Oh, the poor parents, we must pray for them John.'

'What about Miss Black, shall we pray for her too?'

'Of course, we must pray that she sees what she has done and begs forgiveness from God.'

He could not answer her, but he knew he was done praying for God to intercede in someone else's morals. Something more was required. Throughout that journey on the cart, it was as if God was watching with him and railing at the plight of his innocent children. The anger Billy had talked about was in him now. He felt it burn inside his head. The question was whether he should nurture it or try to quench it. If he nurtured it, could he live with the consequences?

The first train out of Grimsby was scheduled for February the twenty ninth. It seemed an auspicious day for the start of a new beginning for the town. Suddenly everywhere was in reach. The children's excitement at the thought of visiting Lincoln infected Emily, who became quite skittish. His daughters had never been further than Bradley Woods and to hear mother and children chatter about this excursion or that, gave John a welcome fillip.

'Can we go and see the train?' asked Edith, she had a slight lisp and her adorable blond curls always melted John's heart.

'Yes, my love. We'll all go, but I'm sure we'll hear it from the house.' The proximity of the station to the house worried Emily.

'Do you think the smoke from the engine will dirty the washing? What if the train comes off the tracks, when the children are passing? Do you think it will be so noisy it will keep Walter awake?'

Everyday a new concern, but at the same time the children's enchantment with the idea of train travel lifted everyone's spirits.

The first train was to depart for New Holland and a day later the service to Louth would begin. By the Autumn Lincoln, then Brigg and eventually Sheffield would be within reach.

John invited his parents and his brother, Tom and his family to watch the departure and then have luncheon with the family. Ada and Mabel declined his invitation, their disapproval of the railway confirmed when it was discovered that the navvies were working on Sundays.

Wrapped up warm against the easterly wind, John stood next to his father on the new railway bridge. Edith's hand squirmed in his as she stood on tiptoe to see over the parapet.

'You're looking pensive, Father. Are you happy this day has come at last? Grimsby is joining the rest of the country.'

'I was wishing that Betsy could be here to see this. She would have been more excited than all of us put together.' He paused. 'As for myself, I'm not sure. Half of me wants to end our isolation but the other half wishes to continue to enjoy our simple life, but this day has been a long time coming.'

As the train began to move away from the station, conversation ceased. John found himself raising his hat in the air and cheering, the children jumped up and down in excitement and Emily, along with his mother, clapped their hands in delight. The train chugged under the bridge and they were enveloped in gritty steam making them cough and splutter. John was pleased they had left Walter with the daily help.

'Well there we are. We've joined the nineteenth century,' his brother, Tom, joked as they walked back to the house.

'Emily may get her trip to London. She longs to see the Queen.'

'Now the railway has arrived, the Queen and Prince Albert may come to Grimsby,' his father said.

What a thought! John was still turning over this possibility as they arrived at his house. There was a letter waiting for him on the bureau which he decided to leave it until after his guests had departed. He recognised the handwriting and hoped it was news that Billy was to become a father, himself.

It was not. Billy, wrote pleading for help with a third attempt at a petition. He had known or suspected this when he had invited John to his wedding, John understood that. As his father told him, before the last Charter petition, Billy was trying to manipulate him. Did it matter, did he care? As always there was only one person he could talk to, his father. John told Emily he had urgent business and walked over to the farm.

'They've tried twice already, why do you think this one will receive any different treatment?' His father looked pained as he finished reading Billy's letter. 'Maybe because of all the trouble in Europe. Perhaps they won't risk anything similar here.'

'So, the French got rid of their King again, that seems like a regular occurrence.'

'It's not just France; the people are demanding their rights all over Europe.

'I don't agree with riots and rebellion; you have to consider what you're stirring up.'

'I don't agree either, but the workers create the wealth of this country and it's only fair that they have a say. Unless we give them the vote and grant salaries to MPs, the working classes will never be able to participate in the way things are run.'

'You sound like you have swallowed their pamphlets.'

'I have been reading everything I can: pamphlets, their newspaper, and I hate how the Tory Press twists and decries them. It's a noble cause but they make it sound so grubby, so laughable.'

'Things take time here; it's not like we're those hot-headed French and Italians.'

'You thought education would make a difference but it's been nearly thirty years since you began Sunday Schools in town. Artisans are more able to read and write now, but how has their life improved? How long is it going to take?'

William sighed. 'Young men are always in such a hurry. I recognise myself in you. Look John, it's not that I don't agree with you, I have a lot of sympathy with what the Chartists are trying to do, but I doubt you will get any more support around here than you did last time. It's your livelihood and family I am worried about. Your work comes from fellow members of the Connexion and Chapel did not like what you were doing last time. Think what you could lose.'

'I know and it has given me many sleepless nights. Didn't you encounter trouble when you were growing our Connexion?'

'Of course, we had things thrown at us, stones, mud and worse. But I never risked my family or my income.'

'But didn't you believe with every muscle, bone and sinew that what you were doing was the right thing?'

His father groaned. 'Yes, I did. Is there nothing I can say that will make you change your mind?'

'The petition is to be presented in early April, so I don't have much time. There are so many more skilled workers here now with the railway and docks being built. The best way is to catch them in the taverns. I will not drink but I may have to buy it.'

'And you want to know if the elders will accept that. I can tell you now that I think they won't. You made a promise to them.'

'Which I broke in Leeds. Father, I have not lost my belief, if anything, I believe God is holding me to account to carry out his work, to take the next step from education which is political reform. Can you try and explain this to the Elders? Last time, I did this work in ignorance but now I know God is guiding my actions.'

'You've already decided, haven't you?'

John realised that he had. He looked at his father seeing love and despair in his face and slowly nodded. 'I'm sorry, Father. I need to follow this path. I can't live with myself otherwise.

'Speak to Emily, Son. Make her understand, please, or I fear for the consequences.' William's shoulders heaved with pain and he clutched John to his chest. 'I will pray for you, Son. Your mother and I will pray that Emily will stand by you.'

'I'll try.'

John knew that this would be harder than anything else.

After the children had all been put to bed that night, Emily picked up her sewing as usual. John looked at his wife in her comfortable seat by the fire. Her sweet face lit by the flames and the oil lamp on the table beside her. Despite her corsets, she had the soft bloom of motherhood written in her body, a body that he loved, even worshipped, although Emily would call that idolatrous. How was he going to make her understand? She, who now that her parents were dead, looked even more to her sisters for moral guidance. Was it too late for her to change? He had been too lax in challenging Ada and Mabel. It was his fault because he had tried to wean her away from them but always gave in to her protestations and entreaties. He loved her too much to see her sad.

'Emily, my love.' She looked up smiling. 'Please put away your work, I have something I need to discuss.' She opened her sewing box and dropped it in, then sat calm and expectant, gazing into his eyes with concern. He moved his chair so that he face her.

'You sound so serious, John.'

'Billy has written to me. There is another petition and he would like me to gather signatures.' He watched her face drain of colour.

'Oh no, please don't get involved. You were so ill after the last one.'

'I am stronger now, more determined.'

'Why you, isn't there someone else? You're a lawyer not an artisan, you already have the vote.' Her voice was becoming shrill.

'I don't know of anyone else who will do it and I truly believe I will be doing God's work.'

She looked puzzled. 'How can it be God's work? What has politics got to do with God?'

'These last months, whenever I pray before bed, I feel him inside my head, telling me to answer when I am called.'

'You do?' Emily's puzzlement creased her brow. 'Isn't it more likely that he wants you to preach?'

'No, I don't feel it when I preach. I feel it when I am helping people gain their rights or often not gaining them. That's the point; he wants me to stand up for his children, our fellow man.'

'So, you are going to go into the villages for your signatures; that didn't work well last time.'

'No, you're right. The men are too scared and too illiterate for that to succeed. I need signatures from the railway and dock workers.'

'But many of them are Irish and Catholic.' A frown swept across her face.

'They are still God's children.' He was determined to be patient. 'It means I will be out most evenings in the next month.'

Her posture stiffened. 'No John, tell me you're not going to break the vow you made.'

'I have to.'

'But you'll be thrown out of Chapel.'

'Emily, God is calling me to do this. Ever since that child died...'

She cut in, 'What has the child got to do with men getting the vote?'

'It shows the contempt the rich have for the poor. If all men get the vote, the rich and powerful will not be able to treat them so badly.'

'Do you think so? You have said it yourself, the banks and rich merchants always find a way to keep the little man down. I distinctly remember you saying that only a month ago.'

'Maybe, but I have to try. If you could have seen some of the sights I saw in Leeds.'

'No, I don't want to hear about them.'

'Children, the age of Dorothea and Edith, children from the workhouse sold to cruel masters to work in the mills.' Emily put her hands over her ears, but John leant over and forced them down by her side in frustration at her refusal to listen.

'I have no choice in this, Emily. In our wedding vows, you promised to love, honour and obey.' He emphasised obey but she shook her head, her hair loosening from its pins.

She stood up and looked at him wildly. 'You can't do this. You can't. What will people say?'

He rose to hold her in his arms but she struggled. 'Emily, it is just for a month. Father is going to try and talk to the Elders to explain. Please give me your support. I love you and don't want to hurt you.'

'Hurt me', she cried. 'You will destroy me, destroy our children and our home.'

'Only if you let it. It's within your power not to let it. If the worst comes to the worst, we can move away. I can set up in business elsewhere.' The look she gave him chilled him.

'I will never leave this town. My sisters and my friends are here. My Chapel is here. How could I start afresh? I couldn't do it.'

She was too timid and she let her timidity rule her. John saw that for the first time. 'You can do it if I support you and I would. You need to trust me.'

She turned away, sobbing. Before he would have tried to comfort her, would have given into her. This time he did not.

'I want you by my side, Emily, but I have to do this. I will get those signatures by any means. Pray for me Emily, by all means, but pray also that you learn to support me in God's work.'

'I don't believe you are doing God's work. Should I put you before God? I don't think He would ask you to risk damnation.'

'I promise I won't drink and I'm convinced God won't punish me. Only you can punish me. Is that what you want to do? And please don't let your sisters poison what I am doing.'

'Poison, is that what you think of them?'

He realised he may have gone too far. She would repeat his accusation to them which would only fuel any argument against him.

'I shouldn't have said that. But sometimes it seems you take their side against me. Emily, we have rarely quarrelled.'

'Then don't do this and we'll quarrel no more.'

He shook his head. 'I have to.'

She turned away, picked up a lit candle and passed him without a glance, but he saw her eyes screwed up against her tears as she left the room. A moment later he heard her soft feet rushing upstairs to their bedroom.

What was he to do? He had loved her since childhood and could not imagine life without her. It was her fragility which had attracted him and made him want to protect her, but he had done too good a job. He remembered the time he had tried to tell her about young girls working in the coal mines with a chain through their legs so that it rubbed away their clothes. She had been most upset that their bodies might be exposed to men's glances. The chaffing sores on their delicate skin or that they were sent down the mine at eight years old seemed to pass her by. A day or so later she had forbidden him from speaking further about such matters. He was sure the words came directly from Ada's mouth; it was unseemly, she said, to talk about young girls in that way. He had swallowed his anger and he blamed himself that she was not strong enough to rebuff her sisters.

His parents were soulmates and he had assumed that he and Emily would be the same. He would always stick by her but would she do the same for him? For her to break her marriage vows was unthinkable, and yet he would not put it past her sisters to twist it so that it seemed he was the one breaking them.

Was he to put Emily and his family before God's work? Increasingly he could not separate his Christianity from Chartism and he felt bound to fight for injustice, if not him, who? He was not prepared to be called and found wanting. John longed for some peace instead of the battle which lay before him but he would not shirk from this fight. In the meantime, he had to sleep and he wondered if Emily would even acknowledge him when he entered the room.

'It's time to find out,' he said, to himself as he banked the fire before retiring.

Chapter 22

Instead of working at legal matters the following day, John poured his soul into the speech he would make in Chapel on Sunday. If he could convince his fellow brethren of the veracity of his case, it could only help his cause. He was far better prepared this time. Six years before he had been a novice orator, now his passion and knowledge of his subject, he reasoned, must sway more men. The congregation numbers had also been swollen by workers pouring into Grimsby, as the new railway progressed. The Freemen held less sway in Chapel as the demographics changed. He hoped the Elders would listen to his father's argument if it became necessary to visit taverns for signatures.

He drew up a plan of action. After morning service, he would attempt an open-air speech on some waste ground near the site for the new docks. He was looking for volunteers to help him, as well signatories. Nothing would give him greater relief than finding other men willing to sign up men in the taverns in his stead. There was barely three weeks in which to gather signatures before he had agreed to meet Billy in Hull with his contribution to the petition.

The only Chartist MP, Feargus o' Conner, was planning a huge rally in London, after which he would present the petition to Parliament. John wished he could go, he tried to imagine the scene, the speeches, the applause, the common purpose. How thrilled he would feel to be a part of it. Increasingly the isolation of his position was affecting his mood, making him by turns despondent and then excitable. He had to warn himself to stay calm. He sighed. He was getting carried away; going to London was not his job. His role was to garner support from anyone he could. He forced his eyes back to the paper and re-read his speech.

At home that evening, he was pleased that Emily made an effort to smile and win him around with his favourite meal of cottage pie, followed by spiced pears. After supper, his daughters ran to him for a bedtime story and he sat them both on his knee and stroked their hair, breathing in the scent of lavender from the soap Emily used. If only it could always be like this, he thought, but soon they'll be young women and too big for my knee. He felt calmer, more certain that Emily would come around. She had as much to lose as him. He caught her hand as she brought him a cup of tea and he kissed it, marvelling at the delicacy of her fingers against his broad, erstwhile farmer's hands. With a sigh, he realised that if they did not discuss what he was about to do, peace would reign. Emily was happiest ignoring what she did not want to know. He wondered at how little they knew of each other before marriage, despite the years of Sundays they had spent together, mostly on their knees in prayer, it had to be said.

After the girls were in bed and Walter sleepy enough to be put down in his crib, he invited Emily to sit beside him on the settle. Normally they sat opposite each other by the fire, but he desperately wanted to put the argument behind them. At first, he felt her body stiff beside him. He put his left arm around her and she sank into it. He felt the tension between them lessen. She turned her face towards his and his heart skipped a beat. Her blue eyes shone with love for him, despite the care and worry in the tiny lines which were beginning to appear around them.

'You know, Emily, that I will always love you and protect you, don't you?' She nodded and opened her mouth to speak. John leant over unable to resist kissing her and stopped the words.

'Tell me we will not argue again,' he begged as he felt her respond.

'I went to see your father today,' she said.

John sat back, surprised. She normally would have gone to her sisters if there was something troubling her.

'He spoke of you with such pride and tenderness that it made me feel disloyal. I did not really give you a chance to explain and I'm sorry.'

Silently he thanked his father, glowing with pleasure that he felt that way about him. 'And I am sorry that I gave you cause to doubt me, Emily. In three weeks, this will all be over. Pray I gain enough names to help the petition, but after that we can get back to normality, I promise.'

'Do you think so, John?' She cast trusting eyes upon him and again he found himself unable to stop his kisses until the quarrel was cast behind and passion overtook them both.

But it was not as easy as he hoped and had promised his wife. The Elders agreed to him entering each tavern once, for the sole purpose of gaining signatures and leaving as soon as he had them. How his father had persuaded them, he did not know and he did not ask. John was pleased with his plea for support in Chapel and some of the railway workers complimented him on his eloquence and reasoned argument as they signed his sheet. Emily kissed him on the cheek afterwards and told him she was proud of him.

That gesture alone gave him the confidence to stand out in the Central Market by the tapering, stone pyramid fountain. Like Silas King before him, he stood, willing men to come and listen. Within spitting distance of Chapel, there were ten taverns and he reasoned that many of them would be filling up after Sunday dinner. He wished he'd had the forethought to print off some notices advertising his meeting. That is what Billy would have done. But Grimsby was never radical, unlike Hull, across the river.

The fisherman and labourers making for the pubs had their minds on drink and not listening to one of them Ranters; despite the fact John was talking about freedom, not God. By his sober dress, they knew him for what he was. He should have thought to don different garb, but these clothes were his normal attire. Only a handful stopped to listen, and although no one threw mud and stones at him, John felt as his father must have done as he began his mission. All that effort put into his speech with no thought to advertising it or the clothes he should wear. His inexperience had let him and the petition down.

Two men remained by his side as he finished his speech and stood down from his perch. He shook them by the hand, their rough hands grasping the smooth, softness of his.

'I signed last time and the time before that,' the clean shaven one said, his accent strange to John's ears.

'Where are you from?'

'Manchester, my father was at Peterloo. I'll help you get some signatures.' John gripped his hand tighter. He wanted to hug the man. 'Look we're just going into the Hope and Anchor. Join us and we can talk.'

It was as though someone had poured a bucket of cold water over John. He stood there, unable to answer, his heart wanting to agree but his head knew it was an irrevocable step. What am I doing, he thought? This task is impossible. 'I can't,' he said. 'I attend Chapel.' It sounded so lame as an excuse and he half expected the men to laugh at him.

'I'll get a jug of ale and we can go back to our lodgings. My name's Ted and this is my brother, Sam.'

'John, I'm John,' the gratitude in his voice threatened to overwhelm him. Ted turned towards the pub and Sam smiled at John. He realised it was an innocent, vacant sort of smile. He was the larger of the two brothers but probably younger. His blue eyes above his straggly whiskers contained the same innocence. 'Do you work on the railway?' he asked.

Sam grinned and nodded.

'Have you always worked on railways?' Sam grinned again but his eyes showed puzzlement. Now John understood why Ted had said 'I will help get signatures', Sam was a simpleton and most likely could not sign his name. All that speech for one name. John's mood deepened.

Ted returned with his jug of ale and seeing John's frown mistook the meaning. 'Sam's a bit daft, but he'll not do you harm. He can dig a ditch as well as anyone, but he's a gentle soul.'

'I did not think otherwise.'

'I keep him with me and we work as a team. If he didn't have me, it would be the workhouse or a lunatic asylum and I'll never allow that. I promised my mam before she died. Our lodgings are in Burgess Street, not far.'

John found himself walking past Chapel with the two scruffy workmen, thankful, that there was no one there to see him and then was ashamed of his thoughts. 'I'm not cut out to be a radical either', he thought. 'I falter at the first hurdle.'

Ted, with Sam close behind, turned to enter a mean looking house. John was reminded of Billy's lodgings in Grimsby. The brothers had one room between them and shared a bed.

'I'm saving for the day when I can settle down and find a wife. I don't like to waste money on lodgings,' he said by way of excuse, as he watched John's reaction to the bare space.

'No, I'm just reminded of my cousin, Billy. He's a Chartist and lives like this. At least it's dry and warm,' he said looking towards the fireplace.

'Ah, it's your cousin who's put you up to this, is it? I hate to say it but you don't look the type to be a campaigner. You're a preacher, aren't you?'

'No, not that even. I'm a lawyer but I hate to see injustice.'

'Sit down,' Ted pointed towards one of the only two hard, spindle-backed chairs. He poured the ale into two cracked mugs and gave one to Sam. 'I'm guessing you don't want any?' he said to John.

'No thank you.'

'Well, I don't recommend the water and I have no tea.' John smiled and shrugged. 'I know a few people who will help get signatures but the thing is, speechifying isn't going to work. These men, they work long hours and when they finish, they're in the ale house drinking, or asleep.'

'I realise that now.'

'It's not a question of just going around the tavern and asking them to sign, either.' He cocked his head to the side and gave John a look to see if he understood. 'My father was a weaver and he was always trying to drum up support for change. The one thing I learnt was that it's a slow process. Men need to trust you for a start.'

'How do you gain that trust?'

'Not by looking like a preacher or a lawyer.' He grimaced at John's clothing. 'Get yourself some second-hand workmen's clothes. Then you need to talk and listen, join in conversations, and get them to listen to you, but gentle, mind. A game of cards and a few rounds of ale, and you'll be part-way there. A sing-song's a good way to break the ice as well.'

John sighed long and hard. 'There's only three weeks to get these signatures and I promised the elders I would not stay in the taverns for longer than it took to ask men to sign.'

232

'Then I doubt you'll get anywhere. It's your choice. Are you serious about this, or is it just a game to you?'

'No, it's not a game. I feel strongly about it.' John told Ted about his visits to the villages and the death of the child.

Ted listened intently. 'It does something to you, doesn't it, watching someone die, knowing it could have been prevented? My father often talked about Peterloo, how the crowd was peaceful, just wanting a chance to listen to Orator Hunt. My father wasn't injured that day but the sight of the hussars laying into the innocent crowd affected him for the rest of his life. You know they went for the women and children first. How could men do that?' Ted sighed. 'If my mother had not been nursing me, she might have been there too, you see. Dad often had nightmares about flashing sabres cutting through a woman holding a babe.'

John knew little about Peterloo, but this account differed from the one he knew where the Riot Act had been read, the thousands of people refused to disperse, and the yeomanry had been congratulated for their actions.

'I'd like to talk to you more about that but I need to get home. My wife will be worrying about me.' He took out his pocket watch to check the time and found it almost two o' clock, confirming his suspicions.

'Does that mean you don't want to go further with the petition?' Ted looked affronted and John backtracked on his error.

'No, not at all. I do, I will, if it's possible. It's just that I told her I will be back for dinner by two.'

Mollified, Ted said. 'Here's what I'll do. Do you know The Rose and Crown?' John nodded. 'Well, the landlady has a back room. I will get some of my workmates there by eight tomorrow evening and see if we can't come up with a plan of action. Only wear something different, will you? They'll think you're one of the bosses, dressed like that. I can't promise anything. It will be down to you to make them trust you.' He stood up. 'Say goodbye to John, will you Sam.'

John stood and gripped Ted by the hand, 'Thank you, Ted. Will you come for supper one evening?'

Ted shook his head. 'Your wife won't want Sam and where I go, he goes, thank you all the same.' Sam stood up from the bed where he'd been sitting and pumped John's hand. He felt the strength in it, despite his gentle, moon-shaped face. Ted walked John to the front door.

'I am so glad I met you, Ted. Thank you for what you're doing.'

'The cause is right, that's enough for me. Until tomorrow, John.' He turned and walked back to his room.

As John walked home along Watery Lane, he mused about Peterloo. It had briefly been discussed at school, where the teacher was also the vicar at Humberstone. A vicar, who, no doubt, depended on his living at the disposal of a wealthy landowner. He knew from his training as a lawyer about the importance of evidence but also how it could be twisted if the need arose. He only dealt with civil matters but he tried to imagine being a barrister in a case such as Peterloo. On the crown side, you would look for the guilt and depend upon the evidence of the magistrates. Those magistrates who had called for the charge against the citizenry and wanted to protect themselves from criticism. On the defendant's side, you would search for innocence amongst the testimony of the crowd and if you were lucky, people of standing. If there were no such people, the odds were stacked against the crowd.

Why would it not be the same in newspapers or in books? Was it not a matter of who owned the newspaper or wrote the piece? And if true about writing, what about thinking? If all your life you had been taught to think in a particular way, was there not also an alternative way, equally valid? A line from Hamlet bubbled up into his mind. 'To thine own self be true'.

Although almost home he stopped at the Abbey ruins and sat on one of the stones, surrounded by silence rather than the resonance of history. The chill of the stone matched the cloudiness of the day, but he scarcely noticed. For hundreds of years, Catholic monks had chanted their prayers here and then Henry VIII changed all that. Was Catholicism any less valid than the protestant religion? Or how about Methodism from the Church of England, surely it was all a matter of interpretation and, he hated to think it, tribalism. His tribe, the Primitive Methodists were better than the Wesleyans because... He knew what his father would say, 'it's because we

234

go looking for people to save and once they're saved they can make something of their lives, rather than spending their wages on sin'. He could understand that, but was it not the greater sin that hard-working men did not earn enough money to feed their families and had no lawful means to change that? John's faith in God was undiminished, stronger even, but the package it was wrapped in, was beginning to matter less and less.

The sun peaked through a cloud and shone on a patch of daffodils in front of him. One was beginning to flower, its yellow trumpet barely visible. I am that flower, he thought, I am a chrysalis opening-up to become a butterfly. Was his hunger making him lightheaded? He looked again at his pocket watch: two thirty. He rose, dusting his coat from the tell-tale sign of stone dust, knowing his life was about to change and the thought both terrified and exhilarated him.

Chapter 23

John presented himself at the Rose and Crown wearing his old farm apparel. Changing into them after work, he felt as though he were shedding a layer of respectability. The trousers were a little tight but not too much despite the sedentary nature of his work. He had bought a second-hand jerkin and a pull-down cap to complete his disguise. He needed no mirror to feel like a different person, a conspirator, his father's worst nightmare. He tried to shrug off this sense of shame as he pulled on his boots, the ones he used for tramping the Wolds. They at least felt familiar.

The most difficult thing had been to lie to Emily. She normally saw him off to work, handing him his coat and hat, before kissing him on the cheek and bidding his daughters to kiss him too. The guilt of packing a portmanteau with his old clothes and boots and telling her he had to visit someone in Market Rasen that day and maybe stay the night, played on his mind.

He felt most guilty for trying to disguise what he was doing from Emily. To spend the whole of an evening in an ale house, maybe even drinking was going much further than he had agreed with Chapel and her. Was it to save her sensibilities or to save his own position that he had begun to lie? Had he more courage, he would announce what he was going to do and be done with it, realising that this dissembling smacked of a lack of commitment. How could he make promises to loved ones that he was prepared to break? He should have been troubled by it but found he was not. Supporting the Charter outweighed everything else.

In an odd hour during the day, he wrote down the names of all the taverns and beer houses in Grimsby that he knew of, and placed them on a street map he had sketched. Luckily the town had scarcely crept out of its boundaries since he'd been born, it was just more overcrowded. He counted thirty establishments, wondering how many men Ted could get to help cover all of them.

Ted was standing, waiting to greet him and he was gratified that he almost did a double-take when John walked through the door.

'This is John, everyone,' he announced. 'We'll just use our Christian names here, it's safest that way.'

John realised Ted was protecting them from him and him from them. Who knew what spies lingered or where? The fug of pipe smoke in the small room reacted on his already nauseous stomach. He knew it was anxiety more than anything he ate, but he was determined to see this thing through. The men sat at tables, their faces shadowed in the weak glow of candlelight, giving them a sinister hue. John gulped in nervousness while they stared expectantly at him. He did a quick count and was pleased to there were nine, not including Sam. He was relieved. It was enough. If each man covered one tavern each week, they should get through them.

'Thanks for coming, everyone. How many of you have signed the Charter before?' All but two put their hands up and they the two youngest. 'So, if you two pair off with someone who has signed before for the first night, then work on your own after that, is that acceptable?' They nodded. 'We want to persuade men to sign by the force of our argument, not by threat or inducement.'

'So, we can't buy them a mug of ale? That's daft.' One of them said.

'Yes of course you can, I meant promises we can't keep.'

'Like getting the vote this side of the end of the century,' the same man sneered, resentment contorting his face.

'If we don't try, we're not going to succeed.' The man seemed like a troublemaker but the others told him to hold his fire. 'I have a crown for each of you to be spent on ale.' The men began to smile and relax. 'Meet Ted back here on Wednesday two weeks hence. I will hand out pages for signatures and please pick three tavern names out of this hat. I have a map of where they are, if you're not sure.

After each had dipped in to select their taverns, John was left with three. He wasn't so bothered by two of them but the third jumped out at

237

him; the Wheatsheaf in Bargate. It was the furthest away from the town, so it would be unfair to ask any of the men to change places with him. But the irony! If there was one tavern he would not have chosen it was this one. He could always leave it out of course. But would that be the right thing to do? Was he serious about this or not? Maybe it was a test of his courage. Yes, that was it, a test he must overcome.

While he was distracted, Ted ordered a round of ale for everyone, which John paid for. He sat down with the men and forced his mind to focus on the Charter. For two hours, he talked with them, wanting to make sure they knew and understood the Charter demands but also asking about their work and why they had volunteered. Most had a story to tell and he quickly got caught up in their conversation. He sipped at the ale, knowing they wouldn't trust him if he didn't drink. It was much stronger than he was used to. The weak ale his mother brewed for the summer months, before he signed the pledge was light, this was dark, bitter and full of flavour. He tried hard not to like it but gave up, although he did not accept another mug when Ted bought the next round with money John slipped him.

By ten o'clock, John was flagging. He made his excuses and walked back to his workplace, his mind buzzing with the conversation he'd left. His clothes reeked of smoke and ale. He was so unused to the smell that he knew Emily would detect it. Once in his office he took them off and slipped them back into the bag, knowing he would have to lose them; there was no way he would take them home. It was going to be an uncomfortable night as he bedded down on the floor. Why on earth had he told his wife he was going to Market Rasen? He longed to walk home and curl up in bed with her. Instead he would arrive home around mid-morning, tired, aching and dirty. At least he had made no appointments for the following day.

It was raining hard the next morning, as it had done for much of the previous month. John was delighted. It meant that he arrived home so wet and dishevelled that Emily was full of sympathy, sending him straight upstairs, while she prepared him a hip bath. His guilt in deceiving her was no less, however. This was going to be the only lie he told her, he decided.

From now he would be truthful, although he knew that Emily would not ask much about his work or the petition.

And so it was. He told her that he would be out in the evenings gathering signatures. He did not tell her which public houses he was visiting and she appeared to accept it with a frown but also resignation. He returned to his office, changed, and set out for the first of his three taverns, The Jolly Sailor in Cleethorpe Road. It was a fair distance to walk, being near the Ropery, but he did not mind. Rather that, than The Wheatsheaf, any day. His last tavern still played on his mind.

Pushing open the door, he was met by noise, a fug of smoke and the hoppy smell of beer. The place was crowded with bodies but he quickly detected there were two factions. The Irish dockworkers kept to one side of the public house and the Lincolnshire ropery workers the other, an invisible line between them. He ordered a mug of ale from the barmaid and turned to survey the room. How was he going to break into a conversation or even hear when anyone spoke to him?

A newcomer tapped him on the shoulder, 'You're new to these parts?' he asked.

John shook his head. 'No, just thought I would try this tavern for a change,' in as good a Lincolnshire accent as he could manage.

'I haven't seen you at the Ropery.'

'I work in an office, clerking,' The man nodded, seeming to lose interest until John offered to buy him a drink. At which point he perked up and invited John to sit with him and his friends at a table. That first evening he did not try to talk politics but listened more than he spoke. Someone brought out a pack of cards and he was relieved that Whist was proposed, rather than Put or any disreputable game. He had never played for money, of course, but was happy to see nothing more than a few pence was required. Somehow that did not seem so wicked. He found himself relaxing and beginning to enjoy himself, aware that his father would have called it a slippery slope to the devil. But this was all in a good cause and he was sure in his faith, he reasoned.

Later that night as he was readying himself for bed, Emily asked him how many signatures he had achieved that night. 'None,' he had to answer.

239

Her face spoke a picture. 'I'll try again tomorrow night,' he said. Her mouth turned down, but she said nothing.

It was not until the third night that he felt comfortable enough in their company to begin to talk about politics. So far, no mention had been made of the government or the state of the land. It was up to him, no point in ducking it any longer. He waited for a lull in the conversation.

'I'm helping a friend get signatures for the Charter, would any of you fine gentlemen be prepared to sign? I know how hard all of you work, should you not be able to vote too?' He held his breath and let it out slowly as the oldest man at the table began to nod. John had noticed how the others looked up to him.

'They're trying again, are they? I've signed before when I was working in Hull. You'd better explain it to these lads.'

John needed no more encouragement, his passion took over. As the men fell silent to listen, the noise elsewhere began to die down until it was just John speaking. He stood and turned to face the bar. 'A pint for every man who signs tonight,' he heard himself saying.'

'Fifty-three signatures,' he told Emily, his face glowing with pleasure. 'Even the Irish signed. That's my last evening out this week.' He wondered how the others were doing.

'Well done,' she said, sniffing the air. 'I can smell the smoke of the alehouse on you.'

He prayed she did not detect the ale he had drunk, although he had washed his mouth out with peppermint cordial before leaving his office. He was only allowing himself one pint a night. He wondered if they would have signed without the promise of a drink and felt a bit ashamed that he had stooped to the level of the Freemen at election time, then shrugged it off.

The Yarborough Tavern, his second inn, was mostly inhabited by the Irish clientele, along with quite a few whores. Knowing that he was never going to establish a relationship with any of the Irish he decided to just ask them straight out. The few of them who could write gladly signed, long memories of mistreatment by the British Government gave them loyalty neither to the Whigs nor the Tories. On the Tuesday of that week, he went in search of Ted, having noted his taverns. He found Sam and Ted in the Mariners on Loft Street.

'I've ninety signatures so far. They're mostly railway men in here, from Lancashire and Nottinghamshire, so not much need to convince them.'

'Maybe it's possible to reach eight hundred signatures, that's better than last time.' He would not be too ashamed to hand those over to Billy. 'Thanks so much for helping me, Ted.'

'From what I'm hearing from the others, it may be nearer a thousand.' They shook hands on it. 'I would offer you a wager, but you wouldn't accept it, would you?' John shook his head with a smile.

'I'll do what I have to, but a wager is a step too far.' It wasn't that much different from playing cards for money in most of his brethren's eyes, but to him there was a subtle difference.

He could avoid the Wheatsheaf no longer. Leaving his old clothes behind for the last time, he walked home, dreading what was to come. Emily was pleased to see him so early.

'It went well, tonight', he said. 'I think we might get over eight hundred signatures. I have some people helping me, so there's only one more public house to visit.'

She looked gratified. Almost idly, she asked, 'Which one is that, dear?'

'The Wheatsheaf,' there, he'd said it, watching her face as the colour drained from it.

'Not Uncle's!'

'Yes, I'm afraid so.' Emily's uncle had been landlord of the Wheatsheaf for twenty years or so, before handing it on to his son-in-law. That side of the family could not abide the Methodist side. As soon as he walked in the door, the news would be sent scurrying to the rest of the family. They would be crowing with delight at Emily and her sisters' discomfiture.

'You can't, you just can't,' she pleaded.

'I have to. It's only around the corner. It makes sense for me to do it.'

'No, you don't have to. Do one of the Cleethorpes ones instead.'

He thought about it, yes, he could do the Dolphin, but he was likely to get several signatures from the Wheatsheaf. It had a more affluent clientele who would be put out at missing out on the vote in thirty-two. 'I'll do both, the Dolphin tomorrow and then the Wheatsheaf. I have a week before I go to Hull.'

Emily burst into tears. 'You 'll shame me, John. I will not be able to lift my head in this town.'

'You're being melodramatic, Emily.' He spoke softly, but his eyes narrowed. 'I will be Master in this house.' He was determined not to be swayed by her tears. 'I gave my word to the men who are helping me.'

'What about your promises to me and to God,' she cried.

'What has God got to do with your family feud?'

'Everything, John. Uncle Plumtree and his family are not saved and you should set an example to them, but it seems you're determined to shame us all.'

Her sadness almost got to him. It would be so easy not to go to the Wheatsheaf. It was the obvious thing to do and he doubted any of Ted's recruits would even notice if he went to other inns outside Grimsby. It was just that he was no longer prepared to compromise his own beliefs. He had to fight for justice and universal suffrage was the obvious step.

Her body was stiff against his that night and he did not try to soften her. He was angry and unable to sleep. She was too at first, but eventually he heard her soft snuffles as she fell into sleep. Was he being unreasonable? He tried to look at it from her point of view but he kept coming back to the dead child, Mary Jane. She appeared sometimes in his dreams; often in different guises, but he knew it was her. Sometimes she was an Irish beggar, sitting on a street in Leeds, once one of the Mr Rack's pitiful chimney sweep boys. She was dressed as a ragged, undernourished boy, with face all blackened, but he knew it was her. Sometimes he looked at his elder daughter and saw Mary Jane's face, accusing him. 'Do something,' it seemed to be saying, 'Do more, you won't save me unless you do more.'

Lack of sleep made him crabby the next day and he stayed at home that night. He spent Friday night and most of Saturday assuaging his guilt in Cleethorpes and Waltham's Inns. On Sunday, he attended Chapel three

242

times, storing up the strength that he needed for the final week. Emily was polite, nothing more, and he to her.

On Monday after supper he left the house in Brighowgate. Emily knew where he was going, she stood stone-faced at the door as he shut the gate behind him. He declined to acknowledge her with so much as a wave goodbye. Turning left into Bargate, he strode the short distance to the Wheatsheaf, past his sister-in-law's cottage, wondering if they were watching but not daring to cast a glance at the window. Once inside the Wheatsheaf he saw old Jim Plumtree sitting on a stool and made straight for him.

'Good grief, I never thought to see you in here,' the old man said.

'I'm here to collect signatures for the Charter, nothing else.'

'No, I don't suppose you are, unless it's to try and convert us from our wicked ways,' he snorted.

'Well not this time, next week perhaps.' John smiled as the old man chuckled. He wasn't so bad as he'd been made out.

'And what does my dear niece, Emily think of this?'

'She's unhappy. Thinks you'll spread gossip all over Grimsby about how I've gone to the devil.'

Jim shrugged. 'I never did understand her and her sisters. Ada and Mabel are mean-mouthed women. I won't say the same about Emily; she's the best of the bunch. Do what you need to. I won't stand in your way, just don't upset the customers. Do you want me to sign? I have the vote but I don't mind annoying the Freemen.'

'Thank you, Jim. I appreciate it.'

'You're good on the piano, aren't you? Why not sit yourself down and play some tunes to stir us up. Leave me your paper and I will get a few to sign. I know my regulars and some are more likely than others.'

John could not believe his luck. There was no way Emily could object to that. For three nights in a row he sat playing whatever the customers asked ranging from Abide with Me to Emily's favourite, I dreamt That I Dwelt in Marble Halls. Some men gathered round the piano singing the words. Every time he played the chorus, he felt a sense of dread and was relieved that by the third night, he had all the signatures he was likely to get. It's done, he thought. That's the end of it. I can get back to normality. But the words of the song lodged in his brain and however he tried to shake them out they would not disperse.

I had riches too great to count, could boast
Of a high ancestral name;
But I also dreamt, which pleased me most,
That you lov'd me still the same...

Emily was asleep when he arrived home. He studied her sleep tousled hair, her milky skin. 'It's over, Emily,' he breathed in her ear but she did not stir. He smoothed the loose tendrils away from her eyes, tenderness flooded his brain. 'It's over,' he whispered.

He left the house before his family had woken. Ted was bringing the remainder of the signed sheets to his office before starting work himself.

'I've counted them, there's seven hundred and thirty-five,' Ted smiled as he handed John the sheets.

'I have nigh on two hundred, so short of the thousand, but good enough. I am so grateful to you Ted.' John grasped his hand.

'Let's hope they take notice down in London. John, don't get your hopes up.'

'We've tried, that's the main thing. I have learnt my lesson about being too optimistic after the last petition. Good luck, Ted.' John passed him a few crowns for the men who'd helped and they shook hands. All that remained was to get the signatures to Hull.

He reckoned without Ada and Mabel. They called on Emily that same morning.

'Three nights, he's been there, Emily. He made a vow to stay only long enough to get signatures. It doesn't take three nights. We've never approved of this whole Charter business. It smacks of sedition to my mind,' said Ada.

'You have to put a stop to it, Emily,' said Mabel.

'He's playing the piano, that's all. Uncle Plumtree is gathering the signatures.' Emily did her best to defend her husband.

'What kind of piano music, that's what I'd like to know? It's not going to be hymns, is it?'

Emily's face dropped at Mabel's accusation. She was trying to hold things together but all she wanted to do was hide from their anger and sneers.

'If you don't get him to stop, Emily, we will have no choice,' Ada threatened.

'No choice but what?' Emily did not think she wanted to hear the answer.

'He's broken his vow; he has to be denounced. We can't stand aside and watch you demeaned.'

'No Mabel, you wouldn't.' Emily shrank into herself. She saw her life disappearing into a void from which she would never escape. 'I love him; you can't destroy him.'

'We will. You should not have to live with a man who breaks his vows. If he goes back to that tavern once more, we will denounce him on Sunday, both of us.' Mabel stared at Ada, who nodded. 'You can come and live with us. The cottage is barely big enough for you and the children, but we'll manage.'

No, Mabel, please. I'll stop him, I will.' Emily collapsed in a heap on the floor.

Satisfied, they fussed around her, ordering the maid to make sweet tea and brought out their smelling salts.

John arrived home from work to a house that was in chaos. The maid met him at the door.

'Thank goodness you're back Mr H, the mistress has been beside herself since this morning.'

He ran into the parlour to find his daughters attempting to comfort their mother. He kissed them both and then sent them upstairs to their bedroom. The maid went back to feeding Walter his bottle in the kitchen.

'What's going on, Emily?' Her bedraggled hair hung down around her face, which was grimy and tearstained. The sight of her clothes in disarray shocked him. It looked as though she had been trying to unpick the stitching in her skirt, the hem ripped and twisted. His wife's face stared at him with incomprehension. He left to find the maid.

'You should have sent for me earlier. We need the doctor. Can you send someone for him, please? Tell him to carry onto to my parents. My mother must come to take charge of the children. Let me take the boy.' John took Walter, who had finished his bottle and was falling asleep. He put him over his shoulder and patted his back, copying what his wife normally did. 'Do you know why she's become ill?' he asked, as an afterthought.

'It was her sisters, Mr H. They came here demanding this and that until the Mistress fell on the floor senseless. I think it was something to do with you, Sir. I wanted to send for you but those sisters wouldn't let me.' She looked shamefaced.

John's brow darkened. 'They are never to be admitted again until I say so, do you hear?' He found himself shouting at the maid, but it wasn't her fault. 'I'm sorry,' he said. She bobbed and sped out of the back door to find a messenger to send for the doctor.

He went back into the parlour and sat next to his wife, talking softly to her. At last she looked up into his face. 'John, you won't go out tonight, dearest. Say you'll stay with me.'

'Of course, my darling. Can you tell me what's happened?'

'They'll denounce you if you go out.' Her eyes stared at him, wild with terror.'

His heart hammered in his chest with fury. 'Mabel and Ada told you this?' He spoke with all the patience and calmness he could muster.

'They say I should not live with you any more, that I must leave you.' Her eyes swam with tears. There was a sharp smell of fear and something else in her breath.

'Have you taken something, my dear? You don't seem yourself.' He noted the pink spots in her cheeks.

She looked guilty and he began to recognise the smell of brandy. The only brandy they kept in the house was for the Christmas pudding and medicinal purposes. He stood and walked to the cupboard in the alcove by the fire. Still holding Walter, he knelt and opened the cupboard. The sole bottle was half rather than two thirds full. Turning around he saw a glass on the table beside her.

He heard the maid return and went back into the kitchen. 'Please make the Mistress a strong cup of tea. I don't want my wife left alone. Can you stay until my mother gets here? I'm sorry to have to ask you.'

'That's no problem, Sir. My husband will understand. Are you going out?'

'I may have to, just for a while. I'll put Walter in his crib first.'

'Bless him, Sir. He's such a darling.'

The doctor took one look at Emily and prescribed laudanum. Taking a phial from his bag, he instructed the maid to add six drops to some cordial, while he and Mr Holtby got his wife upstairs to bed.

John was distressed that the doctor should see his wife like this.

'I believe she has taken brandy after a shock. I have never known her take a sip of anything alcoholic before, not even for a bad chest.'

'Don't worry yourself, John. All women are susceptible to hysteria at times, even the strongest ones. I remember your Aunt Betsy when her friend Alice died.'

If John had been less distracted, he would have asked more. That was the trouble with a family doctor, they knew all the secrets. 'I wish I had known Aunt Betsy. My father admired her so much.'

'I was new to Grimsby when I met her. Good Heavens, it must be nigh on forty years. Time I retired. I'll come and visit Emily tomorrow. What she needs now is a good sleep. If she is still upset in the morning, give her some more drops.'

Mrs Humble brought in the cordial and the doctor instructed Emily to sip it, before bidding John goodnight.

'I'll sit with her a few minutes, while you see the doctor out, Mrs Humble. Have you sent for my mother?' The maid nodded and then escorted the doctor downstairs.

'Sleep Emily,' John held her hand, so tiny in his own broad hand. 'I don't want you to worry about anything. All will be well.' He stroked her hair away from her face. She looked so helpless, his heart turned over at the sight of her. How dare her sisters do this to Emily. They had no business interfering. As soon as she was settled he would beard them in their den. This time he would forbid them to enter his household. He would do anything to protect Emily, even if it meant leaving town.

Mrs Humble came back into the room. Emily's eyes were closed, she seemed to be falling asleep. He placed her hand back on the quilt. She did not stir.

'I will be back in twenty minutes or so,' he whispered. 'Stay with her, please.' Mrs Humble nodded and took his place at her bedside.

He ran down the stairs after looking in on the girls, who were reading quietly. 'Mama's sleeping. She had a nasty upset this morning but will be better soon. Stay here girls and I'll be back to read you a story soon.'

The light had gone from the sky and it was chilly. He put on his coat and hat, opened the door and stepped outside. The wind caught the door, closing it with a bang behind him. Striding quickly to the end of Brighowgate Road, he turned left into Bargate, past Watery Lane. Emily's sisters' cottage was beyond the old hospital, and a come down since their parents died, leaving them little choice but to move to a smaller residence. Outwardly, they bore their straightened circumstances with stoicism. Inwardly, he knew they seethed with bitterness.

He crossed the muddy track which served as a road, his mood darkening by the second. He glanced back and realised it was possible to see the Wheatsheaf on the corner of the next road. They had stood and watched him, he realised. He felt sick with anger to think of them spying on him. Were they there now, waiting to see if he was going to disobey their orders? How dare they interfere. What mischief was in their hearts? Two malevolent spinsters without thought for the heartache they were causing their sister. He wanted to grab them by the scruff of their scrawny necks to show them the damage they had done.

He walked to their door and knocked loudly. A curtain twitched to his left. They were there right enough, watching. It took a minute for the daily help to arrive from the kitchen. She opened the door and peered out. Uninvited visitors rarely arrived at this door and never at night.

'Mr Holtby?'

'The same, Letty. I'll see myself in. If I were you I would go and make them a strong cup of tea. They'll need it and their smelling salts by the time I've finished with them.' He pushed by her making for the tiny parlour on the left, thrust open the door and strode in.

'How dare you barge in here!' Ada began.

'No, how dare you two besoms, attempt to come between a man and his wife. You have no idea of the damage you've done. I came home to find Emily...'

'It's you who are doing the damage,' Mabel interrupted.

'I came home to find Emily drunk on brandy after you bullied her.' He knew that would shock them. As they stood open-mouthed at his accusation, he laid into them for all the hurts they had done to his wife and finished by telling them that the law was on his side. They were forbidden to have contact with her again and they could denounce him to the congregation with pleasure, for all he cared.

'But I doubt you will, now,' he said, finally. Turning on his heel he strode back to the front door, opened it wide, intending to slam it shut.

The sound of a woman screaming and crying on the opposite side of the road meant that he left the door wide open as he ran towards her. Emily stood outside the Wheatsheaf, crying his name. She stood without so much as a shawl against the bitter wind, her hair loose and wild, her cries plaintive and desperate. The door to the Wheatsheaf opened and he saw her Uncle Jim leading out his daughter, Dorothea. What was going on? He stripped off his coat as he ran the last few yards and threw it around Emily's shoulders as he grasped her to him.

'She sent Dorothea in to look for you and to plead with you to come home, John. Get her home as soon as you can. Look your father's here with the cart, let's get her up, she seems feverish.'

John shot his father a grateful look. How typical of the man to come looking for him. He could not bear the thought of how he had let him down.

With Jim's help, John lifted Emily into the wagon and sat cradling her head on his knee. Dorothea climbed in too, her face white with shock and blame.

'Papa, she made me do it, I didn't want to go in there. Will God forgive me do you think?'

'Of course, Poppet. It's all Papa's fault, don't blame Mama. We just need to get her better.' As his father turned the cart around, he saw Mabel and Ada standing in the road, watching. He was thankful there were so few houses in the road. He could not have borne for his wife's shame to be witnessed by more people.

Guilt that he'd allowed this to happen tore at his heart. His anger with her sisters had overcome his promise to stay with her and now her reputation could so easily be ruined. This display of madness, however temporary, could destroy Emily and he was to blame. They had to get away, leave the town, start somewhere new. Was it his own madness that had brought them to this point? Had he been deceived into thinking he could help change things? Was it God or the devil who had been guiding his actions? His brain hurt with the thoughts tumbling around in it. He attempted to take Dorothea's hand in his, but he felt it stiff and unresponsive in his. He looked down at her only then aware that tears were streaming down her face. The poor child looked heartbroken. How could he make amends?

Chapter 24

My darling, Emily

You will know by now that it was all a desperate misunderstanding and my fault entirely. I promised not to leave you that night but my anger with your sisters got the better of me. I feel sure they did not tell you I went to their house instead of the Wheatsheaf. It must show you how they have used the situation to achieve the end they wanted. You and the children weren't in Chapel to hear their damning of me and for that I thank God. But their words were twisted to suit their purpose. My father knows the truth. I can no longer stay in the town. Come with me, my love. Let us start anew. Don't let your sisters win.

John read what he had written so far. How many times had he started this letter and screwed it up? He needed to get through to her how much he loved her and the children and somehow make her understand. He blotted the ink and took up his pen again.

I miss you so desperately. I write this letter in the hope that you will begin to understand what drives me to do what your sisters and others so disapprove of. Perhaps I never explained myself well enough to you, but then I only wanted to protect you. I beg you to forgive me, forgive me for not loving you enough to change. I will always adore you and the children.

Don't blame my father, despite everything that's happened. It's not his fault. He warned me, but I wouldn't listen. The question is, would I have done anything different? Do not think that I have not thought long and hard on this, and I suppose I always will. Maybe there are some things I could have changed or rather, some things I wish I could have changed, because I can't see any way forward for us from here, unless you are willing to understand.

Would you want me to give up my beliefs, my life's work, to suit your family and our neighbours? It's my nature, my temperament to fight for justice; not wickedness which requires driving out. I will never accept that I am wicked or sinful or undeserving of God's love. They would have you think that, but it's they who are driving me away, away from you, my darling. Do you not understand? Can't you find it in your heart to trust me again; will you not come with me? How can I bear to lose you? I only see my future as a vale of sorrow without you and I fear you will find the same. It breaks my heart that you will come to regret this rift.

I don't ever remember not knowing you, but the first time I saw you was in Chapel. Something had upset you and there were tears glinting on your apple cheeks below your speedwell eyes. Was the Sunday School teacher her usual cantankerous self? Had she smacked you for some slight misdemeanour? I only remember taking my handkerchief and dabbing at your tears until you turned your sunny smile on me. Even then my heart contracted at the sight of your rosy mouth; you were all the colours of nature and full of God's blessings. It must have been summer because a light sprinkling of freckles lay on your upturned nose. The way your honeyed hair curled below your cap, entranced me, robbing me of speech. I was probably only seven and you five but I knew then we would marry. I even remember telling my mother and she told yours. They laughed and were delighted with the thought. A Holtby and a Plumtree united in marriage and religion. There has only been you for me, sweetheart. I have never looked elsewhere and never will.

You know what it is to lose a parent, the rawness, the pain. I helped you through those dark days and nights. Do you remember my love, how I held you and comforted you? Who will hold you now; your sisters with their stiff and self-righteous piety? I know you my darling. I know how your body softens at my caress, how you warm to my kisses. Are you truly willing to exchange my passionate love for your sister's cold approval?

Write to me and tell me you don't feel the same, but then I will never believe that. Our destinies are entwined like the honeysuckle and the rose in our small garden; their scents mingling in the summer air. How many times have we sat out under the darkening sky in June and listened to the nightingale's song as we breathed in the fragrant air and thanked the Lord for his generous bounty.

Imagine our children asking for their father and you telling them that you sent him away? What excuse will you give, my darling? That he loved all mankind as much as his family; that he wanted only to rescue children from hunger and poverty; that he saw no other path but the one he took. How do you think they will feel about that? Will they shun me? Will they cast me to the furthest reaches of their minds for the sin of seeing their beloved faces in all the children I have tried to help?

Perhaps I never explained myself well enough to you, but then I only wanted to protect you, and you preferred to ignore what you did not care to know. Do I blame you? No, I only beg you to forgive me, forgive me for not loving you enough to cast aside my beliefs. That I can never do. But I will always adore you and our children. Come home, my darling, please.

John sighed with weariness. The words on the page began to blur. He drew his hand across his face, feeling the stubble on his chin. Had he sat here all day and evening trying to write the perfect letter to bring her home?

He did not understand why Emily had left. According to his mother she appeared to have woken late on the Friday morning with no memory of the evening before and he had told Dorothea and his mother not to mention it, unless she brought it up. He hoped it could be forgotten so that he could go ahead with plans to leave, presenting it as a fait accompli. But while he had been in Hull on Saturday, she had slipped out of the house with the children, having asked his mother to get something from the shop.

'Why not come with me to Hull?' He had asked before leaving. 'I just need to deliver the petition to Billy and then we can see the sights.' She had refused pleading a headache. He should have insisted.

As it was he had spent longer than he intended with Billy. He had poured out his troubles and Billy consoled him before talking about the life they would have in Leeds. So, it was with anticipation and excitement that he caught the packet home to New Holland and then the train, only to be confronted with Emily's note, saying she could no longer trust him.

'Go around there now,' his mother advised. He shook his head. 'At least fetch the children,' his mother pleaded.

'They'll be abed. It's late and I'm tired.' In truth, he was so angry with Emily and her sisters that he thought he might be tempted to lash out. The desire to knock her sisters' heads together was too strong.

He was surprised not to see Emily and the children at Chapel early next morning, a service they never missed. He thought he could persuade her to return, if only he could see her.

But it had all been planned. He sat stony-faced as Mabel and Ada tore into him for breaking his word, for frequenting taverns all evening and drinking. None of it could he deny. His parents stared straight ahead but he felt their shame. All through their diatribe his father gripped his hand tight and he took strength from it. He saw no point in defending himself. The only one who needed to understand was Emily and she was absent. His life in Grimsby was over.

During the week, he busied himself in his office drawing his affairs to a conclusion. Every evening after work he called at the cottage and every evening he was refused entry. He saw his daughters' faces peering down from an upstairs window, Dorothea stared down but Edith's was tearful and sad. Yesterday he left a note under a bush, making sure that Dorothea was watching. In it he wrote that he had not gone to the Wheatsheaf that night and asked Dorothea to tell her mother what had occurred, unconvinced that Emily knew the truth.

Now here he was writing this letter for his father to place in Emily's hands at Chapel tomorrow. If he knew his father, he would insist that Emily read it in front of him. Everything depended on this letter and his father's ability to convince Emily that he meant every word. Father was the best of men and he would miss him sorely.

As tired as he was he began to reread the letter. Satisfied at last, he sealed it, then kissed it, knowing that Emily's fingers would touch the seal to open it. He kissed it again as he longed to kiss her lips, imbuing it with every ounce of love he could muster. He would walk to the Chapel in the morning and hand it to his father to give to Emily.

Tomorrow, she must return. Nay, she would return. On Monday, he planned to travel to Leeds to hunt for a house in Headingly. Could he persuade her to join him? His mother would look after the children. Billy

254

had assured him that Emily would find much to please her there and the children would love the zoological gardens. He longed to share with her the excitement of a new beginning and a life full of friendship and laughter with Billy and his wife.

His mood lightened. It will work, he thought. We will find a new chapel. Billy knew of one frequented by men in the Charter Movement. Their wives would be bound to welcome Emily. As for work, a lawyer could practise anywhere and he had savings to tide them over while he grew his business. He brought Billy's words to mind before they parted a week before.

'If this petition fails, then I'll turn my efforts to setting up unions of workers. We must fight for their rights. Join me, John. As a lawyer, you will be invaluable.'

Was Billy his nemesis as his father thought, or his saviour? Time would tell.

Chapter 25

Epilogue

1860

Edith stood in the doorway, her heart-shaped face up-turned towards his. He would have known her anywhere. She was the reflection of her mother when he'd married her. Blue eyes stared up at him, nervous and imploring, her mouth slightly open as though she had a question but dare not ask.

The shock of her arrival caused his heart to summersault. He took her hand and drew her into the hallway and then into his arms where they silently drank each other in. Her feet barely touching the tiled floor as she clasped her arms around his neck.

'Come,' he said at last, 'come into the parlour and sit yourself down. I need to know everything but make yourself comfortable.' The questions were bursting in his mind. How had she travelled here, had she come alone, why now, where were her brother and sister?

He bid the housekeeper fetch Edith some refreshment, before ushering her into the parlour She walked over to the fire and stretched out her hands towards the heat.

'Are you cold?' He grasped her hands in his, rubbing warmth into them. Where were her gloves? Her hands felt ridged and hard, not soft like Emily's. He studied one, noticing the redness and the chaffing as she removed her shabby, brown coat. And still not a word had she spoken.

The housekeeper entered carrying a tray with a pot of tea and slices of Yorkshire parkin, a favourite of his. She placed it on a table beside a deep-buttoned fireside chair and began to pour. Edith glanced at her and thanked her in a soft voice before sitting down, relief evident now in the half-smile she threw her father.

After the housekeeper left, she opened her mouth to speak. 'You don't mind me coming, do you Papa?'

'Mind? I have longed for you to come, all of you. I have written every month, without fail but never a word in reply.'

'I know. I found your letters yesterday, unopened, all of them.'

'What do you mean? Where did you find them?'

'Dorothea had stuffed them in a box and placed them underneath her bed, where only she would look. Yesterday I decided to clean under her bed while she was out. She doesn't allow me in her room.'

'Why did she hide them?'

'She blames you, Papa. Blames you for Mama's illness and her death. But I don't. Mama died because her heart was broken. She thought you didn't care because you never wrote or visited. Dorothea and I argued tremendously yesterday. I read out some of the letters and accused Dorothea of killing Mama through her own selfishness. If Mama had received your letters she would have been on the next train, I'm sure of it. But Dorothea did not want to leave Grimsby or her Chapel. That's the truth of it.'

John, sitting opposite his younger daughter, put his head in his hands. The waste of it, the sheer waste of Emily's life; pulled between her sisters and him, but then to be betrayed by her own daughter. That was cruel. And he had to bear much of the blame. He should have battered down the door and dragged his family out of that cottage. A ten-year old girl should not have been the one to make the decisions.

His father had told him that Emily was absent from Chapel on that last Sunday in Grimsby but Dorothea had promised to put the letter into her mother's hand. He had waited all that day expecting his family to appear at any moment. How many hours had he waited? He was too proud to walk round to have the door remain shut in his face, after baring his soul. Well then, so be it. He would leave, begin his new life and hope Emily would forgive him, once he had been sufficiently punished.

John had left Grimsby behind, making a new life for himself in Leeds. At first, he had convinced himself that he was working hard to ensure that they would have everything they needed when they joined him. But as the months passed without word, his mind turned towards the friends he made through the Chapel in Holbeck and Billy's contacts.

'When Mama died, why didn't you come for us?'

How could he tell her of the blackness which descended upon him when he'd received the telegram? Emily's sisters had made sure he was informed too late to attend the funeral.

'I was ill myself. An affliction of the mind. Your mother's death almost destroyed me, but when I recovered I wrote to your aunts and told them I wanted you all to live with me. They wrote back that you were all settled and Walter was in school. None of you wanted to come.'

'They never asked us. But you should have come, Papa. You should not have left it like that.'

She was right. The only time he had returned to Grimsby was when his mother died, a year after his wife. By then a chapel had opened in Cleethorpes and his father no longer attended the one in Grimsby.

'Go and see them,' his father had urged, and he had. Ada answered the door and swore that everyone was out.

'I want to see my children. I have the right to see my children.'

'They are away in Brigg, visiting a cousin.' Ada had insisted. He strained to hear any voices but only silence greeted him.

'Why do they not return my letters?'

'If they wanted to, we would not stop them,' she'd said closing the door on him.

The realisation struck him now. Ada knew he was writing letters to them. It had not just been Dorothea conniving against him. Her aunts were in on it too. Well now they had only God to answer to. All the sisters were dead. Dorothea now ruled the roost.

He should have insisted that a lawyer visit them, rather than pay money into a bank account for their upkeep. At least the lawyer could have questioned Emily and the children and reported back. A suspicion entered his mind.

He looked across at Edith, who was nibbling at a piece of the ginger cake. 'Why are your hands so sore, my love?'

'After Dorothea dismissed the maid, she said I must attend to all the chores.'

'Why would she let the maid go?'

'There was only enough money to pay for Walter's education and our food.'

'I have paid an allowance each month for all of you.' Her look of distress on hearing this tore at his heart.

'For three years, I have done everything but cook and shop. I only left the house for Chapel.' Her crestfallen expression as she realised the extent of her sister's duplicity left him bereft.

'When Mama died, I thought no one cared about me and I didn't know where you were.'

'What about Grandpa. He cared.'

'I was not allowed to talk to him. Dorothea said only she must talk with him. That way she might wheedle a few treats out of him. It's true he kept us supplied with milk, cheese and eggs until he left the farm.'

John's fists clenched at the cruelty of his elder daughter. Why did she hate him and her sister so?

'After our row, yesterday, I walked to the farm and Uncle Tom told me where Grandpa lived. I didn't know what else to do.'

'Did he give you money for the train fare?'

'No, he brought me. He's in Leeds, in Hyde Park, but thought you might want to see me on my own. Did he do right?'

'My father always does the right thing. Unlike me, it seems I always do the wrong thing, but with the best of intentions.' Edith was too old to sweep on to his lap and caress her hair as he had last done when she was five years old. Now she was seventeen, and a young lady. 'What about Walter?' He asked. 'How is he?'

'Walter would like a father too.' Edith said.

'I have waited twelve years for you both. Do you think Dorothea will forgive me too?'

'Do you really want to try?'

'I must. I have left it all too long. As your mama would say, I have cared too much for the poor and not enough for my family. But I don't understand why Dorothea hates me, if she knew I was writing and sending money.'

'Mother made her enter The Wheatsheaf, she was only ten and it changed her. She believed that you had caused her to do something sinful and Mama's illness was a retribution from God. I'm sure Ada and Mabel encouraged her to think like that. Yesterday I told her that Mama only took to drinking that medicine because Papa had been driven out of town. For the first time, I saw doubt in her eyes.'

'What medicine.?'

'It was supposed to be for coughs, but she drank bottles of it every day towards the end. We knew she was poisoning herself but nothing we said could stop her.' Edith eyes began to fill with tears at the memory.

'Oh, my dear. What a mess I have made of everything.'

'The last time I saw you, you hid a note in a bush. I got to it first and I asked Dorothea what truth was it that she had to tell Mama. She wouldn't tell me. Later I saw her throw the note into the fire. What did she need to tell Mama?'

'That I never went to The Wheatsheaf that night. I was telling Ada and Mabel to stop interfering.'

Edith stood and walked over to her father, sinking to the floor, she leant her head against him, allowing him to stroke her butter yellow hair. He wanted to sob with happiness but caught his breath not wishing to spoil this precious moment.

'Do you still attend Chapel, Papa?'

Was this the last test?

'I do. Every Sunday I walk to Holbeck. It's about an hour from here. The people are honest and straightforward. Many were Chartists and accept me without judgement. I can be myself and I find that a great relief.'

Edith looked up at him and smiled, her lips slightly parted. An understanding smile, no trace of disapproval.

Awash with love for her, he said, 'It would make me so proud if you would come with me tomorrow.'

'I would like that.'

'I will introduce you to my cousin and his family. You will love them as much as I do.' He could scarcely believe the joy in his heart. He looked down at her, emotion shining in his eyes.

'Papa, can we forget the past and start again?'

John bent his head to hers and kissed her brow. 'There is nothing that would please me more, my love. Shall we go and find Grandpa? I want to thank him for bringing you to me.'

Author's Note

The inspiration for this book came from family history. My three times great grandfather, William Holt became an early convert to Primitive Methodism in Grimsby. He was missioned by Thomas King and eighteen months later they walked to Tunstall and back for the 1821 Conference. Therein lie the bones of the story.

Meeting a distant cousin, also a descendent of William Holt, I found out that her grandfather had been banished from his family and Cleethorpes, for liking a drink and singing in the pub. Needless to say, it was traumatic for all concerned and led to much heartbreak and an early death for his wife who believed he did not care. His letters to her were intercepted.

Primitive Methodism grew exponentially from those first meetings on Mow Cop. It was taken up by the artisan and working classes in their thousands. It became a natural home for those seeking worker's rights and out of it grew Trade Unions and the Labour Party. There was rivalry between the two branches of Methodism but in 1932 they joined together to become one united church.

It is thought that it was Joseph Capper who was ejected from the Tunstall Conference, although no one has been able to prove it.

The 1848 Petition failed as well. Feargus O'Connor claimed it contained over five million signatures, but the government said there were just under two million. The British government simply ignored it, while calling into ridicule some of the signatures, which were plainly forgeries, such as Queen Victoria and Sir Robert Peel. The Reform Act of 1867 gave the vote to many more men in the boroughs but not to landless farm labourers. It wasn't until 1918 that all men over twenty-one and some women over thirty got the vote. In 1928 all women over twenty-one became entitled to vote, thirty years later than their New Zealand cousins.

Conditions for farm labourers continued to decline throughout the century and several fires were set in protest at falling wages and conditions in Lincolnshire villages. http://lacebyhistory.com/node/73

Many Lincolnshire farm labourers from the Wolds were enticed as emigrants to New Zealand in the 1870s where they wrote glowing accounts of being granted land and how their lives changed for the better. http://nzetc.victoria.ac.nz/tm/scholarly/tei-ArnFart-c7-2.html

Others moved into Grimsby and Cleethorpes which became boom towns after the railways were built and the fishing industry took off.

The Revolt of the Field (Labourers' strike) began in 1872 in Lincolnshire but by the winter of 1873/4 the Labour League was well established in the Lincolnshire villages within the Lindsey area. Many of the League leaders were lay preachers from within the Primitive Methodist Connexion.

Bone 'rubbish' was imported into several East Coast Ports from Europe in huge quantities following the end of the Napoleonic Wars. Several sources seem to suggest that this included the bones of the war dead. Certainly, there is well documented evidence that Waterloo teeth were used for dentures.

The incident with the child falling onto agricultural machinery and dying of blood loss, happened to my husband's uncle. The employer refused to let her car be used because of possible bloodstains and the boy died on the journey by horse and cart to the doctor.

If you want to know what happened to the girl who shoplifted in Derby read my book Search for the Light.

Further Reading

Clowes, W. The Journals of William Clowes; 1810-1838. Hallam &
Holliday.

Davidson, J. The Life of William Clowes. 1854.

Dowling, A. Grimsby; Making the town 1800-1914. Phillimore. 2007

Ecob Rev. J T. Primitive Methodism and the Hosiery and Lace Workers.
Christian Messenger, 1921.

Gillett, E. A History of Grimsby. Hull University Press. 1970.

Hempton, D. Methodism and Politics in British Society 1750-1850.
Hutchinson. 1984.

Hobsbaum, E J. Methodism and the Threat of Revolution in Britain.
History Today, Feb 1st, 1957. P115.

My Primitive Methodist Ancestors http://myprimitivemethodists.org.uk/

Patrick, J. Agricultural Gangs. History Today. Volume 36 Issue 3 1986.

Pearson, F.R. The Early History of Hull Steam Shipping. Mr Pye Books.
1984

Price, D. Turning the World Upside Down; Learning from the Primitive
Methodist Movement.

Shaw, C. When I was a Child. http://www.workhouses.org.uk/Shaw/

Uglow, J. In these Times; Living in Britain through Napoleon's Wars; 1793-
1815. Faber & Faber. 2015

If you have enjoyed this book, please leave a review on Good Reads or
Amazon. Reviewers are the author's friends and without reviews our
books may not be found.